## The door behind Bolan was shut with a thud

The warrior faced three leveled guns.

"Come right in," the man at the desk said. "We weren't expecting you here."

"What the hell are you playing at this time? I thought we were going to talk business."

"Look, you and your friend Gage, or whatever his name is. The shakedown won't work. We're onto you."

Mystified, Bolan glanced rapidly around the room. He saw that what he had originally taken as an easy, casual manner was in fact the stillness of a rattler before its strike. This man was deadly. The self-control masked the icy determination of the dedicated fanatic.

Bolan had no idea how it had gone sour. He only knew he had to get out of there—fast.

# MACK BOLAN

## The Executioner

# DON PENDLETON's EXECUTIONER

# MACK BOLAN

## Countdown to Chaos

A GOLD EAGLE BOOK FROM

# WORLDWIDE

TORONTO • NEW YORK • LONDON • PARIS
AMSTERDAM • STOCKHOLM • HAMBURG
ATHENS • MILAN • TOKYO • SYDNEY

First edition September 1987

ISBN 0-373-61105-6

Special thanks and acknowledgment to
Kent Delaney for his contribution to this work.

Printed in Canada

These violent delights have violent ends,
And in their triumph die.

>                    —*Romeo and Juliet*

If the violence in animal man is to be contained,
then the man of peace must at times use violent means.

>                    —Mack Bolan

# THE
# MACK BOLAN
## LEGEND

Nothing less than a war could have fashioned the destiny of the man called Mack Bolan. Bolan earned the Executioner title in the jungle hell of Vietnam.

But this soldier also wore another name—Sergeant Mercy. He was so tagged because of the compassion he showed to wounded comrades-in-arms and Vietnamese civilians.

Mack Bolan's second tour of duty ended prematurely when he was given emergency leave to return home and bury his family, victims of the Mob. Then he declared a one-man war against the Mafia.

He confronted the Families head-on from coast to coast, and soon a hope of victory began to appear. But Bolan had broken society's every rule. That same society started gunning for this elusive warrior—to no avail.

So Bolan was offered amnesty to work within the system against terrorism. This time, as an employee of Uncle Sam, Bolan became Colonel John Phoenix. With a command center at Stony Man Farm in Virginia, he and his new allies—Able Team and Phoenix Force—waged relentless war on a new adversary: the KGB.

But when his one true love, April Rose, died at the hands of the Soviet terror machine, Bolan severed all ties with Establishment authority.

Now, after a lengthy lone-wolf struggle and much soul-searching, the Executioner has agreed to enter an "arm's-length" alliance with his government once more, reserving the right to pursue personal missions in his Everlasting War.

## 1

The mission had started in Athens, Greece.

"The British," Hal Brognola told Mack Bolan, "are designing a supersonic pursuit ship that's going to revolutionize land warfare."

Bolan smiled. "Isn't everybody?"

"This time it's for real," Brognola said. "Naval warfare, too, if it comes to that. The plane's still on the drawing board, but our spies tell us it's a winner all the way."

"Real spies?"

"Let's just say that the intel is encouraging," Brognola replied.

"Okay. What's the pitch?"

"The plane's revolutionary because it's a VTOL supersonic that combines the qualities of deep-penetration attacker, helicopter and pursuit interceptor. With nukes if necessary. And since a vertical-takeoff-and-landing capability means that several of them could be carried by—and launched from—ships as small and fast as destroyers or frigates, I don't need to—"

"I get it," Bolan interrupted. "There's a strike potential there that's much more flexible than you get with a big carrier. Easy to pull back fast in case of danger, too."

"Right. Add that the plane—it's code-named XP-29—is in the Mach 2-plus league, and you'll see why the Pentagon very much wants to be in on the project and share in its development."

Bolan pushed himself out of the low cane chair and leaned on the balcony rail, staring at the thickets of masts and rigging in Piraeus harbor. It was dusk, and the riding lights of fishing boats cast streamers of brilliance across the dark water. What he didn't see was where he fitted into the scenario. "So there's a problem?" he asked over his shoulder.

"There could be." Brognola fished a cigar from his vest pocket and clenched it between his teeth. "Remember the Westland-Sikorsky affair in '86, when the Brits tried to kill a bid by our aerospace people to buy out the ailing Westland helicopter concern?"

Bolan nodded.

"Remember the reasons they gave?"

"As I recall," Bolan said, "there was a lot of media hype—Yankee takeover of British industry, economy becoming the slave of Wall Street, our jobs at risk. Plus veiled threats from the Europeans who put in a rival bid that there'd be no more component orders if the deal went through. That kind of stuff."

"You got it. This time, too," Brognola continued, "there's a strong 'European' lobby urging that the XP-29 remain a strictly independent—and if necessary even unaligned—deterrent."

"You mean not even part of the NATO arsenal?"

"That's what some of them want. With all components, of course, manufactured by a European consortium. This anti-U.S. lobby is unlikely to prevail," he pursued. "In fact, I'd say it hadn't got a chance...unless something happened to undermine this famous 'special relationship' we have with the Brits."

"So?"

Brognola sighed. "Something *might* happen."

"Okay," Bolan said. "What could happen to undermine this U.S.-U.K. special relationship?"

"A projected coup in Northern Ireland."

Bolan whistled. "In Ireland? Why?" He shoved himself away from the balcony rail and sat down again in the chair.

"This is a very sensitive area for both countries. Not because of any real conflict of interest but because of votes. But before I fill you in, you have to take the Brognola crash course on the Irish Problem."

Bolan grinned. "Instant Ulster. Let's go."

"There are parallels with Nam and with Algeria, but they're not too close. Ireland was like a British colony until just after the First World War, when most of the country opted for independence in a referendum. But the northeast corner—six out of the eight counties forming the province of Ulster—voted to stay with Britain. That was fine—the place was self-governing, and it also sent representatives to Westminster."

"Like state and federal with us?"

"Yeah. But there were problems. The guys who voted to stay with England were Protestants, but there were a hell of a lot of others—a sizable minority—who wanted to go the other way. They were Catholics. They wanted a united, independent Ireland."

"So you got a dual polarity—political and religious. Pro-Brit equals Protestant; Pro-unity equals Catholic."

Brognola nodded. "Once the Protestants in the north had the reins in their hands, they fixed it so the Catholics had no say in the government, kept them out of practically everything. When the British proposed electoral reform in the sixties to give them a bigger slice of the pie, there were anti-Catholic riots. Catholic extremists hit back . . . and the British army was sent in to keep the two sides apart."

"And they've been there ever since."

"That's right. At first they were welcomed as saviors by the Catholics. Now the poor bastards are hated by the extremists on both sides. You got booby-trapped cars, gasoline bombs, mob riots and killer ambushes all over. And you got terrorist groups—paramilitary vigilantes on the Protestant side, the IRA on the other. Most of the ordinary folks living there are sick to their stomachs of all the violence, but it's the extremists who make news on television."

"Where does the Republic of Ireland's government stand?" Bolan asked.

"They've always lobbied for a united Ireland, ever since the partition. But they repudiate the IRA. It's illegal in the south as well as the north now."

"You said there was a conflict over votes—between Washington and the Brits, I mean."

"The British government is obliged to support, at least in public, the Ulster cause. A united Ireland over our dead bodies. That's because the Protestants are nonconformists—Methodists, Presbyterians and suchlike. And there's one hell of a nonconformist vote in Britain itself.

"Stateside, nobody dares oppose the united Ireland cause, for which a heap of money is raised by public subscription, on account of the Irish immigrant vote in particular and the Catholic vote in general.

"The British are already sore about pro-Nationalist fundraising in the U.S.," Brognola continued. "They claim the loot is used to buy arms that the IRA uses against the British army in Ulster. Whether or not that's true, anything that worsens this situation is a disaster."

"You haven't told me what *is* going to worsen it," Bolan reminded him. "Okay, the two countries have to back different horses in the race. I don't see what that has to do with your XP-29 project."

"There's this terrorist coup," Brognola explained patiently. "If it worked out, it would inflame anti-British feeling worldwide, and the worst of it is that there's evidence that points to U.S. involvement, U.S. money, U.S. materials and expertise in back of the deal. It's just the kind of catastrophe that would swing British public opinion, and thus Parliament, dead against us, and kill any chance of collaboration on the XP-29 project.''

"What is this coup?" Bolan demanded.

"That's what you're gonna find out, Striker," the Fed said genially, reverting to the code name used by the Executioner when he was taking direct orders from Brognola during the Stony Man operation. "We have the briefest general idea from our man in Belfast, but no details."

"Can't the guy get you the details?"

"No way. He was blown to hell yesterday when he turned the key to start his car."

"What's the general idea, then?"

"Some kind of atrocity or massacre carried out by the IRA on their own supporters. But they'll be wearing British uniforms. 'British Troops Run Amok in Catholic Neighborhood'—that'll be the headline—in revenge for the murder of one of their officers. And some poor bastard will have been wasted two or three days before, just to make the script believable."

"But you don't know when, where or how. Is that what you're telling me? And you want me to go on in and find out?"

"Find out and then terminate the guys masterminding the plan," Brognola said. "Kill the whole thing stone dead at all costs. The whole stinking thing."

"Just that?"

"You're the only guy who fits the scenario, Striker. You must appreciate that the slightest hint of overt action on our part, of American interference in Northern Ireland, would be almost as bad as the plot succeeding. Political maneuvers, diplomatic lobbying, covert CIA activity—they're all strictly out."

"You mean you want someone you can disown if it blows up in our faces, right?"

"Someone we can repudiate if *he's* blown, yes. And are you typecast for the role! You've already been disowned by the U.S. And few people are aware of this. I'm batting without a team. Neither the White House nor the Pentagon are in on the deal. It's just you, me and the admiral."

"The admiral?"

"Richards. Head of Naval Intelligence in this theater. Remember SkyHook?"

"That was a system of stowing Harrier jump jets on small craft, wasn't it?"

"Got it. A robotized crane homed on the jet while it was hovering above the ship and plucked it out of the sky. It was Richards who liaised with the British navy and rowed us in on that project. He figures XP-29 for a better bet—it's faster, and you don't need a crane."

"Okay," Bolan said. "So the mission's kind of a follow-through?"

With the local CIA resident and a man from Britain's MI6, he had been seconded to Athens to track down arms shipments from Eastern Bloc countries believed to be destined for the IRA. The weapons, which included Kalashnikovs and RPG-7 grenade launchers, were rumored to arrive from Black Sea ports via the Golden Horn and the Dardanelles, to be transferred to chartered freighters in Piraeus. It was through Bolan's unrivaled knowledge of Eastern undercover operations that they had discovered the freighter cargos were in fact smuggled overland from state-owned arsenals in Albania.

"At least," Bolan quipped, "I'll be able to check out the way the stuff is used once it reaches its destination. Is there anything else I should know about the Ulster situation?"

"Just remember the labels," Brognola said. "The guys who want Ireland united are Nationalists; The Protestant Ulstermen are called Unionists. Union with Britain, see. They also describe themselves as loyalists—although, if you ask me, I'd say the Brits would be only too happy to do without their loyalty and leave the Irish to sort out their own problems.''

"Why don't they?" Bolan asked. "Why don't they just pull out?"

The Fed favored him with a crooked smile. "Votes."

"THIS VTOL PURSUIT SHIP that interests me," Admiral Richards told Bolan in his usual staccato style. "Want you to remember the stakes here just the same. This IRA plot. If it succeeded, the best that could happen, the very best, would be otherwise peaceable Catholics drawn into a bitter confrontation with the British army; Worst would be actual civil war, with the Brits hated by both sides."

"And in either case," Brognola put in, "some of the crap from the fan would fly our way. If the army is discredited in Ulster, and if there's even the slightest suspicion we're involved, goodbye and farewell to the admiral's hopes for collaboration on XP-29."

"So basically it's another identify, seek-and-destroy mission?" Bolan said.

"Secretly," Richards emphasized. "Check out the details, the timing, finger the organizers and eliminate them before any damage is done. Eliminate. With no leaks—before or after."

"I'll need some kind of cover."

"Cover you'll have. Best you go in from the south, though. Security is very tight at all official entry points in the north. We'll land you from a sub, on the coast between Bundoran and Sligo. Ulster border's no more than six miles from Bundoran, seventeen from Sligo. Dozens of crossing places in the mountains."

"No-sweat landing? No coast guards, police, customs?"

The admiral laughed. "Are you joking? At the creek where we'll put you ashore? Won't be a goddamn soul within miles. There isn't even a village between there and Sligo...."

## 2

Gunfire blazed from the rocks on either side of the narrow stream when the flat-bottom boat was still fifty yards from the shore.

In the dawn light, splinters of wood flew from the gunwales and water spurted through holes drilled in the hull as the boat's stubby bow was raked with a hail of lead.

Mack Bolan dropped the oars and plunged into the water before a second volley could shred the flesh from his bones.

His feet touched the pebbled creekbed. The water was as clear as crystal but penetratingly cold. Angling upright in the shallow swell he saw the dark shape of the boat above him. If he reached up one hand, he could touch the slimed planking.

Bolan planted his palm against the wood, thrusting himself down against the buoyancy of the tiny craft. The ten-pound weight of the immersion-proof Heckler & Koch G-11 caseless assault rifle he carried in his other hand helped keep him vertical and stopped his legs floating toward the surface.

He had filled his lungs before he jumped, but he had no more than ninety seconds before he had to go up for air.

He felt the hull tremble against his palm as a third fusillade cored the timbers. Treading weightless feet carefully on the wrack-covered stones, Bolan began to walk, shoving the dinghy above his head toward the nearer bank of the creek.

Soon the floor began to shelve upward. Ahead, perhaps ten yards away, he could see the wavering outline of a rocky spur that projected from the bank.

If he broke surface there, the spur would shelter him from the gunners on the near side of the creek and the boat would hide him from those on the far side.

But underwater wading without scuba gear didn't come easy. The pressure in Bolan's head and chest was threatening to choke the life from him when at last the dinghy, heavier and lower in the water now because of the water seeping through the holes, nudged the rock wall.

Allowing his feet to drift upward, he lay on his back and broke the surface. He could remember no taste as sweet as the first gulp of chilled air that he sucked into his starving lungs.

When the hammering of his blood had abated, he backed off until he could stand on the creek bottom with just his eyes and nose above the water.

He moved the assault rifle to his shoulder.

The H&K G-11's carrying handle, mounted above the pistol grip at the point of balance, also incorporated an optical sight. Bolan squinted through the rubber eyepiece, thumbing off the safety to the left of the trigger guard.

A dirt road snaked up the incline to a white crofter's cottage just below the crest, and a black, eight-light stretch limo was parked in front of a stack of peat. Bolan couldn't see the frontal treatment or the grille, but he figured the car— out of place in such a wild part of the coastline—for a Mercedes 600, a Fleetwood, or maybe even one of those Russian ZILs carbon-copied from the Caddy.

Further down the slope there was a Jeep, and behind a rock outcrop nearby he could see four or five men armed with submachine guns. At the first outburst of shooting he had taken them for Uzis or Colt Commandos but now, with the sniperscope's magnification, he could see that they were in fact Ingram MAC-11s.

The attackers grouped together, looking out over the creek, staring at the riddled boat rocking empty against the spur. The boat was settling deeper as the water surged in, but where was the boat's former occupant?

Ice-cold hands caressed the underwater trigger. Bolan hosed out three bursts and saw two of the killers topple as easily as pop-up targets in a fairground booth. Two more scrambled up the hillside, dodging between the granite boulders studding the slope.

Bolan flicked the mechanism to auto. The range was no more than two-forty, two-fifty yards. He had never put it to the test, but the G-11's makers claimed the tiny 4.7 mm slugs, each smaller than a .22-caliber round, could drill a steel helmet at five hundred yards.

Firing from behind the flatboat's stern, Bolan permitted himself a three-second squirt, moving the assault rifle's muzzle in a tight figure eight at water level. The death-stream belching from the SMG rocketed away, fanning a network of fine wrinkles across the surface.

One of the runaways threw up his arms, twisted and lay down in the heather. The other pitched forward, rolled, bounced off an outcrop and dropped twenty feet into the creek.

A fifth man had emerged from behind the rock shelf and made the Jeep. Bolan let him go. He was dealing with amateurs here, and the next item to be marked on the card was to flush the gunnies on his side of the inlet and then put them away, too.

He didn't know how many there were; he thought two or three only. But they couldn't be all that dumb. They would have watched the boat, heard the rip-roaring shudder of the G-11, made plans already to encircle the spur in some way and outflank him.

As if *they* knew precisely where *he* was.

So it was time to shorten the odds on that score.

Bolan laid the gun on a rocky shelf, grabbed a couple of handholds and dragged himself out of the creek.

For a moment he lay on the steep rock face, letting the water cascade off him back into the creek—two hundred pounds of muscle hung on a six-foot-three-inch frame topped with a rugged, hawklike face and cold blue eyes. He was dressed in a blacksuit and combat boots, with a watertight neoprene pouch clipped to his waistbelt. Inside the pouch was a Beretta 93-R automatic pistol with a suppressor and several clips of 9 mm ammunition.

Later he would rendezvous with his contact, who would indicate the location of the drop where he could pick up the rest of the gear he needed.

Right now it was a question of a minirecon before he took out the remaining hardmen.

It took several minutes before his circulation was back to normal. It was full daylight now, with a breeze ruffling the surface of the creek and whitecaps daubing the dark line of the ocean beyond. Inland, to the east, the mountains were silhouetted against a flood of gold light that tinged the high clouds moving across the sky.

In the silence succeeding the clamor of gunfire, Bolan heard the rasp of an exhaust and a whine of gears as the Jeep climbed toward the limo on the far side of the inlet. He began to crawl away from the spur, keeping as near the waterline as he could.

Between five and six feet of smooth rock slanted into the water on this side of the spur, which jutted from the hillside as high up again. Above the rock, stony ground floored with scrub rose steeply toward a shoulder of the mountain. Ten yards away in the direction of the creekhead a stunted tree hung over the swell. Bolan squirmed that way.

They would expect him, he guessed, to go the other way, to make the top of the spur and risk peering over the edge to see if he could identify their own position. One guy would have been left down there as a watchman, with a gun trained on the spur, ready to draw a bead and blow Bolan's head off the moment he showed.

The other, or others, would be higher up toward the shoulder, filtering around, hoping to find a position from which they could sight him out in the open, enfilade him and open fire while he was without cover.

Professionals would have a signals routine set up. Expecting him, they would have fixed it so that, if he made either side of the creek, the guys on the far side could pinpoint his position and direct the fire of the killers nearer him. One side would wise up the other on the best time to attack. Someone would have rounded that spur by water.

The way it turned out, instead of maintaining a surveillance through field glasses, the only watchman left on the far side was hightailing it to the crest behind the crofter's cottage.

Bolan made the tree, hoisted himself up a little and sat among the lower branches. A few leaves, yellowed by the early fall, drifted down to the water. From here he could look right over the spur: over and down to the tumble of rocks at the water's edge where a man wearing a cloth cap and a white silk choker crouched over an Ingram kitted out with a bipod. And sure enough the SMG was trained on the spur's jagged crest.

That one could wait. He hadn't spotted Bolan. He was following orders—his eyes were fixed on the spur.

Priority for Bolan himself was the location of the guy's companions. In fact there was only one. He was high up on the hillside, a dimly seen shape flitting between clumps of furze and whin. He carried a double-barreled shotgun, but Bolan's waterside refuge would be way out of range.

Bolan slid down from the tree. Keeping it between him and the spur, he made his way along the lip of the rock that slanted into the creek until he reached a boulder perched above the water. On the far side of this he crouched and raised the G-11 once more to his shoulder, sweeping the sight across the scattered clumps of vegetation two hundred and fifty yards higher up the mountain.

At first he couldn't pick up the man again. Then, swinging the sniperscope eastward, he found him farther ahead and lower down the slope: the guy had quickened his pace, hoping to circle down and take him from behind.

Bolan was pretty sure the killer was onto his present position, but did he know he himself had been spotted?

Reselecting the burst mode, Bolan waited for the killer to show, training the assault rifle on a stand of saplings growing at the edge of a rivulet that ran down a shallow depression into the creek.

After three trio bursts and one three-second blast on auto, there would still be lots of ammo left. He had no compunction about gunning the man down in cold blood: seven of them had opened fire on him with no warning, and only reflexes honed by years of guerrilla combat had saved his life.

A shape, silhouetted against the glare of the sun in the east, moved past the last few saplings thinning out at the edge of the stand. Bolan triggered a burst and then another.

Chips of granite stung his face. A slug screeched off a boulder into the sky. Microseconds later he heard the whipcrack of a rifle.

Correction. For regular shotgun, read "over-and-under" sporting gun with an express rifle barrel beneath the two buckshot barrels.

The rifleman fired again, the high-velocity bullet gouging a sliver of rock from the slope at Bolan's feet.

Bolan dived into the creek.

Swimming powerfully underwater he covered no more than thirty yards, knowing that in such clear water his body would be visible from above.

But by the time he grounded his feet and stood shoulder-high in the swell, he was level with the saplings and the trunks no longer covered the man with the up-and-under.

The gun was already pointing Bolan's way, but the Executioner's sudden submarine-surfacing with the G-11 took the hit man by surprise; he had expected his target to scramble ashore and run for cover. The instant's hesitation cost him his life.

Bolan leaned his finger on the trigger until the assault rifle's magazine was exhausted. Before the harsh echoes of the superfast gunshots batted back from the far side of the creek, the sniper was gone. Hurled sideways by the impact of the deathstream, he tightened his own finger in reflex action and loosed a last shot up among the branches. Then he slumped to the ground, teetered on the edge of a heather clump and began to slide down toward the creek.

Bolan watched him all the way, the limp body collecting twigs, uprooted plants and a shower of small stones as it rolled.

The dead man came to rest with outflung arms at the top of the bank. Blood seeped out from under him to drip down and cloud the water lapping the base of the rock.

The gun followed him, zigzagging the slope in a minor dust storm until it came to rest against the gnarled roots of a leafless bush twenty yards higher up the mountainside.

Bolan left it there. He waded back to the boulder.

Five down, one escaped, one to go.

He climbed out of the water, sat down, unzippered the neoprene pouch and started to ready his Beretta. It was in any case more useful than the empty H&K would have been in a close encounter.

The encounter was closer—and sooner—than he expected.

The watchman had quit his post, scaled the spur and approached the boulder while Bolan was in the water. Given the element of surprise, maybe he figured it would be easier to finish it with his bare hands.

Bolan was surprised, all right. He was slamming a full clip into the automatic with the heel of his hand when the guy launched himself from the top of the rock.

Nail-studded boots powered by two hundred pounds of body weight slammed agonizingly into Bolan's shoulders and smashed him to the ground. The Beretta spun away out of reach. He was facedown on the hard, sharp rock slant with brutish fingers scrabbling for his throat. Bruised and lacerated by the physical shock, he gasped momentarily for air, stifled by the inert mass of the attacker on his back.

Then the years of experience in unarmed combat asserted themselves, and he eeled around to eyeball his opponent.

He saw coarse, blunt features in a red-veined face with bloodshot eyes. He saw hatred in those eyes, and greed, and a mindless cruelty. He flinched from the hot, beery breath playing over his own face...and exploded into action.

An arm block to the neck loosened the grip of those scrabbling, black-rimmed fingernails. He freed a hand to ram the cap down over the thug's eyes and reached for the neoprene pouch to rake the hard metal edge of the zipper tag across the sensitive strip of cartilage separating his nostrils.

The guy yelled as the eyes smothered by the cap were blinded with tears and blood spurted from his nose. He wrenched away one arm and tried to snatch off the cap, but in that moment Bolan slammed in a kidney punch and kneed him savagely in the groin.

The guy jackknifed, and Bolan flexed his leg hard enough to separate them. He dragged himself out from under and rolled on top, chopping again at the throat with the rigid edge of one hand. The killer gagged, but he was tough and he was strong. He whipped across a hamlike fist that rocked Bolan's head and then butted him beneath the chin.

Bolan's teeth clicked together, and he felt the blood flow as he bit his tongue.

He wrapped his arms around his burly assailant, reaching for an ankle lock with both feet, but the guy hit him again and heaved titanically, attempting to reverse their positions. Locked together, gouging and pummeling, they rolled over the lip and dropped into the creek.

The water was waist-deep. For an instant it was thrashed into foam as the two men fought beneath the surface.

Bolan was up first, shaking the moisture from his eyes, seizing one of the thug's ankles and hoisting the leg high up above the miniature whirlpool agitating the creek between the bank the the spur.

The killer struggled frenziedly to sit up, but his head remained underwater. Bolan jerked the ankle higher, up to shoulder level. At the same time he planted one foot beneath the guy's jaw and trod his neck back down to the creekbed.

He leaned his weight on that foot, crushing the windpipe, holding the killer as he lay stretched out, exerting all his strength to contain the convulsive bucking of the body resisting his grasp.

Hands clawed at Bolan's leg; fingernails raked his ankle; the drowning thug's free leg kicked and jerked; thrashing hips creamed the water and thumped against his thigh. But he held on grimly, sweat beading his forehead, until the struggles began to weaken.

Bubbles streaming upward from the silently screaming mouth, distorted beneath the surface, became scarcer and finally ceased altogether. The last one, tinged now with pink, burst silently, and all at once the body went limp.

Bolan released the leg and pushed the dead man out beyond the spur. Facedown in the tide swelling landward from the ocean, he floated slowly toward the shingle beach at the head of the creek.

For the third time Bolan emerged from the water. He brushed the sweat from his brow with a damp forearm and looked across at the far hillside. The Jeep had vanished, but there was still movement below the white crofter's cottage.

As he watched, the black stretch limo backed up, turned slowly and was steered out onto the dirt road. It began climbing the grade to the ridge behind the cottage.

The fiery rim of the sun appeared inland above the distant mountains, striking highlights from the car's tinted glass, the brightwork and the polished trunk.

Was it his imagination, or did he see, just before the limo vanished over the crest, a sudden extra flash of brilliance— as though a fugitive ray had been reflected from the lens of binoculars focused through the rear window?

Bolan shook his head, collecting together his scattered gear.

The ambush had surprised the hell out of him because the landfall had been guaranteed dead secret.

The creek, they told him before he was off-loaded from the U.S. Navy sub, had been chosen because of its remoteness. "It's vital, absolutely vital," they had said, "that nobody knows you're in the country." And the admiral had said, "won't be a goddamn soul within miles. There isn't even a village between there and Sligo."

Just seven killers, a Jeep and a mysterious limousine.

So welcome to the Emerald Isle!

## 3

Bolan's cover was Mike Belasko, a news photographer for the American magazine *World Review*. On a lonely mountain road three miles inland from where he had landed, he made the rendezvous as planned.

A narrow stone bridge carried the road across a stream winding through a shallow upland valley. On the far side of the bridge an old Morris station wagon was cranked up on a jack with a wheel leaning against the rear fender. A short, stumpy man wearing riding breeches and a patched corduroy jacket was crouched beside the car; it "appeared" as though the vehicle had a flat.

He straightened, rubbing his back, as the Executioner's tall, husky blacksuited figure rounded a corner and approached. "You took your time, sure," he complained. "I was expectin' you at sunrise."

"There was a delay," Bolan responded.

The man in black had decided to put aside the whys and wherefores of the inlet ambush. The most important thing was to proceed with the mission. Time was vital.

"I don't want to know about that," the little man said. His voice was hoarse and his mustache nicotine-stained. "All I have to do is brief you on the bloody drop, and then I'm away the hell outta this." He opened the Morris's tailgate. "And hand over this machine."

A Vespa motor scooter lay on its side among cartons of fertilizer, a sack of groceries, an old trench coat and a pair of rubber boots. Bolan lifted the small machine out and set it on the road. "So brief me," he said curtly.

"Bundoran," Bolan's contact said. "The Excelsior Temperance Hotel. Keep on along here. First left, left again, then it's third right an' yous on the coastal road." He went to the front of the beat-up station wagon and opened the passenger door, taking out a worn leather grip, a pair of black denims and a dark blue turtleneck sweater. "Ten-fifteen in the lobby," he said. "You're to ask have they a room, an' they'll tell you no."

Bolan pulled on the sweater and jeans over his blacksuit, strapped the bag to the back of the scooter and rode away. Contacts never wanted to know the details. The less they knew, the less they could tell.

Bundoran was a summer resort, already half deserted at the wrong end of the short season. The dawn breeze had freshened, and waves broke along the empty shore in flurries of foam as Bolan rode past the line of gray hotels and lodging houses fronting the esplanade. The Excelsior Temperance Hotel was three blocks inland, a gloomy Victorian pile across the street from a supermarket, with lozenges of colored glass framed in a fanlight above the front door.

Bolan climbed the worn stone steps and went into the lobby: two potted palms, dark stairs curling upward, a scarred reception desk. Through a half-open door he could see a television lounge with a flowered carpet. The atmosphere in the hallway was heavy with the odor of over-cooked vegetables.

There was nobody in sight. He put the bag on the floor and banged a bell on the desk.

A shirtsleeved man with slicked-back hair came slowly down the stairs. He slid in behind the desk and asked, "And what would you be after wantin', sir?"

"I'd like to have a room for the night," Bolan said.

The man shook his head. "Then yous fresh outta luck, mister," he said, "for although 'tis late on in the year we're full up to here." He drew a forefinger across his throat.

"That's too bad," Bolan said. "Guess I'll have to—"

He broke off as a nondescript man who looked like a traveling salesman hurried down the stairs. He was carrying a worn leather bag that was the twin of Bolan's. He placed it on the floor beside the desk.

"Good day to you, Pat," he greeted the receptionist. "If there's any messages for me, I'll be back around six." He flicked a room key across the desk.

"Very good, Mr. Brogan," the receptionist said, turning to hang the key on a row of hooks behind the desk. "And a good day to you, too, sir."

The man nodded to Bolan, picked up a bag and walked out into the street.

Bolan waited awhile, asking for suggestions where he might find another hotel with vacancies, then he picked up the grip that had been switched with his own and left, too. He returned to the scooter and rode out of town.

Twenty minutes later he dismounted and wheeled the machine into a small coppice beside a dirt road that led toward the mountains southeast of the town. He unstrapped the case from the back of the scooter.

It was much heavier than the one he had been given by the cutout. Inside he found a rolled up raincoat, a jacket, underclothes, a battery-powered electric razor, maps, ID documents, a press accreditation card and a black leather camera case.

The case looked used, but not too used: the stitching of the shoulder strap had come loose in one place; a shiny patch in back of the lid indicated where the case had rubbed against the hip of the photographer toting it. Bolan nodded approvingly. He appreciated good detail work.

There were two cameras in the velour-lined case: a 35 mm Nikon SLR compact that shot real pictures, and a Hasselblad.

The Hasselblad was fitted with a 28-200 zoom lens—at least that was what the lettering around the focus ring said. In fact it had been modified by Brognola's Stony Man armorers for a different kind of shooting.

There were cross hairs within the viewfinder; when the shutter opened it revealed a three-inch gun barrel concealed by the long lens casing and projecting from a 9 mm Beretta breech mechanism with a four-round magazine adapted to fit inside the camera body.

He checked the action, checked that the magazine was loaded and returned the Hasselblad to the case. He took his own full-size Beretta 93-R from the pouch at his waist, screwed on the suppressor and stowed the gun in a special shoulder rig that he strapped on beneath the loose-fitting sweater.

After that it was just a question of waiting around until it was dark.

Possible routes across the border had been marked on one of the maps. This was no iron curtain frontier. There was no one-hundred-yard no-man's-land with watchtowers and searchlights and electrified fences. Certainly there were army patrols and checkpoints on the Ulster side, but dozens of mountain trails, farm tracks and country roads wound across without benefit of customs posts or immigration controls. Smuggling—arms into Ulster, cheap gasoline into the south, where it cost $5.60 a gallon—was a thriving industry despite the warlike situation in the north.

Bolan decided to take one of the southernmost routes marked on his map, over the high ground behind Sligo. The Bundoran area, he figured, where the border ran so close to the ocean, would most likely be more heavily policed.

Compared with the crowded motorways of Europe, the roads were astonishingly traffic-free. In an afternoon spent among lanes wide enough for no more than a single vehicle, Bolan only twice saw drivers having to back up to the nearest passing point.

Later, when night had fallen and there was nothing but stars between the clouds and the lights of an occasional hill farm to pierce the darkness, Bolan coaxed the Vespa through a network of unpaved roads until he was within a mile of the frontier.

According to his maps, the border ran through a depression between two humpback hills that rose a thousand feet above sea level. Most of the depression was formed by a stream that ran into Lough Melvin.

He braked to a halt on the final crest. The night was very still. The wind had dropped, and only a distant sheep bell broke the silence.

Riding down the grade into the valley, he thought, even with the tiny motor switched off, could alert border patrols on either side of the stream: if the dim beam from the single headlight didn't draw attention to him, the crunch of tires on the gravel surface of the roadway would. He left the scooter leaning against a tree and continued on foot.

Soon he could hear the burble of water over the swish of his combat boots through the roadside grass. The lane, he knew, turned west and followed the course of the river until it reached a bridge and the junction with a more important road a mile downstream. He decided to go east.

The bridge, and any place where the current was shallow, narrow and easy to cross, he reckoned, would be the most likely to be under surveillance. He waded across cornfields, pushed his way through thorny hedges and climbed gates for perhaps half a mile until he found a curve where the river flowed swift and deep, channeling a turbulent pool from the rock-strewn earth.

It was an unlikely place to choose for a crossing. He would cross there.

Bolan stripped to his quick-dry blacksuit, packing the jeans and sweater into the leather bag along with the cameras and other gear. With the straps of his shoulder rig, he fashioned a harness to fix the bag on top of his head. Then he slithered down the steep bank and into the river.

The water was ice-cold, numbing him to the bone. The pool was forty feet across.

He struck out for the far bank, his teeth chattering, swimming a head-in-air breaststroke to keep the grip above the seething current.

Bolan was a strong swimmer, but he was carried twenty yards downstream before he could kick his way to shore, grabbing the gnarled roots of a tree growing out of the bank in order to stop himself from being swept around the curve.

Gasping, he pulled himself onto the bank. He unstrapped the bag and exercised his arms and legs energetically until he had stopped shivering and the suit was dry again. Then he dressed and walked away from the river. He had crossed the border: he was in Ulster.

Beyond the bushes lining the bank he found himself in a field waist-deep in some unidentifiable crop. On the far side there was a rutted farm track, and this led to a slant of stubbled hillside over which there hung the sickly stench of flax rotting—the harvested stalks left to rot in shallow water-filled ditches.

The track skirted an unlit farmhouse and joined a country lane. Bolan had traveled perhaps a quarter of a mile before he was surprised by the second ambush.

4

The light blinded him. It blazed into brilliance as he stole around a corner of the lane.

"All right. Stay exactly where you are. Don't move," a voice called sharply from the darkness beyond the light.

Bolan moved.

The accent was clipped, British English. So it must be an army patrol. If it had been a wildcat band of the clandestine Protestant vigilantes who called themselves the Ulster Defense Volunteers, he would have frozen. The army only fired if it was attacked or an armed suspect fled after a warning. The paramilitary UDV shot first and asked questions later.

Bolan moved because of the contents of his bag. No sweat so far as his accreditation, the cameras and other gear were concerned, but among the forged papers were a canceled Manchester-Belfast plane ticket and a passport visa that showed he had passed through security control at Aldergrove airfield—both of them dated the following day.

If he had wanted to establish himself as an "illegal," nothing could do it more surely than showing those papers now, more than twelve hours before the documents were supposed to have been stamped.

There was a thicket of alders and young oak trees between a row of shrubs and the lane at the apex of the corner. The Executioner hurled himself behind the foliage and thrust the grip with its incriminating contents up into the fork of the tallest sapling.

The officer shouted. The searchlight—it was mounted on a Land Rover concealed behind a hedge on the far side of the lane—swung toward the thicket. Bolan heard the clump of army boots approaching, more than half a dozen men, he estimated.

"Sar'nt!" the British voice yelled. "Coming your way. Send two men down each side of the field."

"Sir!" a parade-ground roar replied. There followed a string of orders in ripe cockney. Bolan hoisted himself up a steep bank thick with undergrowth and tangled with briers. He heard the rustle of leaves and the swish of grasses left and right. The engine of the Land Rover burst into life; the searchlight moved out from behind the hedge. Behind Bolan long thin shadows reached for the bank as the dazzling glare penetrated the thicket, probing between the slender trunks of the saplings.

The soldiers advancing along the lane were very near now. At the top of the bank, Bolan dragged himself free of the briers scratching his face and hands, tearing at his sweater, and rolled out on the far side of the shrubs. In the reflected radiance he could see that he was on the fringe of a small cornfield. Light glinted on the barrels of guns carried by the men approaching on either side.

He dared not stand up. He would be silhouetted against the glare from the searchlight. There was no chance of avoiding the soldiers on the perimeter, and behind, the men of the patrol were already pushing their way through the briers.

There was only one route open to him: straight ahead through the standing crop. On the far side of the field a dark bulk, which he thought might be a woods, blotted out the stars. If he could make that, perhaps he could escape the patrol and come back later to retrieve his bag.

Fortunately the height of the bank stopped the searchlight beam from playing directly on the corn. There was a chance that he could crawl through the center of the field without the disturbed stalks giving his position away.

On elbows and knees, making as little noise as possible, Bolan began to force his way between the tough stalks.

The journey seemed interminable. Above him, the searchlight brightened and faded as the operator quartered the area. The soldiers' voices approached and receded. Every now and then the officer called a question.

But at last Bolan parted the final row of stems. There was a strip of rough grass approximately four yards wide separating the crop from the undergrowth at the edge of the woods. In the searchlight beam that split the darkness as he emerged from the corn he could see the headlights gleaming on the polished surface of a pair of regulation army boots.

"All right, lad," the voice of the cockney sergeant said quietly. "This 'ere's a Colt Commando submachine gun. It can put six hundred rounds into you in less than a minute. On your feet then, hands well away from your sides, and we'll take a little walk. I think the officer might like a word."

The officer was short, pink-faced, with a wispy blond mustache and china-blue eyes. There was something about him, just the same, that suggested he was a great deal tougher than his appearance implied. Like his men, he wore camouflage combat fatigues and a clover-red beret. They stood in a circle around Bolan as the young man leaned an elegant elbow on the Land Rover's hood and asked the questions.

"Keep it short," he said. "What the hell are you doing here?"

"Walking," Bolan said. "It's not illegal, is it?"

"American!" the officer observed. "That's a turnup for the book, I must say. What are you, a salesman touting arms for the Provisionals?"

"A news photographer," Bolan said, "if it matters."

"It matters a hell of a lot. Show me your papers—and your accreditation."

"I don't have them with me."

"Well, well. How convenient!" Sarcasm did not suit the young man's character. It made him seem precocious, almost childish. But the Webley in his right hand was no toy.

"Over here," he snapped. "Face the Land Rover. Lean forward, hands on the roof, feet spread. Sergeant . . . ?"

Bolan obeyed. There was nothing else he could do. The sergeant frisked him and withdrew the Beretta from its holster. "Interesting," the officer drawled. He stuck the silenced automatic in his belt. "Journalist, eh? Normal tool of the trade, no doubt."

"I carry it for protection. There are a lot of bad guys around these parts."

"You can say that again. But a *silenced* gun? That seems just a shade professional. Perhaps you'd like to explain what you think you're doing here, armed with this weapon, swanning around in a sensitive high-security area with no papers and no accreditation?"

Bolan decided to gamble. He would bluff it out.

"Come to that," he said hotly, "what the hell are *you* and your troops doing here? You know damn well you have no right to cross over, even if you *are* on the track of some republican fugitive."

"No *right*?" The officer sounded scandalized. "We have every right to be wherever we want to be. We can operate throughout the whole of County Fermanagh if we choose to."

*"Fermanagh?"* It was Bolan's turn to sound horrified. "Oh, hell," he said with well-simulated astonishment,

"don't say I crossed the goddamn border without realizing it!"

"Assuming for the moment that you did," the Englishman said, "what would you have been doing on the other side, armed, prowling around without your camera, your press pass or even a light to show you the way?"

"Prospecting," Bolan said. "Taking the temperature, as we say, of the theater of operations. Seeing how tight security is on the southern side of the frontier, what the chances would be of fugitives from the north getting across undetected. After I'd filed the piece, I figured on making it into Ulster and doing a companion feature on conditions on the other side. But if you're actually following people across with an entire patrol..." He shook his head helplessly.

It didn't work.

"Come off it, chum," the young officer said. "You know bloody well we don't cross the border. In any circumstances. And do you really expect me to believe that if a chap sussing out the ground doesn't *know* the river is the border, he'll strip off, swim across with a pack on his head, when there's a perfectly good bridge a mile downstream?"

For the first time, Bolan realized the patrol must be equipped with infrared night-vision field glasses; they must have been watching him ever since he had put on his dry clothes.

"You're not the usual shot-in-the-back brigand we have to deal with," the officer said. "Why don't you come clean? For a start, where's the bag you brought across with you?"

"What bag?"

"The suitcase, the valise, the grip. Shall we stop horsing around now? Where did you stow it?"

"I don't know what you're talking about," Bolan said.

The young man compressed his lips. "Sar'nt? Take three men and search the hedgerows a hundred yards back. If you don't find it, try the field. Watch out for booby traps, though. You know the drill.''

The NCO saluted and departed with his men. "You and I meanwhile," the officer said to Bolan, "will sit quietly in the Land Rover while we call up HQ on the radio and ask what we're supposed to do with you." He paused, eyeing the Executioner's muscular height. "On second thought, why bother to sit?"

He reached into the army utility and unhooked a microphone from beneath the dashboard. There was a great deal of static, but eventually he raised a response. "Foster here, sir," he said. "Number Three Platoon, B Company, Sector Theta. We have an American. Claims to be a news photographer. Caught him crossing the border. Armed. No papers. He was carrying some kind of case, but he junked it before we could nab him."

"Find it," a similarly clipped voice said through the static.

"Sir. Shall we bring him in, sir? Or do you want us to keep him here until you send the MPs?"

"For God's sake, Foster—" the voice battling to overcome the atmospheric crackle was irritable "—you know the form. Hold your damned American until we contact you. There's a red on here . . . bastards chucked a grenade at one of our jeeps in Cookstown . . . holed up in some farmhouse. In touch . . . you later."

"Very good, sir."

Foster replaced the mike. "More second thoughts," he said to the driver. "You take the rest of the chaps aboard and help Sergeant Williams with the searchlight. I'll keep an eye on this merchant until you've found whatever it was he chucked away."

"Yessir." The remainder of the patrol climbed into the Land Rover, the man with the searchlight swung it down the lane and the driver made a neat three-point turn and steered the vehicle slowly in the direction of the farm and the river. The searchlight beam ranged right and left to pick up the sergeant and his men probing the undergrowth on each side of the lane.

Bolan offered up a silent prayer that they wouldn't start looking upward.

The young officer switched on a flashlight. The Webley was pointed at Bolan's chest. "What's your name?" he demanded.

"John Foster Dulles," Bolan replied. He didn't know why he said it. Maybe it was subconsciously suggested by the Englishman's own name.

"Very droll," Foster said. "Now listen to me, cock. Let's not fool around. If you don't satisfy us, you'll be handed over to the SAS boys. You may have heard of them. They play kind of rough."

Bolan had heard of them. Britain's Special Air Service—the name was a carryover from the formation's beginnings in the Second World War—was an elite undercover unit of antiriot commandos with a reputation for rescuing hostages, handling hijack situations the hard way and eliminating terrorists without the formalities of arrest or trial.

Foster continued. "You'll save yourself a lot of trouble if you level with us—that's what you Yanks say, isn't it?—and tell us what you're really doing here. You may even *be* a clever-clever newspaperman for all I know. But unless you oblige, there'll be tears before bedtime, I promise you. So why not—"

Foster broke off when there was a shout from the sergeant eighty yards down the lane. "I think we found something, sir!" The searchlight was angled into the hedgerow on the opposite side from Bolan's thicket. The Land Rover edged nearer.

"Watch out, Williams . . ." Foster began.

The livid flash of the explosion printed the landscape against the dark in the thousandth of a second before the thunderous blast tore at Bolan's eardrums.

A sheet of flame shot skyward. The gas tank of the Land Rover, wheels in the air on the far side of the lane, erupted in a blazing fireball. Burning debris arched over to drop into the fields on either side. Something soft and heavy thumped to the macadam just out of range of Foster's flashlight beam.

In the instant the young man's attention was seized, the immature mouth open in horrified surprise, Bolan acted.

"Sorry about this, son," he said truthfully. He chopped Foster on the side of the neck, just over the carotid artery, with the hard, flat edge of his hand. As the man crumpled, Bolan slammed a left cross that connected with his jaw. Foster hit the ground.

Bolan ran toward the inferno, his ears still deafened by the explosion.

There was nothing he could do. The Land Rover was a mangled wreck lodged in the far hedgerow and blazing furiously. Corn in the field beyond had been set on fire. Orange light pulsated on the underside of a black smoke cloud boiling upward from the burning tires.

The patrol had been decimated. Bodies and parts of bodies lay everywhere. Some looked like bundles of gory rags, others were no more than shapeless masses of flesh smoking in the flickering illumination. The sergeant's corpse hung like some grotesque fruit among the bare branches of a dead tree.

The Executioner satisfied himself that there were no survivors. Judging from the position of the crater, the mine had been buried at the edge of the road, and whatever it was that had attracted Williams's attention must have been placed there simply as a decoy, to draw the patrol that way. A crumpled imitation-leather valise, lying twenty feet away half covered in leaves and branches ripped by the blast, seemed the most likely bet.

Bolan's flesh crawled as he remembered how close to the mine he must have been when he had crept up the lane from the river. Nauseated by the stench and the useless waste of young lives, he picked his way carefully—the roadway was bright with blood—back to the thicket and maneuvered his bag down from the tree. Then he returned to Foster's unconscious form and retrieved his Beretta, laying the young man down in the grass at the side of the road. He would suffer no more than a bruised jaw.

That wasn't a bad trade against being blown to bits.

Bolan turned his back on the carnage and the guttering flames and got out of there. The mission, as always, came first. In any case, the place would soon be swarming with firemen and salvage teams.

In fact, a half hour had passed before Bolan heard the seesaw bray of sirens and saw, across the fields, the flashing blue strobes of police cars, ambulances and fire trucks. Country folk living near the border knew better than to interfere in the war between the British army and the IRA. Following the explosion, no lights had appeared in the windows of the farm near the river, and the scattered houses Bolan had passed remained dark and silent.

Perhaps it was considered prudent to allow enough time for the terrorists to get away, or return to the far side of the border, before anyone telephoned the nearest town to report the incident.

Perhaps the inhabitants themselves were terrorized.

Perhaps Foster had come to and made the call himself.

In any case the delay profited the Executioner, too. It allowed him to get well clear of the area before it was saturated with security forces.

Bolan walked for ten miles before he rested in a barn on the far side of the hills. At dawn he crossed the narrowest part of Lough Erne at Enniskillen and waited for an early morning bus that would ferry him across the wildest parts of County Tyrone to Dungannon. From there he persuaded a cabdriver to take him around the southern end of Lough Neagh to the airport terminal.

Originally a Second World War field from which the RAF's Coastal Command patrolled the U-boat-haunted waters around Ireland, Aldergrove, on the shores of the lough, is now Belfast's international airport. It boasts every modern navigational aid except good weather. Farmers living in that part of County Antrim will tell you that when you can see the Sperrin Mountains, away beyond the far side of the lake, that means it is going to rain. If you cannot see the Sperrins, then it is raining already.

Bolan saw no mountains.

He pulled the raincoat from his bag and belted it around him, pacing up and down in the rain until the Manchester plane arrived. Then he joined the line of passengers waiting to board the airport bus that would take them into the city.

At last—at least as far as paperwork was concerned—he was "legally" in Ulster.

## 5

The shot that killed Derek Osborne was fired from a stained concrete balcony on the fifth floor of a block of low-income apartments. There was a barricade of overturned cars and paving stones torn from the sidewalk sealing off the street at one side of the block, and an angry Protestant crowd had gathered at the intersection to hurl insults at the Catholics who lived on the far side of the barrier. Stones and bottles, too, had begun to fly when Osborne moved his platoon between them with riot shields and CS cartridges at the ready.

"Belfast is not like any normal city, Mr. Belasko," Captain Simon Gage told Mack Bolan. "Apart from the snob neighborhoods, what the media people call the A and B categories, the whole damned place is divided up into Protestant and Catholic areas. It's like bloody Beirut, except there it's Christian and Muslim . . . Shit, no. It's *worse* than Beirut! There you have the town cut in two: Here they have enclaves cheek by jowl all over the shop."

Bolan held the Nikon up to his eye and shot the crowd scene. He had used his press card to persuade the military authorities to let him accompany an army detail on its tour of the trouble spots. Gage was a tall clean-shaven man with a long upper lip and eyes that often narrowed like those of a helmsman peering through a squall of rain. His own men were being held in reserve, in case the situation worsened to a point where plastic bullets would be needed. They were drawn up behind a line of armored scout cars.

Bolan turned around to frame the view in the opposite direction. The street sloped downhill. The rectangular reflex lens showed him descending terraces of gray-tiled roofs beyond which lay the steely waters of Belfast Lough, that long arm of the sea that was in fact the estuary of the Lagan River.

The hub of the city, where apart from occasional security checks life proceeded much as usual, was grouped around the head of the lough. Through the viewfinder he saw factory chimneys, high-rise office blocks, the cranes and gantries of a shipyard and the long finger of an airstrip that belonged to the Short and Harland aviation works. Behind this the softly rounded hills of County Down formed an undulating horizon.

Hearing raised voices, Bolan turned back toward the barricade. Captain Gage was trying unsuccessfully to persuade a Protestant pastor to use his influence with the mob threatening to swarm across and attack the Catholics.

"...never thought to hear the like," the clergyman said, fuming. "To think I should live to see English soldiers, under the command of an Englishman, take up arms against loyal subjects of the queen on behalf of a gang of hooligan Papish—"

"They are not taking up arms," Gage snapped. It was clear that he found it hard to keep his temper in the face of bigotry. "Their equipment, so far, is purely protective. And as they are only trying to keep the two sides apart to prevent bloodshed, I fail to see how you can argue they're working on *behalf* of anyone. Unless, of course, bloodshed is the aim of your side."

"A soldier's first duty, surely, is to protect Her Majesty's subjects. These people accept no allegiance to—"

"A soldier's duty is to do what he's told," Gage interrupted. "And in this case we have been told to stop the rioting."

"Over and above that, surely, these men have a duty to protect—"

"It's a duty they wouldn't be called on to perform if you, sir, could see your way to fulfill *your* duty as a man of peace," Gage said tightly. "Would you not just walk between them and the barricade? Perhaps say a few words to the more militant ones . . . ?"

"I would not. A man has a right to protect his family and his property if they are in danger," the pastor shouted. He was a thickset man with a small mouth and angry eyes.

Bolan photographed the confrontation, the motorized Nikon continuing to record the development into a battle of what had started out as a routine patrol.

"It is because of that right," Gage said wearily, "that the Catholics have built their barricades—and been permitted to keep them." He had opened his mouth to say something more when the rifle shot cracked out over the brawling of the crowd.

For a moment there was a lull and then an incoherent cry of alarm from someone as Osborne reeled out of the line of helmeted men, spun around, dropped to his knees and then pitched suddenly forward to lie facedown in the road with his arms outflung.

Something moved at the outer, upper limit of Bolan's field of vision. His head jerked around to stare at the apartment block.

A pane of glass in a balcony door caught the light as it swung slowly shut. A silhouette showed momentarily behind a lace curtain and was gone. Blue smoke hazed the air over the balcony, and then a gust of wind dispersed that, too. The mob resumed its baying.

Apart from the khaki figure sprawled in the widening pool of blood, it was as though the shot had never been fired.

Soldiers were grouped around the stricken officer. Bolan was already sprinting across to the entrance of the apartment block. In the instant of action his combat reflexes prevailed.

Simon Gage was close behind, followed by a sergeant and two men. But the apartments were empty. The clock overlooked a Protestant area, and self-styled vigilantes, fearing it would be used as a stronghold against them, had forced the Catholic tenants to leave. There were signs of fire damage around several doors on the street level.

On the fifth floor, four apartments faced the street. At the end of the hallway a door to the fire escape stood ajar. The NCO ran to check it while Gage and the two men did the apartments.

"The doors are all locked, sir," one of the men said.

"Kick them in," Gage said. "I'll take the responsibility."

Except for a few worthless sticks, two of the flats had been cleared of furniture, but the others were still in their overstuffed prime. There were crucifixes and religious texts on the walls, brown velour cloths draping the tables, silver-framed family photos and tea caddies in orange and gold on the cumbersome buffets in cheap mahogany veneer. Bolan pushed aside an armchair and opened the window leading to the balcony. The noise of the crowd was uglier still from up here. They had carried Osborne away and laid him down behind one of the scout cars.

Something gleamed in the pale daylight as it lay in one corner of the balcony. Gage picked it up. It was a spent cartridge case, brass, high-velocity .30-caliber ammunition for a Springfield or Garand express rifle. Near it, two cigarette stubs had been ground out beside pots of dispirited geraniums. Five more butts scarred the parquet-pattern linoleum just inside the door.

"Gallaher's Blue," Gage said, examining the stubs. "Local brand, but it doesn't mean a thing. They sell millions a day. Bastard must have been waiting here some time."

The sergeant came back shaking his head. "Not a chance, sir," he said. "Leads to a vacant lot at the back of the block—but there's a high wall and anyone stepping off the escape would be invisible from the road and from the street behind the barricade."

"Think that's the way he went, Harrison?"

"Could be, sir," the sergeant said. "Unless he came off the escape on one of the intermediate floors, waited for us to pass on the way up and then just walked through, down the stairs and out the main entrance."

"Oh, damn," Gage said. "I hadn't thought of that."

But later, when he was reporting to his CO in the requisitioned country house on the shore of Lough Neagh, he was more positive. Derek Osborne had died before they could get him to a hospital, and Gage was urging that the army should mount a full-scale inquiry to smoke out, with the help of the police, his murderer.

Colonel Alleyn seemed unimpressed. "The police will do everything they can," he said. "They're equipped for this sort of thing. We're not. Besides, we can't start meddling in CID work. Not our cup of tea at all."

"Surely, sir, it's our cup of tea if someone deliberately shoots down our officers?"

"Osborne was a particular friend of yours, Gage, wasn't he?"

"Yes, sir. He was. We were at OTU together. I knew him quite well. But that's not—"

"Look, Gage. Naturally we're all kayoed by this. Osborne was a fine officer. It's a terrible waste. Every man's death diminishes me, and all that. But it's one of the risks of the trade. Can happen to any of us, at any time. Some trigger-happy fool chooses that particular moment to loose off. Derek happened to stop one. That's the trouble with these blasted riot situations—could have been you, could have been me.''

"Yes, sir. But it wasn't. It was Osborne. And he didn't *happen* to stop one. He stopped *the* one.''

Colonel Alleyn got up from his desk. He was a short man with a red face, sandy hair and a neat mustache that was brushed carefully outward. He walked over to the wide window and stared across the sweep of sodden lawn at the lough. "Let me get this straight,'' he said. "Are you suggesting... Do you mean to say you think Osborne was shot *deliberately*? Because he *was* Osborne? Are you saying it wasn't a stray bullet at all, that he was actually a chosen target? Is that what you're saying?''

Gage drew a deep breath. "Yes, sir,'' he said. "It is.''

"But, good God, man—'' Alleyn swung around to fix him with a piercing gaze ''—why on earth should anyone do that? Why? What would be the point? Osborne's only been here a week. He couldn't have fallen foul of these buggers to that extent. What could anyone gain, shooting him?''

"I don't know, sir. That's why I think we should set up an inquiry. To find out the answers to those questions.''

"Captain Gage!'' Breath jetted from the colonel's nostrils as he compressed his lips and sighed in exasperation. "What conceivable reasons have you for making these allegations?''

Mack Bolan stayed quietly in the background. As he was a witness to the shooting, he had contrived—by keeping a very low profile—to accompany Simon Gage back to his HQ, but only on the strict understanding that anything he heard was off the record. The fact that he had promised Alleyn to shoot a photo-feature showing the officers of the regiment off duty, as human beings, may have helped.

"Several reasons, sir," Gage was saying. "The fact that only one round was fired, for a start."

"Yes, but—"

"Once they saw they'd got their man, there was no need for any more. If it'd been some fanatic extremist, a hysteric or any other kind of nutter, he'd have gone on firing. Let the bastards have it! They don't stop at a single shot."

"Perhaps not. I still don't see—"

"And the time factor, sir. Remember the killer smoked seven cigarettes while he was waiting. Allowing for extra-hard puffs because he was nervous, that still means he was there between forty and fifty minutes. And the fuss down below was going on all that time. So whatever else it was, it can't have been a heat-of-the-moment affair, can it?"

"I suppose not."

"In other words, the sniper was waiting for something specific."

"And what," Alleyn asked, "makes you think that something specific was Derek Osborne?"

"Surely that's obvious, sir? The fact that they got him. And the fact that once they had, they didn't fire again."

The colonel switched his glance to the Executioner. "You're outside all this, Belasko," he said. "From an objective point of view, what do you think?"

Bolan, too, had been looking out the window. A breeze trembled the leaves of the lakeside alders, stirring the leaden wavelets into dirty gray foam. On the far side of the water in County Tyrone, the Sperrins rose hard and sharp against a pale sky.

He came to with a start. "What do I think? I think it's odd that the one round fired was a .30-caliber slug. To me that means a Springfield-Mauser or a Garand. From what I hear, the guys most likely to fire at a British officer would be toting a Kalashnikov or even an Uzi SMG."

"That is a point," Gage said admiringly.

"You certainly know your small arms—for a news-hawk," Colonel Alleyn said dryly.

"With all the wars going on these days, you can hardly help it," Bolan said. He silently warned himself to keep to his cover. Bolan was a master at role camouflage, and Alleyn's comment reminded him how easily that cover could slip. Aloud he added, "That seems to me—as an outsider—to support Gage's view that this was a deliberate hit, with that specific target. Maybe even a contract job, when you consider the weapon."

The colonel shook his head. "It doesn't follow, you know. Granted the sniper was there for a special purpose. Granted he had to wait for a long time. Granted, even, that a single shot achieved that purpose—it still doesn't necessarily have to be Osborne."

"Sir?"

"I mean that Osborne's death—the fact that it *was* Osborne and not somebody else—could still have been a matter of chance. An accident if you like."

"I'm afraid I can't see how, sir," Gage said.

"Well, suppose," Alleyn said patiently, "that the aim of the operation was simply to kill a British officer, any British army officer. He'd know there would be one around sometime if there was trouble brewing, so all he'd have to do would be to wait until the unit—any unit—went into action. And the unit happened to be ours, and the first officer to show was Osborne, that's all."

"But what would be the point of killing an officer at random?" the captain objected. "I can't think what possible advantage it would bring either side."

"Can you think of any advantage in killing Osborne *as* Osborne?"

Gage hesitated. "Well, no, sir, not really."

"Then don't try," Colonel Alleyn said shortly. "And that's an order, Gage. I don't want any nonsense about unofficial investigations. I don't want any of my officers messing around playing detective. We'll leave this sorry business to the police, right?''

''Very good, sir.''

But it wasn't good at all, Bolan reflected. Personally he was certain that Gage was right. Brognola's words came back to him. *'''British Troops Run Amok in Catholic Neighborhood'—that'll be the headline—in revenge for the murder of one of their officers. And some poor bastard will have been wasted two or three days before, just to make the script believable.''*

A poor bastard named Osborne?

If so, Colonel Alleyn was right, too.

And if he was, if in fact this was phase one in the plot Brognola had outlined, then time was vital. And there was even less of it available than he had imagined. Two or three days max and this particular hell would break loose.

If?

There was little doubt in Bolan's mind. Brognola had mentioned apparent American involvement, the use of American arms.

Both the Springfield-Mauser and the Garand were American ex-GI issue rifles. The .30-caliber round was rare in Europe.

It looked as if the Executioner had been offered, gratis and by chance, a ringside seat for round one of this particular contest.

How the hell was he going to get up there, in the ring, and take out one of the fighters?

Without anyone seeing him?

Derek Osborne's murder was his only lead. If he was to penetrate the grimy depths of Ulster's terrorist underworld and flush out the scheming conspirators lurking there, the killer's trail would be the only way in.

And whether or not he knew it, Captain Simon Gage, so clearly dissatisfied with official reaction to the death of his friend, was going to help him point his feet in the right direction.

## 6

The guy in the trench coat started the fight quite deliberately. Sipping beer in a booth at the back of the saloon, Bolan and Simon Gage had been watching for several minutes as he worked up to it.

First he attempted unsuccessfully to join in three separate conversations around the bar. He was snubbed again when he tried to attach himself to a party of two men and two girls sitting at one of the tables. Finally he stood, swaying slightly as he cradled his large whiskey, glowering around the low-ceilinged room and muttering to himself. The guy was tall, lean and wiry, with eyes that glittered dangerously.

Then it happened.

Neither the snapping of the stem when it broke nor the crash of the glass on the floor actually made much noise, but the effect was startling.

In the sudden silence, heads turned, people swung around from the bar with tankards halfway to their mouths, a man stood on a chair to see better. Somewhere a woman giggled nervously.

*"Bastards!"* the man at the bar roared suddenly. Without warning, without even looking, he swept an arm backward along the polished bar counter. Bottles and glasses smashed to the floor. A wired soda container toppled, rolled over the edge and exploded against the brass rail below. Water splashed from an overturned jug.

A perspiring shirtsleeved barman ran up. "What's goin' on? What the divil d'ye think you're doin'?" he demanded. "Sure you cannot behave like that in here now! Come on, away out of it...." He seized the offending arm across the bar.

The man in the trench coat shook him off angrily. "Hypocritical bloody bastards!" he shouted, slurring the words. "Think themselves too good to talk to a God-fearin'—"

"Now come on, come on," the barman urged. "That's quite enough of that. Outside, you."

He raised a hinged section in the bar and hurried through. A man in a white linen jacket appeared from a doorway marked Private. Together they grasped the troublemaker by the arms and began to run him toward the exit. He heaved, dragging them from side to side in a series of frenzied lurches. The three of them cannoned into a group of drinkers at the bar.

"Watch out what you're doing, there!" one of them cried wrathfully, dabbing spilled beer from his lapels.

"Ah, leave the feller be, George," another called. "Sure it's only some Papist drunk, for God's sake."

"Throw him out!"

"Would you look at that!"

"Jaysus—do you hear the *language* of him!"

The drunk was swearing viciously as he fought. With his two captors he stumbled into a table and fell over. For a moment there was a tangle of limbs thrashing on the floor, then they rolled against the men around the bar again and brought two of them down. And the next minute there was a free-for-all raging all along the bar. Voices were raised, chairs and tables overturned, fists flew.

By the time two more barmen had run in from the lounge and restored order, the original offender had vanished.

Bolan was not surprised. By any of it.

The guy had been looking for trouble, that was for sure. He was almost a caricature of the fictional IRA conspirator—pale face, belted trench coat, a hat with the brim turned down all the way around. Maybe the role was a little overplayed even. For when you came down to it, this was just one more quarrelsome Irish drunk in a bar.

Or Bolan would have thought so if they hadn't pushed in out of the rain at the same time, and he happened to have noticed that the man was stone-cold sober. . . .

A topcoated fat man who smelled like a wet dog sank into a vacant seat opposite Bolan and Simon Gage. "Well, isn't that the thing!" he said. "Fighting off an afternoon in Geraghty's Wine Lodge! Did you ever see the like?"

"It was certainly unexpected," Gage said.

"It was that. Now if it had been Corcoran's . . ." The fat man left the sentence unfinished and called over the barman. "Hey, Nicholas," he said, "I think you might put down another glass here and a couple of bottles of stout. I don't think they would go to waste, you know."

"Right you are, Mr. McGeehan."

"And you gentlemen? Just a minnit there, Nick. Would the both of you do me the honor of taking a glass with me? For I see by your accents that you're not of the country, and I'd hate you to get away with the wrong impression of this city."

Bolan and Gage exchanged glances. "It's very kind of you, sir . . ." Bolan began.

"Not a word. A stout, is it? The same as meself? That'll be four bottles and three glasses then, Nick, if you please."

"It's very kind of you," Gage echoed.

"Not a bit of it. A pleasure to find strangers here. For it's a quare time, and that's the truth, to run across a tourist in Belfast. Are you long over from the other side? Or perhaps you're in business?"

"As a matter of fact," Gage said, "I'm in the army."

"Ah. Over for the riots, you might say." McGeehan chuckled gustily. "Dear knows how long *they*'ll be going on."

"Not much longer, I hope," the soldier said briefly. Discussion of the political situation was discouraged.

"A hope we all share, sir. And your transatlantic friend? I doubt not he's seconded to the forces of law and order!"

"I'm a photographer," Bolan said.

"Fair enough." The fat man seized a bottle of stout as the barman stooped to unload his tray. Pouring, he raised his glass to Bolan and Gage and drank the contents in a single long draft.

"Cheers," Simon Gage said.

McGeehan sighed contentedly and wiped the froth from his mouth with the back of his hand. "And what," he asked Bolan, "do you make of the fisticuffs, the fight there that we just witnessed?" He poured his second bottle. "I'll bet you wished you had the old Nikon in here with you, eh? Or even a trusty Hasselblad."

"My assignment is for military confrontations," Bolan said evenly. "As for the brawl...well, I guess it was just that the guy was drunk, looking for a chance to pick a quarrel, to accuse the customers of religious prejudice. Guy with an outsize chip on his shoulder."

"Is that so? Do you really think so?" The fat man appeared to be surprised. "Looking for a fight he certainly was, but that he'd taken drink I'm not all that convinced."

"Oh, come on! He was smashed out of his skull, swaying all over the place!" Bolan trailed the bait deliberately. He wanted to know what the fat man was getting at. *Was* he getting at something? Was this after all an entirely chance meeting?

Obligingly McGeehan rose to it. "Stocious you'd think," he agreed. "Falling about certainly. Rolling on the floor and fighting with fellas. Using language. It's my opinion that's what you were supposed to think.''

''You mean he was putting it on?'' Gage said.

McGeehan laid a sausagelike finger alongside his nose. ''Now what do *you* think?'' he said.

''But why would a man do that?''

''Oh, now your guess is as good as mine,'' the fat man replied. ''There could be a dozen reasons. Come that, why would a British army officer in mufti and an American photographer spend a whole day of that officer's leave on a methodic pub crawl across town, first in the Catholic and then in the Protestant areas of the city?''

''Look, I don't really see—'' Gage began.

But the fat man cut him short. ''A dozen reasons,'' he repeated. ''A dozen reasons. I just mention it by way of example.''

He gulped down the remainder of his stout and stood. ''A pleasure, gentlemen,'' he said. ''Let me leave you my card. If ever I can be of any help to either of you . . .''

Bolan stared after him, the pasteboard rectangle held absently in one hand, as the swing doors sighed shut on the rainy afternoon. How had he known? What could he have meant? And that crack about the cameras? Both Nikon and Hasselblad were well-known marques, especially popular with newsmen. But even so . . .

''Very rum,'' Gage said, in agreement with the Executioner's unspoken thoughts. ''And a little worrying.''

For, as a start to their mutual attempt to penetrate the local underworld, Bolan and Gage had in fact spent the whole day going from pub to pub, keeping their ears open, hoping to hear a phrase, a single word, that might give them a lead to Derek Osborne's killer.

The Executioner had not revealed the reasons for his own interest; since Gage, with a seventy-two-hour leave due him, had vowed to disobey orders and try his hand at a murder inquiry, Bolan had offered to help all he could on the excuse that he might get a story out of it.

This of course was the answer to the fat man's final question. But there was no answer to the one that prompted it.

Why would a guy made up to look like a revolutionary feign drunkenness in order to start a fight in a saloon—and then disappear?

There might, as the knowledgeable Mr. McGeehan had suggested, be a dozen different reasons. Bolan didn't give a damn what they were because he had seen the man in the trench coat before.

Less than twenty-four hours previously he had been drinking at the bar of Gage's own lakeside mess in the uniform of a British artillery major....

## 7

It was the explosion that wrecked the facade of the bank in Royal Avenue, or more precisely, the excited conversation in the pub across the road after the bomb had gone off, that really gave Bolan the idea.

He was to meet Gage in a place called McNulty's Cellars at ten-fifteen in the morning. Walking through the city center on the way from his hotel, he glanced up High Street toward the Albert clock tower, leaning every year a little more to one side in its precarious position on the clays at the side of the Lagan River. It was five after ten: he was early.

Crossing to Royal Avenue, he waited for a bus to swish past him on the wet roadway, and started moving toward the gold curlicues surmounting the double doors of McNulty's Cellars, when suddenly the force of concussion knocked him to the pavement. He spun around on his butt, let go of his camera case and then rolled over and over until he came to rest in the gutter, with his shoulders jammed against the curb. The noise of the detonation was only just registering as he scrambled upright again.

A dense cloud of brown smoke masked the sober facade of the bank building across the street. Brickwork and fragments of broken glass were still showering to the ground. People milled around on the opposite sidewalk; there was a lot of shouting. Bolan shook his head to try to clear the ringing in his ears and went to retrieve the camera case.

The bus had been blown over as it had taken the corner, and all its windows had been shattered by the blast. Passengers were extricating themselves through the empty frames, picking broken glass from their clothes. Blood streamed from a superficial cut on one woman's forehead, but miraculously nobody appeared to be seriously injured.

At the bank, the bomb had blown out a few windows, buckled a length of iron railings and destroyed one pillar of the ornate portico, whose coping and balustrade had then crashed to the ground. Again, nobody appeared to have been hurt.

Bolan shouldered his way through the fast-growing crowd and proceeded to the saloon. McNulty's Cellars was one of those instant-ancient places, with seats fashioned from sherry casks and lovingly preserved spiderwebs screening the light from lead-pane windows. It was filling up with eyewitnesses of the explosion, all talking at once.

"If I'd not changed me mind and gone back for that second pack of Gallahers..."

"Not a bloody peeler to be seen! Where are they at all?"

*"Hey, Paddy! Another John Jameson, two Bush liqueurs."*

"I'm thinkin' it'll be them university fellas up to Queen's. Them student fellas. Awful uppity, some of 'em are."

"Och, away outta that! Students don't throw bombs!"

"Some did today, but."

"Man, dear, those were no students. That bomb was put there by the Papists..."

*"Three by the neck, two half ones and three glasses."*

"Students or bloody Papists, what's the difference?"

"Want your head examined? This was an Army job. I'm tellin' you. One of Rafferty's specials."

"If I'd passed that way just five seconds earlier...!"

"Whoever fuckin' put it there, the bloody Republicans are goin' to be out of bombs by the end of the month. That was the fourth this week!"

*"A port-and-lemon, two Scotch, and a Black Velvet for Mr. Rothschild here in the corner...."*

Bolan lowered his glass of beer slowly to the table. But that was the answer, of course! Out of the mouths of babes and whoever. Somebody had said the bomb was "an Army job," and in the context that had to mean the IRA, the Irish Republican Army. Another guy had said they'd soon be out of bombs, the rate they were going.

Whether or not they were right, whether or not the bank bomb was an IRA job, the principle held good: underground organizations had to have arms and ammunition; the extremists were always looking for weapons.

Bolan signaled the waiter calling out the orders that he was ready for a refill.

He remembered Foster, the young British officer whose men had been decimated by the buried mine in Fermanagh. What was that crack he had made?

*"What are you? A salesman touting arms for the Provisionals?"*

Yeah, that was it.

And why not?

If terrorists had to have arms, they must always be on the lookout for fresh supplies. And you couldn't just buy them over the counter, even in Ireland.

According to Hal Brognola, this threatened IRA coup that would wreck the XP-29 negotiations involved "U.S. money and U.S. materials." The caliber of the bullet that killed Derek Osborne suggested that at least the latter part of that was true.

If the coup was successful and a civil war was provoked, the terrorists would need more weaponry. If it was squashed, they would be eager to replace the stuff they had lost. And since Bolan's own work in Athens, along with his CIA and MI6 colleagues, had at least temporarily dried up one source of supply, they should be in the market for another.

Right now.

And who better placed to approach them as a possible supplier than another American? An American using press assignments as a cover.

If he *was* an arms salesman—perhaps not a salesman but someone with a grudge, a guy with weapons available and a reason to allow the IRA to get hold of them—wouldn't that be the best way to contact the bosses of the illegal organization? And this guy Rafferty, whoever he was, that the drinkers in the saloon blamed for the bank bomb?

"Rafferty's kind of a wildcat leader," Simon Gage told Bolan ten minutes later. "You're familiar with the storyboard?"

"Tell me again," Bolan said.

"The IRA was originally the paramilitary wing of the Republican Sinn Fein party. When the party achieved independence for Ireland in 1921, it continued by legal and diplomatic means to press for the return of Ulster. That wasn't good enough for the Army. They continued by illegal, military and terrorist means. There were bomb outrages in Britain before the Second World War. During the war, they helped the German intelligence services. Afterward, when we decided to give Ulster Catholics a fairer crack of the whip, they hotted up their activity again."

"And the Provisionals, if I read you right, claimed the Dublin-based old guard wasn't hotting it up enough and broke away to form a rival HQ in the north?"

"Right," Gage said. "But for the real tearaways, the lunatic fringe, even they were too soft. Rafferty's the man who recruited this wildcat breakaway cell that's causing all the trouble. There's a parallel with the split between Abu Nidal's random killers and Arafat's original PLO."

"I don't know that I'd call the Provisionals soft," Bolan said grimly. "If we're talking about bombings and brutality and multiple murders, they've pulled off thirty major outrages in the past fifteen years, against thirty-three by Carlos and the PFLP, nineteen by Baader-Meinhof and their followers, and a dozen each by Abu Nidal and Black September. And that doesn't take into account the scores of individual 'executions' they're responsible for here."

"Including the murder of Derek Osborne," Gage said. "If that was an IRA affair. But it could just as well have been the Unionist extremists. Don't forget we were protecting a Catholic area when he was shot."

For a moment Bolan did not reply. He was in a difficult position. The Englishman was determined to track down the killers of his friend—and for his money they could be either side of the political-religious fence. Bolan had every reason to believe it was an IRA murder, the first step in the conspiracy he had been told to stamp out. All the evidence pointed that way. But he could not tell Gage this.

He dared not reveal the details of his own assignment; he was stuck with the role of news photographer, helping out in the hope of a scoop.

There was a risk, therefore, that time and energy would be wasted trying to penetrate the Unionist underground.

The Executioner could see no way of avoiding this without revealing his real reasons. He decided therefore to try out the arms salesman idea on Gage . . . and after that play it by ear.

"Hey, I think you've got something there!" Gage exclaimed when Bolan broached the subject. "And it happens, in the circs, to be a damn sight better idea then you realize!"

Bolan frowned. "Come again?"

The Britisher narrowed his eyes, staring through and beyond the drinkers at the bar. "I know of an arms dump, a secret army cache, that could be used as bait," he said at last.

"That can't be bad," Bolan said.

"It's strictly a reserve," Gage said. "Part of a contingency plan that would only be actuated in the event of a total breakdown in the rule of law. If there was to be an escalation of civil strife, for instance, with the whole bloody country split on a religious basis. Or if one or the other of the extremist factions tried to seize power. That kind of thing. Not to be used in any other circumstances. But all officers above a certain rank have been briefed about it so that they could make use of it if the chain of command was broken in an emergency."

"Where is it?"

"In the Mourne Mountains, not far from the border. I don't know if Whitehall expects the south to invade, to protect their sympathizers here! But that's where it is, and damned inconvenient, too."

"How secret is it?"

"Well, of course, the locals know of its existence, which means for sure the opposition will know, too. But they have no idea of its extent. And they don't know the most important thing about it."

"Which is?"

The man's eyes slitted again. "I shouldn't be telling you this." He shrugged. "But what the hell, I'm disobeying orders playing shamus anyway. The fact is, there's a small, heavily guarded perimeter with two blockhouses halfway up one of the mountains, and an elevator housing for the ammo lift that brings the stuff up from the underground stores. But all of that, the whole bit, is a blind, a fake. The real entrance to the dump is from the sea."

"The sea?"

"You know the old song? 'The Mountains of Mourne run down to the sea.' Well they do—steep slopes that plunge straight under the surface, and no coastal strip at all."

"You mean you have some kind of camouflaged landing stage?"

Gage shook his head. "Old smugglers' caves. There's a cutter on permanent alert in Newcastle harbor, ready at a moment's notice to run down to a fault breaching the cliffs near Kilkeel and get the stuff out."

"Do the IRA know your blockhouses are just a front?" Bolan asked.

"They might. They might even know or suspect the way in is from the sea. But they won't know how or exactly where. There are a lot of caves, and it's a hell of a tricky route."

"I agree with you," Bolan said. "That's a good bargaining chip. In a land as full of divided loyalties as this, the militant Republicans probably know better than you do the extent of this arsenal—how many assault rifles, how many SMGs and grenades, what kind of explosives. An illustrated guide to the way in would be an offer no IRA leader could resist."

"Of course I couldn't actually tell them that," Gage said hastily, "but I think I could make out an interesting enough case at least to tempt the leaders of both sides into talking. After that it would just be a matter of keeping one's ears open until one picked up some hint, some passing reference that would give one a lead to Derek's murderer."

The Executioner nodded his agreement, although the lead he would be looking for was in quite a different direction.

Gage chuckled. "Tell you one thing," he said. "There's not a chance in hell of any cross-checking between the two sides, so we could safely hold out the bait to the IRA *and* the Unionists!"

Great, Bolan thought to himself, and half the time available for the genuine job! But the idea gave him an opening, a way he could keep in touch with the British captain and make use of his local knowledge and leave himself, at the same time, free to follow up his own secret trail.

Aloud, he said, "This has got to be believable. There has to be a surefire reason for the offer to come from a British officer stationed here. D'you reckon you could convince an IRA fanatic that it wasn't part of some intelligence trap?"

"It wouldn't be easy," Gage admitted.

"Here's what we do, then," Bolan said. "You *could* convince the Protestant extremists by telling them you were pissed off with the army command, that you were an anti-Catholic yourself who wanted to see some tougher action. You could say there was nothing you could do personally, but you could given them a tip-off to this arms dump if they cared to make use of it."

Gage nodded. "I think that would work."

"Okay. As far as I'm concerned," Bolan said persuasively, "I'd be more likely, as an American, to ring true to the Republicans, right? I could sell them the idea that I was some kind of middleman. A guy on the make. Or, better still, a go-between talking for some Englishman with a chip—maybe a soldier who wanted to get even with the army but didn't dare come out in the open himself."

"Why would he want to get even?"

"I don't know. Something personal, I guess. His boss pulled rank to get into the sack with the solder's girl. He was passed over for promotion. He carried the can for a superior's screwup. Some kind of injustice that would make a guy sore as hell."

"I like it," Gage approved. "That line would allow you to stall, too. You couldn't supply any details at an initial meeting—you'd have to check back with the soldier. Because, you understand, I can't give you any details anyway. Security and all that.''

"Understood. The important thing," Bolan said, "is that they'd accept me as a Republican sympathizer. Irish immigrant relatives stateside, that kind of thing. But they wouldn't accept you. So I suggest we split the job down the middle: You concentrate on the Unionist extremists, I'll handle the IRA.''

"Fine." The captain hesitated. "There's just a couple of things...."

"Yeah?"

"I don't know why you should be doing this...going to these lengths to help—"

"I told you why. If we track down the killer or killers, there's a story, an exclusive. With pictures. Inset, Superintendent What's-it, who arrested the accused man. It's not just because I like the color of your eyes, buddy.''

"Well, I'm grateful anyway. But the other thing...Hell, it's all very well to say I'll concentrate on the Protestant underground and you'll do the IRA. But how do we actually *get* in touch with them? I mean they don't exactly wear lapel badges.''

"We have a mite too much to drink," Bolan said, "in the right kind of clubs and saloons. We're a little indiscreet. We brag, say something like, 'If those bastards knew what *I* know,' and we let slip a few key phrases. After that, the way the bush telegraph works in this town, we don't have to call them. They'll contact us.''

Gage nodded. "We'll give it a whirl," he said.

They parted with an agreement to meet again that evening and exchange intel—Bolan to try his luck in the predominantly Catholic Falls Road and Shankill neighborhoods, Gage to stay nearer the city center in the reactionary Unionist Sandy Row area.

GAGE WALKED THROUGH A NETWORK of streets flanked by identical terrace houses whose slat roofs were silvered by the rain. It was the only sign of brightness in a drab neighborhood. Laurels blackened by decades of soot dropped against the grimy brickwork in each mean front yard. Vandalized traffic lights at each intersection stared with dark, unwinking eyes at the empty roadway.

Gage crossed a main road twisting up toward the hills that sheltered the city from cold winds blowing from the north. The remnants of tramway lines set in granite blocks gleamed dully through the patched pavement.

On the far side, the frosted windows of a saloon overlooked a cul-de-sac littered with stones, bottles and broken bricks. He lurched across the sidewalk and went inside.

He saw at once that it was the wrong kind of place.

There were only half a dozen men in the bar, undersized, pinched-looking men in collarless shirts with white silk mufflers tucked between the lapels of their greasy dark suits. As the door opened, the heads in their flat caps turned as though attached to it by wires, and all conversation ceased.

Gage glanced quickly around the dingy room with its sawdusted floor. He noted the narrowed suspicious eyes, the small mouths. Someone spit noisily into a cuspidor. The distrust in the air was a palpable thing; he could feel it boring into his back as he contrived to walk a little unsteadily to the bar. It was clear that no conversation was going to start again until he left.

There was no point trying to get on boozily confidential terms with anyone here, and then raising the question of arms. He'd be lucky if the surly bartender asked him what he wanted.

Just the same, he'd have one drink. It might prove useful as a link in a chain if he wanted to establish a pattern of drinking all over the area. He ordered a half pint of porter.

At the sound of his voice, slurred just enough to be noticeable, a low muttering broke out behind him. Gage was wearing tweeds, stout leather shoes and a trench coat. Before he spoke, he could have been taken for a Belfastman—from the other side of the tracks certainly, perhaps the "haw-haw" district on each side of Malone Road, but at least no foreigner.

But it would be useless for him to attempt the local accent, in particular the genteel pseudo-Mayfair variety of it affected by the anglicized upper crust of the city. His Englishness condemned him as soon as he opened his mouth.

And yet, he reflected as he swallowed the drink and stumbled out, if they had known he was an army officer, paradoxically, they might even have welcomed him. Yon wee soldier man with his shooter to blast the bloody Papishers.

Gage turned up his collar and buttoned it against the rain. A bus swished downhill, spraying a fan of water across the road as its double rear wheels jolted into a deep pothole pitting the surface. Cursing the driver, Gage skipped to one side as the cascade of liquid mud lashed the leg of his pants. He cannoned into a chest-high electrical transformer box at the edge of the sidewalk and swore again. Then his eye registered the lettering on a handbill that had been posted on the green metal of the box.

It advertised a "loyalty" rally that evening in the Ulster Hall, to be addressed by Charles Mulligan, MP, and the Reverend Kevin McComb, two of the most rabidly anti-Catholic diehards from the right wing of the Unionist party.

There, Gage reckoned, among as many as two thousand fervent supporters, he would be more likely to find receptive ears for his let's-get-together line than he would in a hundred saloons filled with men for whom suspicion was second nature.

He turned around and retraced his steps toward the center. The posters, orange with black lettering, urged him to attend the Ulster Hall meeting from every fence, mailbox, parlor window and brick wall that he passed.

MACK BOLAN TOOK A BUS labeled Floral Hall and dropped from the running board as it turned right along Antrim Road, which paralleled the northern shore of Belfast Lough. He traversed a grid of low-income residential streets crisscrossing the lower slopes of the hills, passed the Royal Hospital and a couple of abandoned mills, and finally headed for the notorious Falls Road district.

If he couldn't make contact with the clandestine forces of the militant Republicans in this most rebellious of the city's wards, then he couldn't do it anywhere.

The rain fell more heavily. Beyond the blackened chimneys of ugly workmen's cottages, wisps of low cloud masked the cross that surmounted the escarpment above the Floral Hall and Bellevue public gardens.

Drawing a blank in three saloons, Bolan moved into a better neighborhood. Here the houses were taller, brick-built with sandstone facings serrating the window bays. The sidewalk widened a little farther on, and there was a run of small stores: a dairy displaying pyramids of canned food, a Laundromat, a cigar store, a boutique with sheets of amber cellophane protecting the clothes in the window from the heat of some mythical sun.

There were cars parked against the curb, and then the double doors of an ornately decorated nineteenth century pub. This one, Bolan thought, might be a better bet.

Beneath the painted inn sign on its bracket, a young army lieutenant and two corporals with shouldered arms paced the sidewalk in company with a couple of heavy red-faced men in the greenish-black uniform of the Royal Ulster Constabulary. Inside, a jostling throng crowded the place from wall to wall.

A white-clothed lunch counter loaded with sandwiches ran along one side of the room, and most of the clientele, intent on an early lunch, were competing for the attention of a huge man in a chef's hat who presided over the joints of beef, pork and ham. Most of the patrons were already provided with drinks, and the bar counter was relatively free. Bolan eased himself in beside a group of three men and two women who were arguing heatedly about some horse-racing catastrophe the previous day.

It was odd, the Executioner reflected, how you were always aware of the violence just beneath the surface in an Irish pub. He recalled the cracker-barrel philosophers back home who said the Irish treated their noisy disputes, and the fights that often followed, almost as a sport, as natural to them as it was to the crowd at a ballpark to taunt the players...and how they were always as friendly afterward as though nothing had happened. He wondered if it was true.

Take the party beside him, for example. The fury of their argument seemed to him to be out of proportion to its content.

"Bloody ridiculous," a little man in a hard hat was saying. "I never heard the like. Sure nobody but a half-baked idiot woulda considered layin' *another* tenner before the results were up. Yet here's herself gaily lashin' out with *my* winnins..."

"Ah, Barry, cut it out," one of the women snapped. "For Jay's sake..."

"I will not. When I see this kind of tomfoolery—"

"Cool it off, Barry," a stocky bald man interrupted. "Don't be an idiot all your life, man. Sure it's over and done with."

"Idiot, is it!" the man with the hat stormed. "I'll thank you to repeat that outside of here. And I'm in the right, but. The bloody jock at Leopardstown told us to leave the second race alone. But does she listen? Does she, hell!'' Fuming, he choked into his drink.

''What's eatin' him, then?'' the barman asked, leaning over the counter to swab away wet rings with a cloth.

''Dropped a packet on that animal of Deegan's yesterday afternoon,'' the third man said, smoothing his mustache with a nicotine-stained finger. ''And now he's taking it out of Moira here because she bitched up some deal he had with a rider.'' He jerked his head toward the woman who had not spoken, a faded blonde who scowled into a pint of Guinness.

''Bitched up?'' the little man exploded. ''Did you say *bitched* up? The stupid cow only—'' And then his anger was drowned in a chorus from all sides.

''Why don't you leave her alone, for God's sake?''

'' . . . not as if it was a bloody accumulator, man!''

''Shuddup, you! Just leave it be.''

''Haven't I been tellin' you these fifteen minnits past—''

'' . . . if Kevin would just shut his gob for half a second.''

*''Piss off!''* the blonde suddenly shouted, banging her empty glass on the counter. ''Piss off, the lot of you. You think I care? I'm away outta here an' the hell with you. You can piss off, the whole sodding lot.'' She slid off the bar stool and weaved an unsteady path toward the doors. At once there was pandemonium.

''Moira!''

''Don't be like that, for God's sake!''

''Come you back here, darlin'. Have a drink.''

''Moira . . .''

The barman looked inquiringly at Bolan. He was grinning. ''Would you look at that!'' he said. ''What'll it be, sir?''

Bolan ordered a whiskey on the rocks. By the time it was served, the three men and one of the women had returned and started a discussion about something else. Mysteriously the blonde was with them and it was the other woman who had left. The man in the hard hat was off again. "As Moira says to me last Saturday," he began, "you simply cannot—"

"It was Sunday," the blonde cut in.

"You're right, darlin', it was Sunday. No...wait a minnit, but. It *was* Saturday because I remember... Well, never mind. As Moira says to me, you can't trust a bloody soul." He turned to the barman and added, "Not these days, not a bloody soul. We'd better have the same again, Sean. Divil a man you could trust in the whole country!"

His bloodshot eyes swiveled around to seek confirmation, caught and held the Executioner's gaze. "Isn't that right?" he demanded accusingly.

"Right," Bolan said.

"There you are, then," the little man said. "What'd I say?"

Bolan leaped in with both feet. It was too good an opportunity to miss. "Too goddamn right," he repeated in a louder voice. He swayed toward the party and added thickly, "Wouldn't trust...a single bloody...one of the bastards. Not one. I ask you, would *you*?"

"Who's that then, squire?" the little man asked amusedly.

"Why, what you said. Would'n trust one of 'em... All against you, eh?"

"They are, and that's a fact."

"Bastards," Bolan said.

"Aye. I was just after sayin' to Kevin here—"

"An' the worst are the ones nearest to you. Worst of all."

"That's just what I was sayin' to—"

"You know what happen' to a frien' of mine?" Bolan asked sepulchrally, leaning so far forward that his face was almost touching the little man's hat brim. "English officer and gen'man. He was betrayed by the bloody army, the bloody British army. Let down with the biggest bump of his life, he was. What do you think of that?''

"But you're not in the army yourself, squire? Not the British army anyroads.''

Bolan shook his head. "'Merican myself. My frien' is . . . was. But he walked out. Left the bas'ards in the lurch. They lef' him inna lurch, so he lef' them inna lurch!'' He smiled foolishly and pushed his empty glass across the counter toward the barman. "Have a drink,'' he said to the party as a whole.

"Ah, no thanks, mister,'' the bald man said quickly. "We're after startin' on one a few minnits since, and then we have to be away. . . .''

"But he's going to get his own back,'' Bolan went on loudly. "They can't treat an officer and a gen'man like that. He's going to tell everyone he meets about their silly bloody arms dump. Tha's what he's gonna do.''

"Well, I don't know about that,'' the bald man began uneasily.

"He tol' me already. You wanna hear about the arms dump?''

"Well, no. To tell the truth I don't think I do. Here, Barry, isn't it about time we . . . ?''

"You're right, you're right,'' the little man said. "Drink up, Moira. We're on our way.''

"Why don't you wanna know?'' Bolan demanded truculently. "Bloody Rafferty would wanna know. I'm gonna tell Rafferty. . . .''

But the name of the IRA's wildcat chief in the north only made the party more anxious to leave. They swallowed the remainder of their drinks hastily and buttoned up their coats. Bolan started to speak again, but the blonde snapped, "Ah, save it for the Prods!'' And, sliding from her stool, led the way to the doors for the second time.

Looking around after they left, Bolan saw that the bar had all at once lost more than half its customers. The barman was looking at him—hard. Bolan asked for a refill.

"I think you'd do well, sir, to have a sandwich with it," he said politely, gesturing toward the lunch counter.

"I'm not hungry. You better make that a large whiskey."

"The sandwiches are very good indeed," said the barman, staring at Bolan expressionlessly.

"I tell you I don't..." Bolan picked something out of the air, something tense in the man's manner, that activated the sixth sense he had developed in combat situations over the years. "Maybe you're right at that," he said. And he carried his drink across and waited by a glass cover shielding a pile of ham sandwiches garnished with sprigs of watercress.

The big man in the chef's hat came to stand inquiringly before him. "You're the gentleman who wanted the turkey sandwiches," the chef said. "I'm sorry, sir, but we're fresh out of turkey sandwiches. Now if you was to go just down the road to Ballygarry Arms, I'm sure they could fix you up."

"But I didn't ask—"

The chef leaned forward. "Excellent, their turkey sandwiches are, sir," he said smoothly. "I'm sure you would appreciate them. Do you a power of good, they would." He looked meaningfully at Bolan and repeated, "A *power* of good."

Bolan hesitated. "Where did you say this place was?"

"The Ballygarry Arms. Over toward the top of the Falls Road. Three blocks along this street and then first left. You can't miss it."

"An' you think I'll be . . . satisfied there?"

"You tell them Seamus, the chef from the O'Donnel Hotel, sent you. I'm sure you'll find everything you want," the big man said.

Bolan shrugged. Whether this was significant or not, what could he lose? He drained his glass and left.

The chef went into a back room and picked up the phone.

The Ballygarry Arms was a two-story building with one immense bar. Four shirtsleeved barmen worked behind a counter that projected into the room like the rounded prow of a ship, and there were others whisking loaded trays up and down a row of high-backed booths along one of the walls. A group of overpainted girls giggled at one end of the bar.

Bolan slid into an empty booth. The man who had followed him from the O'Donnel Hotel whispered a few words into the ear of a florid individual in a blue suit who stood by the door to the cellars, then went into an office behind the bar.

"Yes, sir? What can I get you?" Blue Suit was standing at the entrance to Bolan's booth.

"Seamus, the O'Donnel Hotel chef, sent me," Bolan said. Now that he felt he might be onto a lead of some kind, he played down the slurred speech. "He said you had real neat turkey sandwiches. He said I could get anything I wanted here."

"Turkey, is it?" the man in blue said. "Right you are, then. With you in just one minute." He turned and went away.

Bolan slumped back against one corner of the booth and opened his wet raincoat. The drunk act had been put on for the benefit of his audience, but with the amount he had actually taken, and the lack of food, he was genuinely beginning to get a buzz on. He shook his head, staring at his rain-wet legs and hoping the sandwiches would be on brown bread. Outside the booth, waves of conversation crashed down wall to wall and echoed down from the plaster moldings of the high ceiling.

A few minutes later there was a swish of nylon and a pair of feminine thighs slid along the bench on the far side of the scarred, knife-initialed tabletop. Bolan frowned. Surely he couldn't have gotten the whole thing wrong? Surely the man in the blue suit couldn't have been so dumb as to think he was on the lookout for . . . ?

"Look, sweetheart, just beat it, will you," he said irritably without looking up. "You're on the wrong pitch. I don't have the time or the inclination—and anyway I never pay for it on principle."

There was a gasp of outrage and a muffled exclamation opposite him. Bolan's head jerked up.

The woman had honey-colored hair that fell to her shoulders, and enormous sea-blue eyes that were blazing now with anger.

"Just who do you think you're talking to?" she demanded icily. "I was evidently misinformed, but I was given to understand there was a possibility you might have a message for a Mr. Rafferty. . . ."

**8**

Her name was Deirdre O'Mara. She had "heard somewhere" that he had information that could interest Rafferty, and she might be able to fix a meeting if the material proved to be of the right kind. But that was the only information she herself would give before she had put Bolan through an interrogation as searching as any debriefing he had ever experienced.

After ten minutes, she suggested they move on somewhere else. Bolan followed her out to a side street, and she led him to a shabby gray Volkswagen Beetle parked by a half-completed barricade of flagstones, old bedsteads, sandbags and huge beams of wood that looked as though they had been raided from a railroad marshaling yard.

The woman didn't speak as they splashed toward the center of the city. It was only because Bolan wanted to get the layout of the place fixed in his mind that he glanced several times over his shoulder and out the VW's small, rain-spotted rear window, but again it was his fighter's sixth sense that warned him to pay special attention to the yellow-and-black taxi that was following them.

He was not one hundred percent sure it *was* following them until Deirdre O'Mara took a fourth shortcut, and the cab was still there, hugging their tail about fifty yards behind. Then he noticed there was a guy sitting beside the driver, even though the For Hire sign above the windshield was still illuminated.

Bolan unfastened his raincoat and loosened the front of his jacket, checking that the silenced Beretta slid easily in its leather. "Slow down," he said peremptorily.

She glanced at him sideways. "Slow down for a hundred yards and then speed up for another hundred," he repeated.

She braked obediently to a crawl, flicking a glance at the rearview mirror, and then accelerated. At the end of the maneuver the cab was still fifty yards behind them.

The attack came as she avoided a busy intersection controlled by traffic lights by driving down a narrow lane that cut diagonally through a block.

On one side of the lane, a high wall pierced by doors blanked off the backyards of a row of tenement houses; on the other, seventy yards of twelve-foot wooden fencing separated a warehouse from a red brick, tin-roofed church hall. The fence was covered with spray-can political slogans and torn posters advertising long-gone concerts and movies.

The VW was halfway along when a battered 1950s Buick sedan pulled slowly out of an entry beside the church hall and blocked the roadway.

Behind them, the cab was closing fast.

"Put your foot down hard!" Bolan said urgently. There was a gleam of metal above the open front window of the sedan; the cab's passenger door was already half open.

The woman obeyed his command without question. The clatter of the air-cooled engine turned to a roar. The old VW leaped forward.

At the last moment, when the needle on the dial hit fifty miles per hour, the sedan was less than thirty yards away and the first eruption of flame blazed from the submachine gun, Bolan seized the wheel and cranked it violently to the left.

Wrenched off course, the tail-heavy VW lurched, dipped and almost overturned, then smashed through the wooden advertisement hoarding in a storm of splintered planking.

The murderous stammer of the automatic weapon was lost in the rending crash as they burst through the fence, but Bolan heard several deeper reports from a heavy-caliber revolver fired through the open doorway of the taxi.

Deirdre O'Mara was showered with nodules of toughened glass as the driver's window imploded; the windshield starred; metal shrieked on stone as the offside front wheel, its tire punctured and ripped away in shreds, ground its steel rim on a stretch of cobblestones.

They were in a vacant lot. Bolan took in the scene in a single swift glance: rough grass sprouting through broken bricks; rusted piping and refuse in untidy heaps; hummocks of earth separated by puddles of yellow water pitted by the rain.

At the far end of the lot, near another fence hiding the backyards of drab houses in the next street, he saw the wreck of a burned-out panel truck.

The waste ground was closed in on one side by the high blank wall of the warehouse; on the other, wire grillwork protected arched windows set in the brick facade of the church hall. There was nowhere to go but straight ahead.

"Make for the wreck," Bolan rapped. "Keep as low as you can." The silenced Beretta was already in his hand.

Yawing crazily left and right on its damaged front suspension, the Volkswagen zigzagged away from the hole smashed in the hoarding. Flicking a glance at the rearview mirror, Deirdre saw that the Buick had pulled up on the far side of the gap.

Framed by the ripped posters and splintered planks, the man with the SMG and three more men armed with revolvers were crowding into the lot. Deirdre saw flame stabbing from one of the guns, and then the image vanished as the rear window disintegrated and fragments of glass pulverized by a heavy slug cascaded over her knees.

The lot was a demolition site that had never been redeveloped. The cobblestones from which the car's naked wheel rim struck sparks had once floored a factory entrance. Near the burned-out truck, the remnants of a loading bay raised a weathered concrete shelf above the weeds.

The VW staggered as a burst of lead from the SMG slammed into the body above a rear fender. Deirdre wrestled with the wheel as it spun almost from her grasp.

Bolan had smashed the window on his side of the old sedan with the butt of the Beretta. Now he leaned out and let loose a trio of three-round bursts at their pursuers.

With the car bucketing over the rough terrain it was impossible to score a hit, but the deathstream bought them precious seconds as the gunmen flung themselves full-length behind clumps of grass, discarded tires, any cover they could find.

The sedan was almost level with the truck when the hardman with the stuttergun rose to his feet long enough to spew a long burst of 7.62 mm skullbusters their way. And this time the killer struck pay dirt. Penetrating the louvered rear hood, the slugs wasted some vital part of the mechanism, and there was a scream of tortured metal as the engine seized up.

Driving wheels locked, the Volkswagen skated sideways across the wet pavement, rolled the other front tire off the wheel rim and came to rest broadside-on, ten yards from the old loading platform.

Bolan flashed a glance behind him. The hardguys were up and running. He leaned across the woman and hit the driver's door. It burst open, and he shoved her out. "Run for the concrete shelf," he commanded. "I'll cover you until you're down."

Again she complied unquestioningly.

Bent double, she raced for the remains of the bay while the Executioner leaned over the back of his seat and aimed the Beretta two-handed at the attackers.

He fired single shots, the suppressor censoring the messages of death until they were no louder than a butler's cough.

The lack of noise took the killers by surprise. One of the guys toting a revolver, cored through the center of the chest by a 9 mm boattail, jackknifed on the run, tripped and pitched forward, the weapon spinning out of his hand. He fell to his knees, keeled over and splashed into a pool of stagnant water. His head, sunk beneath the slimed surface, remained submerged.

Seconds later another man spun around clutching his left arm above the elbow. It couldn't have been more than a flesh wound, because he dropped behind a pile of garbage and continued firing. And now the heavy with the SMG was sheltered behind a stack of three tires.

Bolan heard him shouting orders before the stunning multidetonations of the gun sent more slugs thunking into the body of the stalled VW.

He looked over his shoulder. The woman was out of sight.

He himself was in an untenable position; he had to move fast. Squeezing out hip-level hellbursts as he ran, he sprinted for the wreck of the panel truck.

From there, protected by the metal bulk of the old engine block, he could shoot through the gap where the windshield had been.

But his targets were moving, fanning out sideways in the classic urban guerrilla enfilade. Run...drop...fire... scramble up while the enemy's head is down and run again....

Deirdre was unarmed. Crouched behind the concrete ledge—he could see her now—she would be a sitting duck if they spread out far enough left and right, for Bolan couldn't cover both flanks at once, not with the submachine gunner pinning him down in front.

For the moment, however, there was no more gunfire. In the silence he heard the rain drumming on the wrecked truck's roof.

Bolan was saving his ammunition. Not expecting trouble, he hadn't packed spare clips, and he had used most of the rounds in the Beretta's twenty-round box magazine already. The man with the injured arm was fifty or sixty yards away, half hidden behind a pile of bricks, working his way around until the woman was between him and Bolan. Soon she would no longer be hidden from him, although the range would be dubious for what looked like an old-fashioned service Webley.

The other guy was someplace behind the Executioner, temporarily hidden by the rusted rear doors of the truck.

But where was the machine gunner?

He was running, veering from side to side, weaving between obstacles to hurl himself down behind the VW. He was already inside the bullet-riddled body.

And from there, at extrashort range, he could effectively cover every move Bolan made, force him to keep out of sight while his two sidekicks circled around to take out Deirdre and finally close in on the Executioner himself.

Bolan bit his lip. The woman was defenseless, and he was damn near surrounded.

It was then that his mind registered what his nose had already sensed for some time: another odor, acrid yet aromatic, that cut through the charred, oily smell hanging around the panel truck.

Gasoline.

Raising his eyes to peer through the empty windshield frame, he saw that one of the early shots must have drilled the Volkswagen's curved frontal trunk and pierced the gas tank.

The inflammable liquid was splashing out and welling across the wet roadway beneath the car; rainbow colors, refracted from the greasy surface by the gray afternoon light, showed the extent to which it had already spread.

Muzzle-flashes blazed from the VW's window, and a hail of slugs sheared away one of the truck's windshield pillars and drilled the doors in back. Bolan had to duck hastily out of sight as the echoes of the blast died away.

But he knew what to do now. It wasn't that easy, but he had done it before, and it was possible. In any case it was his only chance.

He crawled out of the doorless truck on the side hidden from the VW and belly-crawled his way through the mud until he could sight the lower half of the sedan between the brake drum and a battered fender.

If he was going to make it, he'd have to fire from a prone position, with a low, flat trajectory, so that the slugs would glance off the cobbles instead of flattening themselves or gouging a furrow.

Because there were smoothed flints among the polished granite stone . . . and a well-placed ricochet could strike a spark.

Very slowly he brought up the Beretta and aimed. Sighting just beneath the VW's front axle, he held his breath and squeezed the trigger.

The silenced self-loader coughed in his two-handed grasp once, twice, three times.

Metal clanged as one of the slugs flew high. Another splatted against the pavement. Sparks leaped from the third . . . and at once the vapor concentrated in the damp air beneath the sedan's floorpan ignited with a *whoomp!* that cracked the Executioner's eardrums.

Flame enveloped the vehicle. The half-empty gas tank exploded, and then there was nothing to be seen but a seething column of fire marbled with black smoke, a raging scarlet hellball that boiled up toward the scudding clouds.

Detonated by the heat of the inferno, the rounds in the SMG's magazine exploded at firecracker speed, and then a fiery scarecrow figure erupted from the holocaust. He was a human torch, flopping horribly, rolling to the wet ground in a vain attempt to extinguish blazing clothes and hair, his screams sawing through the roar of flames.

Bolan was on his feet beside the panel truck, knees flexed in a combat crouch as he folded down the front handgrip and arced the Beretta at arm's length in search of the unwounded killer.

He saw movement fifty yards away behind a dented oil drum that was lying on its side half buried in garbage. Two hands grasping a large-bore revolver and the head of a prone man edged into view at one side of the drum.

Bolan didn't wait for the guy to rise and try a snap shot. He fired a single lethal round.

The 240-grain killer took away the top of the gunman's head, spraying the raindrops with a cloud of blood and brain tissue. The revolver choked out a shot in reflex as the man's death spasm tightened the finger curled around its trigger. The sound of the report was snatched away in a sudden squall of wind, and the slug demolished the remaining shard of glass in the panel truck's rear window.

The Executioner whirled to face the other way, standing in the open to do battle with the last adversary, as proud and solitary as an ancient duelist.

But the man with the shattered arm had had enough. He turned and fled, scattering drops of blood as he sprinted for the hole in the fence and the beat-up Buick beyond it.

Bolan let him go. The Volkswagen was still flaming, but the carbonized figure lying beside it had stopped twitching. He leathered the Beretta and walked over to the concrete ledge.

Deirdre straightened slowly. She was shivering. "Who were they?" Bolan asked.

"Protestant illegals, who else?" she replied. "The man with the...that man there—" she nodded toward the charred corpse with a shudder "—was a thug working for a racecourse gang leader called Connolly. Our enemies are not above hiring professional help whenever they want to keep their own hands clean."

"*Your* enemies? Were they following you as a matter of course, or me?"

She shrugged. "Me, I guess. The old car is...was...well enough known. My sympathies are no secret."

The injured hood had made the Buick. Slamming it into Drive, he steered one-handed out of there.

"We were going to talk some more," Bolan reminded her. "But we can't make an entrance like this, not in any respectable place." He gestured from himself to the girl. She was soaked to the skin, her honey-blond hair in rats' tails; he was covered in mud from shoulder to ankle.

She nodded her agreement. "Go back to your hotel," she said. "I'll go home and meet you in the Grand Central in one hour."

Bolan took her arm, but she shook him off. "I can manage quite well, thank you," she said coldly as they picked their way across the lot. And then she said frowning, "Maybe that's running it a wee bit close. We're a good mile and a half from the center, and dear knows how we're going to get there in this state."

"No sweat," Bolan said. He nodded toward the gaping hole in the hoarding and the driverless vehicle behind it. "We'll take a taxi," he said.

"YOU CERTAINLY HAVE A FLAIR for a combat situation," Deirdre O'Mara said, "for a news photographer."

"My assignments have taken me to a lot of tough places," Bolan said evasively.

They were sitting in the lounge bar of the Grand Central Hotel, a lofty room whose faded carpet and odor of cigar smoke and after-shave could have belonged to any good hotel in Europe. "Is this another Nationalist stronghold?" Bolan asked as the tailcoated waiter swooped away with their order.

She stared at him. "Ah, be your age, do," she said. "Sure, the whole city is not divided up like a chessboard! It's only in special areas like the one we just came from, like the Falls, the Shankill or Sandy Row, that there are special folks for special places. The rest of the town is just like anywhere else. You go where you want, whoever you are. And you don't have to keep up that pretense that you're stocious," she added later when Bolan was staring absently at the brandy swashing around in his glass. "Especially after that performance in the vacant lot. You're as sober as I am."

Bolan grinned. "Sorry," he said. "It seemed the best way to attract the right kind of attention, to make contact. As a reason for being indiscreet, I mean. Who'd listen to a normal guy who'd stand up and yell, 'I have a buddy with secrets to sell'? I didn't realize my acting was so bad."

"Don't worry. We're trained to tell, after all."

"We?"

"The Army," the woman told him. "You never said anything about selling."

"Figure of speech. He doesn't want any money. Me, neither."

"What do you want? In return for what?"

"I told you. There's this underground arms dump—"

"If you mean the one in the Mournes, we know about it. We know about the decoy unit and the phony entrance. We know you get to the place from the sea—"

"Okay. But do you know which cave, which route? Do you know how many guards there are, where they're posted, when they change tricks, what their orders are in case of a raid?"

"Maybe not," the woman admitted, "but we know more about it than we do about you. What's your friend's name?"

"I told you that, too. Gage. Captain Simon Gage."

"I see." There was disbelief warring with something stronger, something even less pleasant, in the way she looked at him. Her full lips turned down at the corners as if she had suddenly come across a disagreeable odor. "And how old would you say this Captain . . . Gage is?"

He shrugged. "Thirty. Thirty-five. I don't know."

She nodded slowly several times. "Simon Gage. A captain—so presumably he must have been in the army some years. Yet it is only today that he decides to betray it and his country. What has been keeping him?"

Bolan sighed. If only she wasn't so damned attractive. He kept his eyes away from the ripe curves of flesh contouring the sweater she now wore with a heather-colored tweed skirt. "It's a personal matter I can't discuss," he said. "You can ask him yourself if things don't go wrong—but he's not pretending suddenly to believe in your cause or anything like that."

"What does he believe in? And why would he ask an American newspaperman to speak for him?"

Bolan ignored the first question. "He felt an offer from an American would be more likely to be taken seriously by . . . your party," he said. "But he gave me his word—"

"His word!" she said passionately. "His *word*? The word of an officer in the English army? Do you realize what that means to me? Do you know how much it's worth to someone in my position? Do you?"

"Look," Bolan began, "all I said was—"

"I'll tell you. My grandfather was with Collins in the Easter Monday rebellion in Dublin in 1916. He was killed by the Black and Tans later, murdered by the dregs of the British prisons that they fitted out with army uniforms and let loose on the patriots they were trying to suppress. My father died of the pneumonia after six years in the Crumlin Road Jail here, along with McAteer and a host of other brave lads that'd done nothing wrong but speak up for their country that was being ruined by foreign politicians. Does that give you some idea of the way I feel and why I feel it?"

"All right," Bolan said. "So you hate the British. Lots of the Irish do."

"I hate the English. And why wouldn't I hate them? Would you tell me one good reason why an Irishman or an Irishwoman should do anything else *but* hate the English? Would you have us lick the boots that have been kicking us four hundred years, for God's sake?"

Bolan said nothing. There was nothing to say in front of such conviction.

She sipped her drink and said in a calmer tone, "I'm sorry. Your friend cannot help being English, I suppose. But there is one thing worse than that in my book: being a renegade, a deserter. As a guerrilla—for that is what we are in the Army—I rate disloyalty to one's cause the meanest crime of all."

Bolan grimaced. "Can't win, can we?" he said. "Okay, if that's the way you feel, let's get out of here. I'm sure there are others—on one side or the other—not quite so, what shall we say, purist?"

"Don't mistake me," Deirdre O'Mara interrupted. "We need your damned arms dump. But it doesn't mean I have to like you or your traitorous friend for putting it our way."

He shrugged. "Well?"

She picked up her purse, opened it, looked inside and then, as if she had suddenly come to a decision, snapped it shut again and met his eyes. "I have to make a telephone call," she said. "Wait for me here." She rose and went out of the room.

Bolan was tempted to follow her and try to listen in on her conversation. He knew the layout of the phone booths—and the thinness of the partition walls—and he would have given a lot to have heard what she was going to say. But he decided the risk of discovery was too great, and she was, in any case, back so quickly that he wondered whether perhaps she had contacted somebody already in the hotel and not telephoned at all.

"Very well," she said. "Just so I know I have it straight. You're offering us this total rundown on the Mourne depot, in return for what?"

Bolan and Gage had spent some time discussing the point: which would be more convincing, pretending to make them a gift of the whole deal, kind of a revenge action, or asking some kind of price, as a deserter might be expected to do? "We're not looking for money," he said. "I told you. But there may be something you can do for me...."

"Ah!"

"Something in the way of special and exclusive news facilities. An inside view, talks with your leaders, that kind of thing. But we can discuss that later. If your principals are interested, that is."

She nodded. "It's a possibility. No pictures, of course. In the meantime, some friends of mine would like to meet you this evening. Take a Ravenhill bus, get off at Ormeau Park and go into St. Stephen's Church, near the river embankment. You are to be sitting in the back row, on the left as you face the altar, at exactly seven-fifteen. Understood?"

"What happens then?"

"You will be contacted." She looked at him oddly for a moment, and then added, "What's this you say your friend's name is? Gage? Simon Gage?"

"That's right. What of it?"

The woman shook her head. "Nothing. Make sure you are on time."

A HALF HOUR LATER he met Gage at a small, comfortable one-room saloon called the Club Bar, near the university.

"Drawn a complete blank, old boy," the Englishman said. "After the fifth pub, I didn't even have to pretend playing the jolly drunk. If you plotted my course through the Sandy Row area, the map would look like a knitting pattern for a cable-stitch fisherman's sweater!"

"But no takers?"

"My calculated indiscretions were sowed far and wide," Gage said, "but nobody wanted to know about a secret arms dump in the . . . you know where."

"The Ulstermen weren't spoiling for a fight?"

"Oh, sure. Lots of the types I talked to were full of praise for the UDV. Most them seemed to harbor what seemed like a personal grudge against us—the army, I mean—for what they called protecting the Catholics. Nationalists about to be given the vote after generations of gerrymandering should be rubbed out before they could use it. That was the general idea."

"But they weren't interested in doing the rubbing out themselves?"

"Actually, a lot of them were." Gage frowned. "But they were talking of fists and boots, of clubs and bottles and stones, and not of your genuine shooting irons. At least the chaps I met seemed to be thinking that way."

"Maybe you should try a more up-market neighborhood." Bolan grinned.

"You can say that again. There's a big Unionist rally downtown tonight at the Ulster Hall. Addressed by the Reverend Kevin McComb, no less! I thought I'd drop in and pass the word around a bit while the boys were in the mood."

"Good idea," Bolan agreed. "You may find it hard to believe, but I'm going to church myself."

## 9

There were a few people waiting in the pews near the carved-wood confessional boxes, but apart from a fat woman in black halfway down the center aisle, the church was otherwise empty. Bolan slipped into the row nearest the Gothic door with its padded draft-excluders and settled down to wait.

As always in countries where the Church took sides, he felt uneasy. The heavy, chill atmosphere, the poor light, the musty odor and the contrast between the richness of the decorations and the poverty of the congregations combined to produce in him a kind of mental indigestion that became more acute each time he remembered the unChristian sentiments so often expressed by preachers.

Soon somebody sat down at the far end of the pew and slid along the polished oak until he was beside him. Bolan glanced sideways. A ferret-faced man with red-rimmed eyes—who still, surprisingly, wore a shallow hat on his head—looked at him inquiringly.

"Mr. Belasko?"

Bolan nodded. The hat and the head beneath it jerked briefly toward a small door on the far side of the church, and the man slid himself back toward the other end of the pew. The Executioner shrugged and followed.

Ornate iron hinges spread three-quarters of the way across the door. Beyond it a short flagstoned passage led to a cloister overlooking a square of wet grass flanked by gravel paths and dispirited plane trees whose remaining leaves drooped sadly in the humid atmosphere. Beyond the trees were bushes, and someplace on the far side of the bushes was the river.

A red brick wing of the church blanked off the far end of the cloister. At one side a concrete stairway led to a lower level. The ferret-faced man crossed the path and, beckoning Bolan to follow, shuffled down the steps.

Most of the basement was taken up by a boiler room. They crunched across fragments of spilled coal, ducked beneath a nest of water pipes and found themselves in an arched crypt that had been part, Bolan guessed, of an older church that had once stood on the same site.

Two candles stuck in beer bottles dimly illuminated an alcove on the far side of the crypt. And in the alcove stood two men.

Both wore belted trench coats with shoulder straps. Both were tall and well-built. But one had a large head with dark curling hair, a blue chin and wide brown eyes, and the other's head was small, with flat, pale hair slicked across the scalp. It was the second guy who spoke.

"Michael Belasko? You have a message from a man named Gage?"

"Right," Bolan said. "Are you Rafferty?"

The fair man ignored the question. "Captain Simon Gage, from Somerset? Presently stationed on Lough Neagh?"

"For God's sake!" Bolan exclaimed. "What is this? I don't know how many times… Shit, anyone would think the guy's name was more important than the product!"

"Perhaps it is in a way," the fair man said. "We understand you're acting as a go-between, that this man is offering certain information we may be able to use. *You* tell us now: why is this British officer making such an offer? Why are you acting for him? What are the both of you going to get out of it?''

"I'll tell you one thing," Bolan said shortly. "This eternal questioning makes me mad. I'm not a candidate for a goddamn oral examination. I'm passing on an offer. Take it or bloody leave it." He turned as if to go. The ferret-faced man moved quickly to block the archway leading back to the boiler room.

"Ah, c'mon now." The dark man spoke for the first time. "Sure, you have to see our point of view. We have to satisfy ourselves that you're the genuine article. You could be part of a trap intended to catch us out, to make us commit ourselves, else. Can you not see that now?"

"I guess so," Bolan said reluctantly. He turned back to face the two men.

"Well then… There's this underground arsenal, and your friend is going to be kind enough to provide us with the plans of the interior, and tell us how we can best get into it. is that the way of it?"

"That's it."

"When can you give us the full details?" the fair man asked. "Tonight?"

"Well, not tonight," Bolan said, stalling. "They change from day to day, you see."

"What do?"

"The routines, the times of guard changes, the passwords, that kind of thing. Captain Gage is duty officer the day after tomorrow. He could check then on the latest system."

"And you could pass on the intel the following day?"

Bolan nodded. "I guess so."

"When could we make the raid then, to get the stuff out? We'd need, let's see, twenty-four hours to set the thing up. Would Gage be free to lead us in there then, four days from now?"

This was a complication the Executioner hadn't bargained for. "Hell, I don't know about *lead*," he said slowly. "He wouldn't want to be recognized. There's such a thing as treason, you know. But we could show you."

"Sure, sure, sure," the dark man said. "A figure of speech, just. What we'd want to know, specifically, is how many men there are on guard, how many in reserve, where they are situated and how far away the nearest reinforcements are. Plus the times of shift changes, the signals routines, any alternative ways of getting in and, of course, a list of what's stored there."

"Yeah, well, that's the information we're offering, isn't it?"

"Why are you offering it?" the fair man asked suddenly.

"I thought I'd been all through that. Which one of you is Rafferty?"

"Rafferty doesn't enter into the operation at this stage."

"We'll only tell the full story to Rafferty."

"We can arrange for you to see him later," the dark man said. "Just tell us in the meantime—what's your price? What do you and your . . . friend . . . want in return for this information?"

"I just told you. I'll only deal with Rafferty direct."

The dark man sighed. "You're a desperate difficult fella to bargain with, Mr. Belasko! Very well, you shall meet Rafferty tonight."

"When and where?"

The two Republicans exchanged glances. Finally the fair man said, "There's a place called the Ambassador. Kind of a nightclub. You'll find it in a cul-de-sac called Mullen's Passage, off Ann Street. It's the third door on the right, up a flight of stairs. Be there at fifteen minnits past one o'clock tomorrow morning."

"Who do I ask for? Rafferty?"

"Ah, be your age! You ask for Mr. O'Connell, at the reception desk just inside the door at the top of the stairs. Tell them...tell them Mr. Callahan sent you. Rafferty will be in the manager's office."

"The Ambassador in Mullen's Passage, at one-fifteen. Okay," Bolan said.

"And you'll bring Captain Gage with you?"

"Not at this stage. Later, if we come to an agreement."

"Fair enough. There's just one other thing," the dark man said.

"Yes?"

"You understand, we have to take certain... precautions. In a sense we are marked men, especially in the city center. We can afford to take no risks."

"Sure," Bolan said, wondering what was coming next.

"I just want you to know—" it was the fair man speaking now "—that in spite of these precautions, aimed mainly at making absolutely certain that we are not tailed in any way, we shall still expect you at one-fifteen. The action we are obliged to take in no way invalidates our arrangement."

"What the hell are you talking about...?" Bolan began.

"Our apologies, Mr. Belasko," the dark man said. He raised his eyebrows and nodded, looking over the Executioner's shoulder.

Ferret-face, who had stolen up behind him without being noticed, raised his arm as Bolan swung around. Bolan saw the glint of candlelight on gunmetal and tried to hurl himself sideways as his right hand flashed toward the holstered Beretta.

For once in his life he was too slow off the mark.

The barrel of the revolver slammed against his skull behind the left ear, and the crypt exploded into black flame. Bolan leaned forward into the darkness and dropped slowly into its center, turning over and over.

## 10

There was an air of tension about the city that evening. It crackled like an electric current through the downtown bars, animated the faces of loyalists crowding to the Ulster Hall rally and found a voice in the rumble of armored personnel carriers bringing troops into the center along Antrim Road. Beneath the domes of the wedding-cake city hall, administration clerks and secretaries streaming from their offices hurried more quickly than usual to the buses that would take them home.

Night-helmeted RUC patrols with their military escorts paced the wet sidewalks outside dance halls in Divis Street and Donegall Place. Welders on night shift showered sparks on the rooftops from the stocks of the shipyard across the river, and a tall man with glittering eyes started a fight for no reason at all in a Catholic pub on Corporation Street.

Identity checks and other security measures were stepped up in railroad stations, cinemas and certain restaurants.

But nobody expected a full-scale riot.

Soon after eight o'clock the rain stopped. By nine, the curtain of cloud had withdrawn to the west, and the moon rode out into a clear sky. A wind blew suddenly down Lisburn Road, stirring the banners held by a group of students assembling between a Methodist high school and the university.

Mack Bolan recovered consciousness on a bench in the Botanic Gardens. His head ached like hell, and his clothes were once more damp from the rain, but otherwise he seemed none the worse. He swung his feet to the ground, wincing as a shaft of pain lanced through his skull. He felt the tender spot behind his ear where the ferret-faced man had struck. It had been professionally done: there was a fair-sized lump, but the skin was not broken.

He staggered to his feet and stumbled groggily toward the lights of a street showing through the trees. A man and a woman walking toward him made an ostentatious detour to avoid passing too close. "God help us, would you look at that!" the woman said disparagingly. "And it not yet half-nine!"

"Ah, it's just a fella has taken a sup too much," the man replied. "I saw the same person sleeping it off on a bench there when I came through the wee park fifteen minnits ago on my way to look for you."

She sniffed. "It's a pity of him indeed."

Bolan grinned to himself. When he'd played the part of a drunk, Deirdre O'Mara hadn't believed him; now he was being condemned when he wasn't even trying!

The students were on the far side of the street. There were about one hundred of them. Their banners and placards read: Civil Rights for All and End Unionist Gerrymandering!

What an irony, Bolan thought, that the civil rights movement in this country, which attracted largely left-wing sympathizers, should be championing the Catholic cause, which the left normally associated with reaction!

A long-haired young man with a muffler around his neck was addressing the marchers before they moved off. Their intention was to picket the Ulster Hall and chant slogans at the audience as they came out after the rally.

"But no violence, mind," the young man shouted. "We are *not* to be provoked. That would be playing into their hands. They'd beat the bejasus out of us and claim it was self-defense."

"What if the fascist stewards strong-arm *us*?" someone demanded.

"We sit down. We wait out the half hour as arranged, and then we move on to picket the GC."

"What about the polis, but? Suppose they use violence?"

"Or tear gas?" another voice called.

"They won't if we remain calm. We decided already," the leader yelled, "if the police take action, you go limp and let them drag you away. You don't fight, and you *don't* knock off their fucking helmets."

"Above all," said an older man beside the leader, "if the army asks you to move—move. We're showing our rejection of the police, so we must make the point that if any *reasonable* authority orders us, we obey."

"Mind you, though, if anyone happens to find a bloody steward, individually, behind the hall, I'm not saying a black eye or two would come amiss...."

"Ah, for God's sake! Nonviolent is nonviolent. Is this to be a demo or a bloody free-for-all?"

Eventually, after much argument, some ribbing and ironic laughter, the procession moved off with its banners toward the city center. Waiting for the bus that would take him downtown, Bolan could hear them, far down the road, singing "We Shall Overcome."

He shook his head. Did the nonviolent civil rights kids' adoption of the Nationalist cause extend to approval of the violent IRA? Did their condemnation fo the Unionist paramilitary units apply equally to terrorists on their own side?

You tell me, Bolan said to himself.

The important thing for him, the essential thing, was to stay clear of any sectarian engagement. This wasn't his war. His war was to expose and destroy one particular terrorist operation planned by one specific group: it didn't matter a damn which side the group was on; apart from the cold-blooded callousness of the action, its importance lay in the fact that it could ruin military negotiations vital to his country.

Trouble was, he had yet to locate and identify beyond any doubt the plotters who *were* his target. Even if Deirdre O'Mara's contacts brought him face-to-face with Rafferty, he had so far no positive proof that the wildcat leader was the man he wanted.

He returned to his hotel to collect the camera case and then headed for the rally at the Ulster Hall.

THE ULSTER HALL WAS a building as solid and as gray and as old-fashioned as the values of the people who hired it for their meetings and rallies.

The student demo was not yet in place, and when Simon Gage arrived, twenty minutes still remained before the meeting was due to end. The side street leading to the "stage door" was therefore uncluttered with supporters, opponents or sightseers. Two RUC policemen shared a cigarette in the shelter of a doorway. Half a dozen others joked with a detail of soldiers at ease a hundred yards away beyond the parked cars.

Gage had discovered years ago that doormen were a suggestible race. The man who comes in diffidently, hesitates, and then looks around inquiringly will receive the full force of the little-Hitler mentality; the man striding in arrogantly as though he owned the joint, scarcely deigning to glance at the guardian, will probably get away with it.

Probably.

Gage walked briskly past the policemen, pushed open the door and marched confidently past the doorkeeper's box toward a short, steep flight of stairs that led to the rooms behind the stage. "Evening," he said as he passed.

The old man must have put down his newspaper and moved fast. He was already barring the way before Gage had his foot on the lowest step. "Where the hell you think you're goin'?" he demanded.

"Urgent message for Charlie," Gage said peremptorily. Charles Mulligan, Member of Parliament, was known to his friends as Charlie, according to a Sunday supplement columnist.

"Charlie who?"

"Mulligan, of course," Gage said pleasantly. "New here, aren't you?"

"Not so new I can't spot a flamin' try-on when I see one."

"For God's sake! This message has to get to him before the rally's over. It's important."

"So are they all. Beat it."

"He'll need it before he makes his final speech."

"Give it me. I'll see he gets it when you're gone."

"I dare not write it down. I told you. It's important."

"And *I* told *you*. Outside!"

Gage's hand dived into his pocket. It emerged with a five-pound bill between two fingers. "Look," he said, "I don't want to put you to any trouble, but..."

"Well, now... Of course, if you put it like that, sir..." The bill vanished. "Very kind of you, sir, I'm sure. If you would just turn right at the top of them stairs there, and through the door marked Private, you'll find him in there on his own."

Gage looked up the stairs. Two bulky men in cloth caps, long black overcoats and white mufflers stood shoulder to shoulder barring the passageway. "It's all right, boys. Genuine caller for the wee man," the doorman called.

The strong-arm men moved aside, and Gage squeezed between them, on his way to hard-sell the boss of the ultra-reactionary breakaway wing of the local Unionist party.

MULLIGAN ON ONE SIDE, Rafferty on the other, Mack Bolan thought, approaching the Ulster Hall from the front. One preaching intolerance and violence, the other practicing both. Who was to say which was worse?

With the Nikon and the modified Hasselblad slung around his neck, he joined the small group of photographers and reporters waiting on the steps. The students were forming two lines between the steps and the sidewalk so that people leaving the hall would have to walk between them.

PA speakers above the ticket windows beyond the open glass doors of the entrance lobby were relaying samples of the Christian ethic as served up by Mulligan's tame pastor sidekick, the Reverend Kevin McComb.

*"These so-called progressives, these Papist tools,"* the unctuous voice intoned, *"do we even need such people in our society? Does not St. Paul say, in his Second Letter to the Corinthians, 'Enter not into relations with those who reject the Faith'? Does he not add: 'For what partnership can there be between righteousness and lawlessness?'..."*

"That seems to be a direct tilt at our student friends," Bolan said to a young man who was standing nearby with his hat on the back of his head and a notebook in one hand.

"I wouldn't be surprised," the reporter said dryly. "Wait'll you hear the follow-up. I know this speech—I don't even have to take notes!"

*"St. Jude had a word for the kind of men who would hand over your religion and your security to foreigners across the border. Men who malign what they do not understand, he called them, while they use what they do know for their own corruption... leafless trees with no vestige of fruit... wild sea waves, foaming with their own shame... wandering stars for which the blackest darkness has been reserved forever. Is it into the hands of such men, brethren, that you would allow the politicians of Westminster to deliver you?"*

"Who the hell *is* he getting at?" Bolan asked. "The Brits, the civil rights people, the students, the Dublin government?"

The reporter shrugged. "What does it matter, so long as the boys come out fighting mad, rarin' to have a go at *someone*?"

Now, suddenly, the rabble-rousing voice in the PA speakers was drowned by an uproar that seemed to come from the rear of the building. Bolan thought he heard another verse of "We Shall Overcome." He hurried around to the side street, firing off a series of shots from the Nikon as he ran. The 35 mm SLR was loaded with superfast ASA 1000 stock, and the street lighting was bright enough for the emulsion to record images without a flash.

There were more students crowding the stage entrance. They were dressed like the young men and women out front; they carried similar banners; they chanted the same slogans. But there was a difference—something ugly in the tone of these voices, a menace that the Executioner sensed but could not quite place. And these demonstrators were a lot older than the kids he had seen.

The police were shouting. Army men advanced from behind the parked cars with riot shields. Some of the students began to throw stones.

In a temporary lull, Bolan heard McComb's voice from a loudspeaker just inside the open stage door.

*"What did the First Letter of St. Peter say? It said—no beating about the bush, and I quote—it said, 'God's will is this: that you should silence the ignorance of foolish people by doing what is right.'"* He paused for effect. *"Silence the ignorance of foolish people, brethren. Silence them. I wonder if there may not be a message there for all of us here..."*

Bolan exposed another run of film, trying to shoulder his way through the throng to the entrance. This was the most open invitation to sectarian violence he had ever heard. Simon Gage should be in there someplace; maybe he could do with moral support.

Beefy RUC men shoved the Executioner away from the door. The police nightsticks were out and swinging; between them and the riot shields, the demonstrators had been contained on the far side of the street.

Another voice rasped from the PA speaker now. Bolan could only hear snatches of the tirade. Mulligan was winding up the evening in his usual near-hysterical fashion.

*"...God-fearing Protestant community...rule of law set aside by a handful of callow youths directed from Eastern Europe... vicious Republican elements trying to endanger our way of life... Why give them votes when all they do is vote to cut us off from the Mother Country...? No Popery...conspiracy to undermine...refuse to tolerate... Smash them down if they try..."*

The police moved in to deal with concerted jeering from across the road. A patrol wagon backed up from the main drag, and there were fights as some of the demonstrators were dragged toward it. Figures sprawled on the sidewalk, covering their heads with their hands. Bolan profited from the confusion and slipped through the door.

There was a burst of cheering and then the shuffle of thousands of feet as the audience began to leave the auditorium.

Bolan ran up the stairs and headed for the stage. There were voices coming from behind a door on the right, among them the clergyman's persuasive baritone and Mulligan's more staccato delivery. As the Executioner passed, the door opened and Simon Gage came out.

His eyes widened. "Hello! I didn't expect to see you there. I though we were to meet—"

"Change of program," Bolan said. "How did it go?"

"I think they've bitten. Not the place to discuss it here, though." The Englishman glanced toward the stairway and the noise of the disturbance outside the stage door. "I have to see them again in some pub at Craigavad."

"Okay." Bolan led the way to a pass door at one side of the high stage. "Let's get out of here."

They passed the table, the chairs, the water carafe and the microphone on the platform, dropping down to the lofty auditorium. Most of the house lights had been switched off, and the place smelled of stale cigarette smoke and too many wet topcoats.

Beyond a dense crowd jamming the lobby, they came to a halt on the fringe of another battle ranging beyond the hall's somber entrance.

The inflammatory advice dispensed by Mulligan and the cleric had clearly taken hold of a section of the audience. Emerging from the rally with their hearts stirred by this dialectic, they had seen before them the student demo—what appeared to be a textbook example of the very evil against which they had been warned. The enemy was even flaunting banners urging adoption of those same measures—devices of the devil—which would result, they had been told, in the destruction of everything they valued.

Such a challenge could not go unanswered. "Silence the ignorance of foolish people," they had been advised. "Smash them down," the wee man had said.

Right then, if there was one thing young loyalists could do, it was obey orders. With fists and boots and bottles they sailed in to teach the demonstrators a lesson—and these *were* the same people Bolan had seen outside the university: he recognized the long-haired leader, backed up against a doorway with his placard held high, and several other kids under attack.

The ugliest thing about the riot was the noise. Mulligan's followers were baying for blood, and the students, trying vainly to deflect vicious multiple assaults without hitting back, were themselves hurling insults at their enemies and at the large crowd cheering on the mob from the top of the stairs.

Many of the students were on the ground, their banners torn and trampled. Bolan saw one girl felled with a rabbit punch and a simultaneous blow over the heart. Another ran blindly from side to side with blood streaming from her nose and the clothes ripped from her back. There were no police to be seen.

Bolan was about to dive in and do what he could for the beleaguered demonstrators when there was a screaming of sirens, and an army patrol pulled up on the fringe of the struggling crowd and deployed a water cannon.

The Executioner and his companion ducked back inside before the stunning jets separated the contestants. The students would be saved: nobody could remain standing, let alone keep on fighting under the relentless pressure of that water.

"We'll go out the rear entrance," Bolan said. "There's something strange going on here, and I want to take another look."

He hurried to open the pass door in back of the stage, jerking it with such speed that a large man who was about to open it from the other side was pulled off balance.

The two of them collided with some force and staggered against the wall of the passageway. "God save us!" the big man exclaimed. "Where are you away to at-all in that much of a—Well, well, well! If it isn't our transatlantic friend and the wandering subaltern himself!"

Bolan stared. The man he had bumped into was the portly Mr. McGeehan, the stout-buying know-it-all who had attached himself to Gage and Bolan after the brawl at Geraghty's Wine Lodge.

"Pardon me," he said. "Didn't know you were there. What are you doing here, anyway?"

"I might well ask you the same question," McGeehan responded.

"Trying to find a way out without getting soaked," Gage said.

"Well, then, that's exactly me own objective. Are the soldiers there yet, out the front?"

"Yeah," Bolan said. "None too soon. Those kids were getting the worst of it out there."

"Well, now, there are some would agree with you," McGeehan said, "and some would say that provocation deserves what it gets."

"Animal violence of the kind those young thugs use is never justified," the Executioner said shortly.

"Is that a fact? Were you in the hall this evening, sir? Did you hear what our friends had to say?"

"I wasn't in the hall. I heard some of the speeches through the PA speakers. For my money they were a damned sight more provocative than anything those students say."

"You don't say!"

Maybe, Bolan thought, he shouldn't have made that last remark. The guy could be a buddy of Mulligan and the pastor. "Were you in the hall?" he asked.

"Well, yes and no," the fat man replied. "Yes and no."

Bolan made a move. "We're on our way," he said. "Are they still throwing punches around the stage door? If you're heading for the entrance, there's a water cannon to get past."

"Oh, I've seen the performance at the back," Mr. Mc-Geehan said oddly. "I reckon I'll go out the usual way just the same. Good night to you, gentlemen." He paused, and then added to Bolan, "A word in your ear. I'd watch what I say if I were you. There's folk very quick to take offense these days, you know." He smiled and ambled off toward the lobby.

Bolan and Gage exchanged glances. Gage shrugged. "Nut case, would you say? All this conversation full of veiled warnings and hidden meanings! Is the man just an amiable eccentric, or isn't he what he seems at all? D'you think he could be tied in with Mulligan's crowd?"

"Search me," Bolan said. "What I'd like to know is, how did *he* know so much about our movements before he met us in that bar?"

Gage was about to reply when the bullet struck the wall six inches from his head, scoring a long furrow in the plaster. He jumped involuntarily as the chips stung his face, jerking his head back so that the second slug fanned his forehead instead of penetrating his temple.

The two shots cracked out whiplike over the roar of the crowds on both sides of the building. Before the third echoed among the scenery racked in the flies high above their heads, Bolan had hurled himself at the captain and pulled him down behind a metal sandbox, which was part of the hall's antique fire-fighting system.

The gunman, Bolan reckoned, was using a fairly small caliber automatic, perhaps a 7.65 mm Walther PPK. The reports lacked the deep, thunderous quality of a Combat Master or a .45 Magnum. There weren't many theatrical productions at the Ulster Hall—an occasional pageant or specialized concert was about it—but there were a number of permanent flats stored up there in the stagehouse. Someplace among the Gypsy encampments and Ruritanian village squares and classical pastorals, nevertheless, a killer was waiting for them to make a move.

Who or why could wait until later. Right now the important thing was to get out alive.

Gage was in civilian clothes; he would be unarmed. Bolan unleathered his Beretta, flipped off the safety and handed the gun to him. "Yes, but what are you...?" he began.

Bolan patted the Hasselblad slung around his neck. "I have other means," he said.

There were two more shots in quick succession, and then a third. The slugs penetrated the metal but stalled in the sand filling the box. Bolan jerked his head at the dark rectangle of flies far above them. "There are two of them," he said. "The last of those shots came from farther over. They're up there somewhere and they ain't gonna be hanging from the scenery. There'll be an electrician's gantry, a catwalk running along above the back of the stage, and they'll be on that."

"Are they... You reckon my salesman routine tipped them off that I was looking for Derek's killers, and they thought they might as well get rid of me?" Gage whispered.

Bolan shook his head. "They're not Mulligan's men," he replied. "It's me they're after." He glanced toward the stairs. They were about fifteen feet from the back wall of the stage. "The nearer we get to that," he said, "the more acute their angle of fire. Fire a coupla shots to cover me. I'm going on over there, make myself a tougher target. Do nothing till you hear from me, okay?"

Gage nodded. He was obviously familiar with the gun.

He folded down the foregrip, selected the three-shot auto mode and loosed off a burst into the darkness above the stage. One of the flats moved slightly as a bullet traveling at 1,230 feet per second slammed into the batten stiffening its base.

At once there was answering fire. And this time, as Gage ducked back behind the sandbox and Bolan sprinted for the wall in back of the stage, they saw muzzle-flashes in the gloom above.

Gage pumped out two single shots, one aimed at each flash, firing this time from low down, around the edge of the sandbox instead of over the top.

Bolan gained an iron ladder that spiraled upward. He began to climb. From here the catwalk itself protected him from the nearer of the two killers: the iron grillwork was too thick and too close-meshed for a gun barrel to be shoved through and angled toward the spiral.

The guy at the far end of the walk, where it curved around above the wings, was pinned down by Gage. Bolan thought he must have opened up again, but with a flash-hider and a suppressor fitted to the autoloader he couldn't be sure. What was certain was the sudden scrape of feet from the far side of the stagehouse, and the sound, much nearer, of a heavier tread approaching the staircase.

The gunman on Bolan's side of the stage had suddenly realized his best chance was to wait at the top of the spiral, from where he could fire directly down on the big guy as he circled into sight.

He was too late.

He was still fifteen feet away when Bolan rested his elbows on the catwalk, his feet half a dozen steps down the spiral, and raised the Hasselblad to eye level.

In poor light conditions, a built-in mechanism actuated the flash for one-fifth of a second immediately before the shutter release was pressed. If a man already had a line on his target—Brognola's armorer had pointed out in the instructions that came with the camera gun—he should have enough time to move the cross hairs and zero in on the guy.

It was enough time for the Executioner.

In the dim light, before the hardman racing along the catwalk was aware that his prey had already surfaced, Bolan applied pressure to the button.

The moment the flash galvanized an eruption of light up there in the dark, splashing steel-hard shadows in among the old canvas flats, Bolan shifted the cross hairs fractionally, already homing the viewfinder on the hood, and pressed the button all the way down.

The shutter opened, and the squat barrel concealed behind it spit flame.

To the Executioner, the report was shockingly loud, and he had not allowed for the powerful recoil. The camera body smashed back against his face, blinding his eyes with tears and initiating a stream of blood from his nose.

The killer didn't notice. The 9 mm slug caught him high on the left shoulder, punching a fist-sized exit hole through his scapula, spinning him around with the force of the impact so that he hit the catwalk rail with the small of his back, flipped over it and fell.

The sound of the body hitting the stage boards seemed to shake the building.

Without the gunfire, there was nothing to hear but the distant, sullen roar of the rioting crowds, which from this height appeared to originate not from two sides but a single explosive point.

Bolan pulled himself up onto the walkway. Nearby, a loop of heavy-duty rope curved away into the dark from a bolsterlike shape leaning against the rail. It was, he imagined, a counterweight, connected with the raising and lowering of scenery in the flies.

He picked it up. It was filled with sand and heavy— something around three hundred, three-fifty pounds, he guessed. Sweating, he heaved it up until it was balanced on the rail.

If he was right...?

The hell with it. Why not try?

"Keep shooting. Draw the fire," he shouted down to Gage. He didn't reckon the danger of the remaining hood catching on: he knew that he was dealing with amateurs again. Dangerous, ruthless, callous—but when the chips were down, just careless local talent.

Gage must have made it right away, because the gunny opened up again at once. The sandbox rang as the slugs thumped in.

Bolan pushed the counterweight off the rail. It plunged like a stone for a few feet, stopped, shuddering on the end of the rope as the slack was taken up, then eased on down at a moderate speed. At the same time, the plain backcloth behind the table onstage rose slowly up toward the flies. When the top of it was level with the catwalk, Bolan dashed to the far corner, shielded from the killer.

And the killer, as he had hoped, had emptied his magazine at Gage and was reloading.

Bolan, hurling himself forward, saw a brutish face with pig eyes and a thick-lipped mouth beneath the inevitable cloth cap. The mouth opened in astonishment, and then they were grappling on the narrow iron walkway.

The Executioner opened with an arm block, chopping down at the same time on the guy's wrist with his free hand, so that the reloaded gun dropped out of sight.

The Irishman was big, taller than Bolan and going around two-twenty. He was strong. He might have aimed a mean PPK, but he had drawn the short straw on fighting skills.

With surprise on the Executioner's side, plus anger, it was really no contest. The gorilla landed one short-arm punch that felt as if it had drilled right through Bolan's diaphragm and out past the spinal column. But by the time Bolan had backed off and coaxed breath back into his savaged lungs, the hood was swinging a roundhouse left and all the warrior had to do was get up off his knees, grab the wrist as it sailed past his ear, twist and pull.

They used to call it judo.

The guy, projected forward by his own speed and weight, sailed over Bolan's shoulder and broke the catwalk rail.

Simon Gage stood up behind the sandbox and put two shots into the man before he hit the stage.

"Nice little gun," he observed, handing it back to Bolan two minutes later. "Super balance, even with the silencer."

"You sure know how to use it," Bolan said.

The army captain smiled. "Had a little practice at Bisley, actually," he said offhandedly. "My God! They didn't wing you, did they? You're covered in blood!"

Bolan shook his head. "Punched myself on the nose," he said, pressing a forefinger hard against his upper lip.

"You're about as much a news photographer as I am a bishop," Gage said. "Come on, Belasko—give. Just who are you? And why are you helping me?"

"Tell you later," the Executioner promised. His nose had stopped bleeding. "Let's get out of here while we can."

He didn't want to talk. There were too many questions clamoring for an answer. Such as, who the hell were the gunmen? They wouldn't have been Rafferty's men: they could have killed him in the church if they had wanted to. Mulligan didn't know his connection with Gage's crazy private eye scenario. In view of the gorillas' amateur status the attack must have been related to the original ambush in the creek. Though who the hell *they* were . . .

He shook his head. That still left a wild card in the form of the mysterious Mr. McGeehan.

He'd have to wait. Right now so much noise was coming from the stage door area that thinking was out.

The door marked Private was open, and the room was crowded. A huge man in a RUC uniform, with a peaked cap set squarely on his head and silver barring his shoulder straps, was trying to make himself heard. "Hold it, boys, hold it!" one of the white-scarved bouncers was yelling. "The DI wants a word."

The policeman addressed himself to a shambling, raw-boned man with a large jaw, a small forehead and pale hair plastered across his scalp. "Sorry to interrupt, Reverend," he shouted, "but I'm thinkin' you'd best be quittin' the hall as soon as you can. There's this gang of young hooligans outside with their banners and all, and some of our fellas are shapin' up for a bit of a bash at 'em. It could turn into an ugly situation...."

He broke off as the window disintegrated in a shower of glass. A brick crashed onto a table littered with empty beer bottles. From outside, the angry tumult was punctuated by the soft detonations of CS gas cartridges.

Bolan and Gage stopped in the passageway by a helmetless constable slumped against the wall with a gory handkerchief held to his gashed temple. A sandy-haired man with spectacles, a toothbrush mustache and a creased neck was shrieking hysterically at the reporter Bolan had seen before. "You see? You see what I mean? *There* are your bloody civil rights campaigners. *There* are you nonviolent demonstrators! Nonviolent be damned! Forcing their way into a private meeting, viciously attacking the staff—armed hooligans trying to impose their will with a reign of terror!"

"All right, Mr. Mulligan, all right," the reporter said.

Bolan looked down the stairs at the commotion raging around the stage door. Demonstrators, attacked by police from behind and a squad of Unionist strong-arm stewards in front, appeared to be trying to force their way into the hall. The area around the doorkeeper's box was littered with broken glass.

Beyond the splintered hutch, the invaders lost ground as the CS gas in the street depleted their ranks from behind. Oaths and insults, mingled with the thud of blows and the panting of struggling men, filled the air, and from time to time the concrete walls echoed thunderously as fists or feet crashed against the entrance doors.

But eventually the police, angry and red-faced, their nightsticks swinging, forced the demonstrators far enough back to slam one of the barred doors and shoot the bolts. From then on it was only a matter of time before the other, too, was shouldered home.

Bolan watched through the narrowing gap as the leader of the attackers, still shouting defiance, was hammered back under a hail of blows and the door closed.

He turned to Gage. "I wish someone would tell me," he said bemusedly, "what the hell's going on!"

For the contorted, blood-streaked face of the demonstrators' leader was the face of the pseudodrunk who had started the fight in Geraghty's Wine Lodge....

## 11

Bolan and Simon Gage walked through the back streets to the Executioner's hotel. Somewhere not far away trouble was still brewing. Over the rooftops they could hear the ugly growl of a hostile crowd and the bark of orders through a bullhorn. Farther away police whistles shrilled, and there was a blare of sirens.

After Bolan had changed his bloodied clothes, they had a quick meal before he set out for his date with Rafferty. "We left two dead men back there," Gage reminded him over coffee. "You said they were after you. Reporters from a rival newspaper, perhaps?"

The big guy laughed. "Okay, I owe you an explanation. And, yes, the news photographer number is a cover."

"A cover for what?"

Bolan gulped coffee. Clearly he must come up with a believable story, but he wasn't prepared to risk giving away the details of his mission, especially to a Brit. And an officer in the army, at that. In any case, less said the better. "I can't tell you," he said. "It's a government job. But I can promise you it's in no way directed against your people. And it's, well, only indirectly connected with Ireland and Irish politics."

"Your own government? CIA? Narcotics Bureau?"

Bolan hesitated. "I'd rather not say at this time," he said finally. "And I'd like you to know that my offer to help you personally is on the level."

The Englishman had to be content with that.

They were walking toward the city hall cab rank, so that Gage could get a ride back to the parking garage where he had left his car, when a heavy hand fell on his shoulder.

"Simon!" a hearty voice enthused. "The hard man himself! What are you doing here? I thought you'd be living it up in Dublin for your seventy-two!"

The two men swung around. Swaying slightly on his feet, a mustached brother officer in the uniform of a major was surveying them genially.

Gage introduced Bolan. Then, "You're stealing my lines, Courtney," he said. "What on earth are you doing in town at this hour?"

"Looking for crumpet, old boy. Tail, as your friend would say. There's a place just around the corner full of the most smashing birds. Come and have a drink."

Gage shook his head. "I have to get back to the billet. Busy day tomorrow."

Major Courtney looked expectantly at the Executioner. "Sorry," Bolan said. "I already have a date."

"Oh, come on. Just nip in and have a quick one with me. Toast the special relationship an' all that, hospitality to our gallant allies. In any case, by the time you see some of these birds you may change your mind and chuck your other date altogether."

"No, really, I—"

"Mind you, some of 'em cost. On the bash, you know. But that's up to you to find out first, what!" Courtney was clearly the kind of drunk it was hard to shake off. "Where's your bloody date, anyway?" he asked.

Bolan sighed. "A place called the Ambassador." He glanced at his watch. It was not yet twelve-thirty. He had time.

"The Ambassador!" Courtney exclaimed. "But that's the place I'm talking about, dammit! We'll go together. But what are you doing, waiting here?"

"Gage is waiting for a cab. I'm going to the other side of the square. The place is in Ann Street."

"Don't be bloody silly, old man. It's the other way— down Royal Avenue and in toward the market."

"It's in Ann Street." Bolan tried to master his irritation. "Or rather an alleyway off Ann Street called Mullen's Passage."

"Up Mullen's Passage," the major said coarsely. "It's in there by the market."

"Must be another place with the same name."

"Look, old man, if anyone knows the night spots in this blasted city, such as they are, it's yours truly. And I swear by the spirit of Jack Daniel's there's only one Ambassador, and it's—"

He broke off as Gage saw a cruising taxi and hailed it. Bolan turned his back and walked across to two RUC men standing outside the city hall.

"Pardon me," Bolan said. "Could you direct me to a place called the Ambassador Club, in Mullen's Passage, off Ann Street?"

"In Mullen's Passage?" one of the cops echoed.

"That's what I was told."

"Somebody's been having you on, sir," the other policeman said. "There's no nightclubs in Mullen's Passage! It's not but fifty yards long, and one side's Newell's fish warehouse all the way. The other's a row of empty houses waitin' to be demolished."

"There *is* an Ambassador Club, but," the first man offered. "In by the old market, off Royal Avenue there."

Courtney was cawing with laughter. "She's sold you a pup, old boy. You've been stood up," he said. "What did I tell you? Now the first round's bloody well on you!"

Bolan was puzzled. He didn't get it. What was the point of decoying him to a dark cul-de-sac if it wasn't to kill him or screw some information out of him? And those things could have been initiated at the church. In any case, as far as the Republicans knew, he *wanted* to give them the information.

He decided he would go along with the drunken Brit. Bolan would play out the script as it had been written, and the guy might be useful as a cover.

Okay, the club wasn't in Mullen's Passage. But once they were in the right street, it *was* the third door on the right, as the fair man had said; it *was* up a long, steep flight of stairs; and there *was* a reception desk at the top. Behind it sat a brightly painted blonde in scarlet knee boots and a plastic miniskirt.

They paid the entrance fee and were heading for the hatcheck counter when Bolan decided to make his run. It wasn't one-fifteen yet, and if he had deliberately been given phony directions it was unlikely the rest of the scenario would be played as scripted. Just the same, he'd give it a whirl. "You go ahead," he said to the major. "I'll be with you in a minute."

Back at the desk, he leaned across and murmured to the blonde, "I'd like to see Mr. O'Connell. Callahan sent me."

The penciled eyebrows scaled the smooth cliff of her forehead. "Mr. *O'Connell*?" She seemed astonished. Perhaps it was a code name, used at the wrong time in the wrong place. "Just a sec. I'll have to see."

She slid her tight sweater, and the braless breasts beneath it, out from behind the desk. The red boots creaked away down a corridor.

Bolan looked around him. Cigarette burns scarred the dove-gray carpet in the entrance lobby. Behind him was an empty snack bar with the obligatory low key lighting in red. Ahead were quilted double doors with portholes from behind which came the jangling blare of hard rock played competently but without imagination. Guys in sharp suits drifted to and from the hatcheck counter to buy clandestine fifths of liquor, and there was a constant parade of women and girls with too much makeup and too few clothes.

The receptionist was back by his side. "Would you come this way, please?"

Bolan followed her down a short passage opposite the washrooms. She knocked on a door, opened it and gestured for him to go on in.

Bolan went in and found himself facing three men with leveled guns: the dark-haired IRA man he had met in the church basement and two wide-shouldered characters who looked as though they could be racecourse toughs. The guns were short-barreled American .38 Police Specials.

Lethal in a confined space.

The door thudded shut. Hands patted his pockets, buttocks and the inside of his thighs. The Beretta was tweaked from its holster. "Clean now," a voice said.

The room was small. Three tall gray filing cabinets by Chubb. Red leather tub chairs. No windows, another door. A black steel desk with two telephones and an intercom.

The pale-haired man from the church sat behind the desk. Bolan glanced over his shoulder. Ferret-face was leaning against the door, with Bolan's gun held loosely in his right hand.

"Come right in," the man at the desk said. "We weren't expecting you here. You're early, anyway. My two friends were about to make it to Mullen's Passage and prepare a welcome for you."

"In a condemned house or the fish store?" Bolan asked.

"The third house on the right," the fair man said humorlessly. "We don't make detail mistakes."

"Just king-size, jumbo, economy-size mistakes," Bolan needled, "like shooting down Derek Osborne."

"Derek who? What are you on about?"

"The Englishman murdered on patrol near the Falls Road."

"That? That was nothing to do with us," the fair man said indifferently. "Ask the local Westminster lickspittles if you want to know who did that."

"Or like this little performance," the Executioner pursued. "What the hell are you playing at this time? Anyway, you'd never dare shoot in here."

"Don't bank on it." He pointed at a corner of the desk, and Ferret-face stepped forward and laid the Beretta down between the two phones. "Seeing as how we have a nice silenced weapon to play with. But in any case we don't need to shoot. Not here. This door behind me leads to a yard hidden from the street. There is a covered hearse there, ready to go. All we need do here is give you another wee tap on the head."

He leaned forward and flipped the key of the intercom. Over the sudden harsh jangle of the band, a voice called something unintelligible. "Listen," the fair man said, "have Eddie tell the drummer take two choruses at the end of this number. Good and loud. We have business in here."

He snapped the switch off again.

"Why?" Bolan asked. "What's the point? I thought we were going to talk business. We had a deal. I want to see this Rafferty—"

"I am Rafferty."

"Then why not say so, for God's sake?"

"For my sake," Rafferty corrected. "And I was right, was I not? No matter though, now that we have you. You will do us no more harm."

"Harm? I was going to help you. What is all this crap?"

"Look, man, you and your friend Gage, or whatever his name is. Don't insult our intelligence: the shakedown won't work. We're onto you, is all."

Mystified, Bolan glanced rapidly around the room. The three guns were rock steady. Ferret-face was behind him, to one side; Rafferty was relaxed at the desk. And Bolan saw now that what he had taken originally for an easy, fairly casual manner was in fact the stillness before the strike of a rattler. This man was deadly. The self-control masked the icy determination of the dedicated fanatic.

Bolan had no idea what had gone wrong, what he was supposed to have done, but he knew he had to get out of there, fast.

Once through that second door, it would all be over. So 'Act fast' was the golden rule. The longer you delayed, the more the roles of captor and captive became established, the less likely you were to put the guys with the upper hand off their stroke.

He had only advanced a single step into the room when he entered. Now, making a performance of it, he edged warily back, eyeing the gunmen apprehensively. His hands, which he had automatically raised to shoulder level when he'd first seen the weapons, clenched themselves lightly.

Suspecting that he was going to try and jump them, the dark man spoke for the first time. "Stay where you are," he rapped. "Don't make it hard for yourself now."

But Bolan was already where he wanted to be. His shoulders were brushing the wall at one side of the door, and behind them were the four flush-fitting switches controlling the lights in the room. Imperceptibly he flexed his knees.

The distant yowling of the rock band ceased, and a fusillade of percussion effects filtered through the walls as the drummer launched into his unexpected sixty-four-bar solo.

Rafferty got to his feet and nodded to Ferret-face. The three gun barrels raised warningly. From his pocket Ferret-face drew something short, sausage-shaped and covered in leather, and turned toward the Executioner with a grin on his narrow face.

Now.

Bolan flattened his shoulder blades hard against the wall and straightened his knees with a jerk.

The moment his rising body tripped the switches, plunging the room into darkness, he threw himself down and sideways, toward Ferret-face.

Flame lanced the dark, the roar of the three reports stinging his ears. He hit the little man below the knees, bringing him down. Rafferty shouted something, and one of the guns fired again toward the door. A finger of light probed the darkness as the slug smashed through into the bright passageway beyond.

Bolan felt a numbing blow on his left shoulder as Ferret-face swung the blackjack. He snatched the tiny flat-bladed knife that was strapped, beneath the sock, to his right ankle and struck upward.

There was a cry of pain. Homing on the sound, Bolan picked the little man up bodily and slung him across the room in the direction of the desk.

The body thumped to the floor, Rafferty's chair crashed over backward, voices cursed. A telephone fell from the desk with a jingling smash as a fifth shot plowed into the ceiling.

Bolan reached and swept his Beretta from the desk. He fired once toward the voices, heard a choking grunt, another stumbling fall.

He was crouched on all fours, reaching for the door handle, when the door slowly opened and light flooded into the room.

Major Courtney, looking decidedly drunk now, peered shortsightedly at the tangle of men unwinding themselves from the wreckage of the desk. One of the gunmen remained facedown on the floor, and Ferret-face was holding a bloodstained hand to his left upper arm. The Police Specials had miraculously vanished.

With a single movement, Bolan got to his feet and slid past the major into the passage.

"Oh, there you are, old man," Courtney said. "I was looking for you. Silly bitch at the desk said you'd left, but I knew you wouldn't do that without saying—I say! Whatever's going on here?"

"These gentlemen have been having a little difference of opinion over a matter of business," Bolan said, taking his elbow and steering him back to the lobby. "I think it's time we split."

## 12

"Leave? Don't be an ass, we can't leave now," Courtney expostulated. "I just found myself the most fabulous bird. You, er, there's booze available from the hatcheck feller, you know."

"So I see," Bolan said.

"No license of course, but you know the Irish."

"Have one for me," Bolan said. "I'm on my way."

Easy to say; harder to do. He might have gotten away from the immediate danger in the little office, but quitting the whole place was something else.

Two guys in broad-brimmed hats were standing by the reception desk, blocking the way to the stairs. They could have been twins of the pair in the office. Ferret-face scuttled across the lobby with a blood-soaked handkerchief pressed to his arm. He muttered something to a hard-faced giant behind the hatcheck counter, scowled malevolently at the Executioner and disappeared into the men's room. At the end of the passage the bullet-scarred office door was closed, and the dark-haired IRA man stood sentinel by it with folded arms.

Bolan stared past the jigging dancers through the porthole in one of the padded doors. The drummer was still thrashing away at the far end of the room. Beside the stand was an archway blanked off with velvet draperies. As he watched, the remaining thug from the office pushed through and sat down at a vacant table nearby.

Bolan was surrounded. If they couldn't shoot at him in this crowded joint, neither could he fire back. He was safe as long as there were customers in the club, but he couldn't leave, and once the dancers had gone home they would close in on him from all sides. End of story.

Courtney was lurching toward him, towing a red-haired woman in a fringed Charleston dress and gray suede boots buckled above the knee.

For a moment Bolan thought of asking for his help, but the guy was too far gone, and anyway the hardmen guarding the entrance were approaching, one on either side. "We'll have a word with you, sir, if you don't mind," said one, reaching for the big guy's arm.

There was a crash of cymbals and a burst of applause from the far side of the quilted doors as the drummer completed his marathon. At once the rest of the band attacked an old-fashioned two-step.

"The ladies' choice, for God's sake!" squealed the redhead, who was clearly a little smashed. "What I've been waitin' for all my life! Come on, you, and dance with me!"

Staring appraisingly at Bolan, she skipped forward, grabbed his other arm and whirled him away toward the dance floor.

Her name was Ginny McDade. When they were dancing, he saw that she was older than he had thought. Pushing thirty, maybe, with tired lines under her eyes. But there was humor in their green depths, and the corners of her full-lipped mouth turned up.

"Don't get me wrong," Bolan said as he steered her toward the bandstand, "but do you come here often?"

"Oh, brother!" the woman said. "Often enough to have heard that one before!"

"I'm not kidding. I really want to know. How well do you know the place?"

She looked up at him, sensing from his tone that the question was important. "Well enough, baby," she said. "But what's the pitch? I don't get it."

Bolan looked into her eyes. She was dancing lightly but voluptuously, her waist pliant against his palm, large firm breasts lying against his chest, heavy thighs hugging his own.

"I have to get out of here," he said. "Fast."

"So go then," Ginny McDade said. "But no so fast that I'm letting you skip before the end of this number." Her hand rose from his shoulder to his nape, and she swung her hips sensuously against him.

"No, I mean get out without anyone seeing me go."

She leaned back against the curve of his arm and stared at him. "You're on the run?"

"In a way. Not from the law."

"But whoever it is, they're in here? Now?"

Bolan nodded. "A man called Rafferty," he said.

"*Rafferty?* The breakaway Army boss? That's tough. He's a bad man to be running after a person. He never lets up. You say he's here tonight? In the club?"

"In the office. There's half a dozen strong-arm guys blocking the main staircase, the washrooms, the back stairs from the office, that arch beside the band."

She glanced around as they circled the close-packed floor. "They'll be from Connolly's racecourse gang. They work in with the Army lads sometimes."

"I've got to get past them, find some other way out," Bolan said. "Would you know of one?"

She was clinging to him, her breath warm and winey on his cheek. "I might," she murmured. "It depends where you want to go afterward."

"Meaning?"

"To put it bluntly, do you want to come by my place, to come home with me?" Every curve of her soft body, draped languorously against him as they danced, pleaded for him to say yes.

"Nothing I'd like better. But I guess I have to—"

"Ah, c'mon," she said, abandoning the pseudotrans-atlantic effect and dropping into her normal voice, "give us a while of your time. I'm a wee bit stoned, I know, but you're a fine-lookin' feller and I fancy you, but."

Abruptly she disengaged herself and sat down at one of the small tables bordering the dance floor, pulling him down beside her. "Have a drink of lover boy's whiskey," she said, pouring from a fifth standing on the table.

Bolan looked across the crowded floor. Courtney seemed already to have made good the loss of his smashing bird. He was propped up in the center by a tall brunette with enormous false eyelashes and a blue-rinse wig, barely moving in time to the music. There was a foolish smile on his face, and his eyes were closed.

The Executioner grinned. "You're right," he said. "The major won't be needing any more. What's with the brown highball glasses?"

"Custom of the house. So the scrubbers don't catch on when they pour in meths. The brown glass hides the mauve color, and then they add ginger ale to hide the taste. Not to worry though. This bottle is for real."

He raised his glass. "Happy escapes," she said.

Bolan drank. "If I read you right," he said, "you'll only let me in on the secret if I agree to come home with you. Is that it?"

"Hole in one, handsome."

"And you are, pardon me if I'm indelicate, what they call a business girl?"

She giggled, eyeing him over the rim of her glass. "A girl has to live, sure. And I was never a dab hand at the typing machine."

"How much?"

She looked him in the eye. "To you, darlin', a pony. And that's only because I have hot pants for you. Most times I take half a century. But it is for all night, mind."

"I couldn't just give you the money here, and you explain how—"

"No!" she interrupted angrily. "You could not. Didn't I say I had a thing for you, for God's sake? What kind of a person do you think I am . . . All right, don't answer that."

"I'm sorry," Bolan apologized. "I didn't mean—"

He realized suddenly that he had no place to go if he did get out of the Ambassador. He couldn't take the risk that his hotel might be watched. He couldn't make any more progress on the mission until tomorrow. In any case, the woman was his only chance of getting away. "When do we leave?" he asked.

She squeezed his hand, her eyes bright. "That's me boy! Don't look specially, but when you get a chance take in the wall these tables are against. You'll see it's a row of plaster pillars with alcoves in between. Shallow alcoves to take the chairs, like the one we're at."

"So?"

"So you'd think it was an outside wall, with no windows. But it's not. The alcoves are deeper than they look. The wall behind us is false. They had to put it in a few years back when neighbors complained of the noise. But behind it there are windows still there."

"Are you telling me there's a way through? That we could get to those windows?"

Ginny nodded. "These tall panels in each alcove are hinged. They open like doors. Next time they play a bossa nova or a samba, the lights will dim. If we were real quick, we could jerk open a panel and slip through before anyone could get to us. The floor's always crowded, anyway."

"What's beyond the windows—if they still open?"

# Terrorists, anarchists, hijackers and drug dealers—BEWARE!

In a world shock-tilted by terror, Mack Bolan and his courageous combat teams, *SOBs* and our new high-powered entry, *Vietnam: Ground Zero* provide America's best hope for salvation.

Fueled by white-hot rage and sheer brute force, they blaze a war of vengeance against a tangled international network of trafficking and treachery. Join them as they battle the enemies of democracy in timely, hard-hitting stories ripped from today's headlines.

## Get 4 explosive novels delivered right to your home—FREE

Return the attached Card, and we'll send you 4 gut-chilling, high-voltage Gold Eagle novels—FREE!

If you like them, we'll send you 6 brand-new books every other month to preview. Always before they're available in stores. Always at a hefty saving off the retail price. Always with the right to cancel and owe nothing.

As a subscriber, you'll also get…
- our free newsletter *AUTOMAG* with each shipment
- special books to preview and buy at a deep discount

## Get a digital quartz calendar watch—FREE

As soon as we receive your Card, we'll send you a digital quartz calendar watch as an outright gift. It comes complete with long-life battery and one-year warranty (excluding battery). *And like the 4 free books, it's yours to keep even if you never buy another Gold Eagle book.*

## RUSH YOUR ORDER TO US TODAY.

PRINTED IN U.S.A.

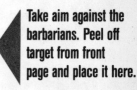

## Meet America's most potent human weapons

*Mack Bolan* and his courageous combat squads—
*Able Team & Phoenix Force*— along with *SOBs*
and *Vietnam: Ground Zero* unleash the best
sharpshooting firepower ever published.
Join them as they blast their way through page
after page of raw action toward a fiery climax
of rage and retribution.

If offer card is missing, write to: Gold Eagle Reader Service,
901 Fuhrmann Blvd., P.O. Box 1394, Buffalo, NY 14240-1394

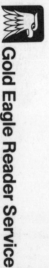

## BUSINESS REPLY CARD

First Class    Permit No. 717    Buffalo, NY

Postage will be paid by addressee

**Gold Eagle Reader Service**
901 Fuhrmann Blvd.
P.O. Box 1394
Buffalo, NY 14240-9983

NO POSTAGE
NECESSARY
IF MAILED
IN THE
UNITED STATES

"They do, they do. There's like an old-fashioned balcony: we used to go out there, summer nights, and smoke a cigarette before they blocked it. The balcony joins up with the regular fire escape that you get to through the snack bar."

"Where does the fire escape come down?"

"An alley behind the building leads into the old market."

"Ginny, darling," Bolan said, "I love you."

A few minutes later, wall lighting dimmed, a faceted globe revolving in the center of the ceiling slung spots of colored light spinning around the room, and dancers began to bounce to the sibilant rhythms of a samba. Bolan craned his neck to spy out the disposition of the enemy forces as people crowded in from the lobby and snack bar to jam the floor.

The two hoods who had been approaching when Ginny had whisked Bolan away had followed them into the room, but advanced no farther than the doors. They were still there, one by each porthole. Beyond them, each time the doors opened, Bolan saw Ferret-face and the dark man in the lobby. The gorilla by the bandstand was still at his table.

The woman plucked a camel hair coat from the back of her chair and slung it over her shoulders. While she was doing this she contrived to reach behind her and feel for the crack between two of the wall panels. "This one doesn't budge," she told him over the rattle of maracas. "Must be the hinge side. Try the one behind you."

She stood up and reached for her purse. Bolan remained seated. Anyone taking in the scene might think she was about to leave—perhaps after some disagreement—and he was going to stay. He tilted his chair back against the wall, letting his arms drop to either side.

The gap between the panels was wide enough for him to insert his fingers. He flexed the top joints, trying to lever the edge toward him. A moment later there was a loud crack. Bolan tensed, glancing swiftly right and left; in the excitement of the samba nobody had noticed.

He brought his other hand across and added more pressure. The leading edge of the panel shuddered a half inch into the room.

Bolan looked at Ginny and nodded. "On your way," he said.

She stepped farther into the alcove, leaning over her chair as if she were picking up something she had left behind. Bolan now had both hands curled around the panel edge, gripping it hard. He jerked it toward him.

The panel swung open, revealing a tall, thin rectangle of darkness that released a breath of stale, musty air.

The dancers whirled and jumped as the music got louder. Ginny McDade straightened up and slipped through the narrow gap into the night. Bolan thought he saw the hood by the bandstand come to attention and stare his way. He slid off his chair and eased himself, bent double, into the opening.

A shout from the porthole doors pierced the racket of flutes and brass and electric guitars. "Hurry!" Bolan shouted. "They're onto us!"

Beyond the panel he found himself in a narrow space between the false wall and a huge, leaded window. The woman was wrestling with an ancient iron catch that operated a locking rod. "It's stuck," she gasped. "Hasn't been opened . . . in years. Here, see what you—"

Urgency lent Bolan a manic strength. He seized the catch and wrenched it powerfully. At last the bolt withdrew from its sockets. He shoved the window open, and they stepped over a low sill onto a railed iron grid that ran the length of the building. Opposite them, a high wall studded with lightless windows rose toward a strip of starry sky. Below was the narrow yard where the hearse was parked. Bolan imagined the three hoods forcing their way through the press of dancers to make the breached alcove. "Come on," he urged, grabbing her hand. "We've gotta move!"

"Not that way!" Ginny cried. "If they saw us leave, they only have to run up to the snack bar and use the emergency exit, and they can cut us off before we get to the fire escape." She pulled him in the other direction, and they clattered off toward the back of another building blocking off both the alleyway below and the balcony they were on.

Bolan looked over the iron rail. She was right. A band of light lay across the far end of the walkway, and two men stood at the top of the fire escape. He thought he recognized Ferret-face and the dark guy. There was already somebody in the yard below. Nearer, in the diffused light from the opened window, a bulky silhouette emerged.

Ten yards father along, Ginny stopped by a dark window and swung her purse on its strap. The pane imploded with a crash. At once flame lanced the dark from the top of the iron escape ladder and the entry below. The sharp explosions reverberated between the walls. The woman gasped as her purse was shot from her hand. One of the slugs passed so close to Bolan that he felt the hot wind of its flight on his neck.

Ginny knocked away shards of glass that tinkled to the iron floor of the grid and raised a booted leg over the sill of the smashed window. Bolan was flat on the grillwork, the Beretta in his hands.

Between the railings, he pumped three, four single shots down into the entry, aiming at the near side of the hearse's dark bulk. Glass smashed, metal sang, a slug glanced off a hubcap and shrilled away. The hood below aimed up at the balcony and fired twice. One, two, the muzzle-flashes reflected in the polished black panelwork of the hearse.

That was when the Executioner's 93-R sneezed out the one that mattered.

Betting his entire stack of chips that the gunman was right-handed, he shot inside and a little above the darts of flame, to the right for him, left for the killer.

He scored. He heard a hoarse cry, a stumbling fall, a metallic slither that could have been a gun skating across a brick-floored yard.

"Hurry!" Ginny called from the window. "Or they'll be round the front and stop us leaving."

The gorilla who had been sitting by the bandstand, flattened against the wall, was sliding toward Bolan. He couldn't see the gun, but he knew it would be there.

What he could see was the bird beak of a hat brim, the curve of the man's belly against the light streaming from the emergency exit at the far end of the balcony. He was a big man, but he wasn't too hot on cover. He was fifteen feet away, and he didn't even get a chance to fire.

As the gun arm came up, fist, chamber and hammer silhouetted, the Executioner stowed a slug six inches inside the upper curve of the belly.

Over the subsonic *chock!* of the Beretta, Bolan heard the actual thwack of the impact, and the hood gave a heavy sigh. He took a step forward across the balcony, and buckled slowly until he was kneeling with his arms folded on the rail and his head on his arms.

Then he keeled over and lay spread-eagled on his back. After that he didn't move anymore.

Bolan used him as a cover, inching his way forward until he was behind the corpse. He could hear blood dripping through the grillwork onto the yard below.

Ferret-face and the dark man had retreated down the fire escape until their heads were level with the walkway. Bolan approved of the maneuver: he had used it himself on the spiral at the Ulster Hall. But there was a difference: at the

Ulster Hall the guy on the walkway was approaching the stairs; here he was retreating.

The two IRA men were safe, but they weren't in an attacking position. Bolan fired a three-shot burst designed to ricochet from the ironwork just ahead of the stairs. Make the bastards keep their heads down just long enough for him to run and dive through that window before they could rise high enough to lay an accurate shot on him.

The 9 mm slugs screamed their farewell. Bolan leaped up, raced hunched forward to the window, and took a header into the dark room beyond. They got off two rounds, one splatting against the brickwork framing the window, the other nicking the heel of his combat boot as he dived.

Not bad. Not quite good enough, but close.

He picked himself up from the floor. His left arm was giving him hell where Ferret-face's blackjack had landed. "Where to now?" he panted, aware that here he was dealing with professionals, and there were still the two hoods who had been standing by the porthole doors to be accounted for.

"Out," Ginny said. "Quick. This is an office block. Empty at night. Just follow me."

They bumped their way across a roomful of desks, found themselves in a corridor and opened a door leading to an upstairs hallway. From here they stole down a huge, curving stairway to an entrance lobby that was illuminated by the street lighting that slanted in through a semicircular fanlight above the front door. The lobby had a marble checkerboard floor.

"Cross your fingers and pray this baby's not mortised," Bolan told Ginny, staring at the massive mahogany paneling. He was imagining those two porthole hoods footing it around the block from the side street where the Ambassador was located.

But the door was secured with a normal Yale-type lock. He turned the milled brass knob, opened the door cautiously and peered through the crack into a deserted Royal Avenue.

Not entirely deserted. A cab was turning the corner from High Street. And its For Hire sign was lit.

Bolan jerked open the door and ran out into the street, waving his arms. The woman followed, leaving the door open. The cab angled in toward the curb, and stopped with a squeal of brakes.

Bolan shoved her in the back seat and slammed the door.

Ginny gave an Antrim Road address, wound up the glass partition and sank back on the seat with a sigh of relief. "A chase is a chase," she said, "but I hadn't reckoned on getting shot at. Suppose now you tell me just what all this is about?"

The Executioner felt he owed her something. What he told her was Simon Gage's story, beginning with the death of Derek Osborne, ending with the scene in the nightclub before he had met her. He admitted they were making a pretense of giving away the Mourne arms dump...to both sides. He told about the Ulster Hall ambush. He said the aim of the operation was to track down Osborne's killer. As an explanation for his own interest, he plugged the possible photo-scoop line. He said he had no idea why the whole city seemed to be gunning for him.

"Maybe it was a crazy idea of my friend's," he said. "But there's one thing that puzzles me more than the murder itself." He paused, trying to crystallize his thoughts. The woman watched him gravely, leaning back in her corner of the seat.

"We wouldn't really have told them the secrets of the dump," Bolan said. "But we did get in touch with the militants of both sides. Shit, they weren't to know we didn't intend to go through with it, and they must all be crying for arms. Yet the suspicion, the open distrust that my offer provoked..." He shook his head. "In a way, my friend, too. They kept on asking his name. As if that mattered. I mean, you'd think either side would damned well jump—"

"I think I can explain that," Ginny interrupted.

"*You* can? But how?" Bolan was astonished.

She was looking out the window. Red brick walls and slate roofs sped past. "You meet a lot of different folks in my business," she said. "I know some of the fighting boys on both sides. Some of the girls take sides, but I prefer to stay in the middle. It's safer that way. But of course you have to be hell's own tactful, because you hear gossip from all over." They had stopped for a red light. She fell silent and gazed at the darkened windows on the far side of the intersection.

"Well?" Bolan prompted gently as the driver let in the clutch and they started off again. The green light tinged her face with an unearthly pallor.

"It's understandable they were suspicious," she said. "You see, you were just a wee bit too late."

"Too late?"

"Sure. Somebody else has already been around, touting the idea of breaking into that arms dump. Only a few days ago. And he went to both sides, too, but he was doing it for real. He wanted money. And he was playing off one side against the other so that he could get the best price possible."

For a moment Bolan said nothing. The street, dried by a wind that was now scouring the city, sang under the wheels.

And then, "Good God!" he exclaimed. "No wonder they... They must have thought we— But *who*? Who else would be going around trying to sell a deal like that?"

"I never saw him myself," Ginny McDade said. "But I heard the boys talk about him. It seems it was an English army officer, name of Simon Gage."

## 13

The house looked as if it belonged to somebody's aunt. Stiff silk brocade covered the fat cushions of the easy chairs in the parlor; there were white antimacassars draped over the back of the couch. Opposite the front door, a grandfather clock ticked loudly once every second, each time the pendulum swung.

A stout, high-busted woman in a jump suit led them in. She was about sixty years old, and her lacquered hair reminded the Executioner of the steel swarf that curled away from a factory lathe.

"You can have number four, dear," she said to Ginny. "But no slapping, please. Bridie's in six with the old colonel, and you know how light he sleeps." Flashing gold-rimmed spectacles momentarily toward Bolan, she added in a low voice, "I hope you know what you're doing."

Bolan, taking in the gilt-framed Irish landscapes that punctuated the striped wallpaper, was suddenly conscious of his appearance. He could see her cash-register eyes taking inventory of his mussed hair, his lack of a raincoat, the missing heel of one combat boot, the damp soot from the balcony that grimed his face, hands, elbows and knees. "I'm one of the more eccentric millionaires," he said with a bow.

Ginny laughed. "Don't worry about me, Mrs. Mac," she said. "Could we have something to drink, please?"

"I'll send the girl in," the woman said, turning to leave. "All the same—" with a glare at Bolan "—I'd get the cash in advance if I was you."

Bolan laughed as he pulled two chairs close to an electric heater presiding over artificial logs pulsing with a plastic glow. "You're the only person in town who seems to know anything about anything," he said. "Tell me more about my buddy's namesake and the guys he deals with, okay?"

The "girl"—a woman of about fifty with a sour expression—carried in a tray loaded with ice, soda, highball glasses and a bottle of John Jameson. She placed the tray on a walnut veneer occasional table, took money from Bolan and went away. Somewhere upstairs a door closed with a solid click.

Bolan poured drinks while Ginny talked. It seemed that the fake Gage had appeared about a week ago, ironically enough following much the same technique as Bolan and his companion to find his way to extremist elements on both sides. He had talked to Mulligan and the pastor; he, too, had offered the secret of the arms dump to Rafferty and his gangster sidekicks. He had, in addition, contacted Citizens' Defense Committee members and spokesmen for the People's Democracy, all of whom had refused to have anything to do with him. Where he was one step ahead was arranging a meet with a Protestant racecourse gang leader who sometimes worked with the ultraright wing of the Unionists. Man by the name of Connolly.

Correction. Bolan had met, if not Connolly then at least some of his men. At the wrong end of a Russian-made SMG in a vacant lot near a burned-out panel truck.

Could the Belfast underworld grapevine have worked swiftly enough for that ambush to have been set up for him and not for Deirdre O'Mara?

That didn't matter anymore, Bolan thought. What was certain was that the impostor had been in the middle of negotiations with both sides, each unknown to the other, when he and the real Simon Gage had made their play.

Was it such a surprise that the use of Gage's name had provoked such mistrust and raised so many questions?

No way.

But the most vital question of all was the one that Bolan himself now raised.

What stage had the negotiations reached and where was this impostor now?

Did he really know the secrets of the Mourne dump? If so, had he sold them, and to which side? How would this affect the IRA plot Bolan had to destroy?

Or were the arms in the depot *part* of the plot? Had the whole deal been predicated on gaining control of this dump? "They'll be wearing British uniforms," Brognola had said. It could figure.

One more question. Was the impostor wise to the fact that there was now a real Simon Gage on the board, and if he was, would he retreat back under cover? Or bluff it out and let the suspicion rest with the latecomers?

It depended on whether the deal had already been concluded—and whether he actually knew Gage.

Bolan sighed, then swallowed his drink. Too damn many questions and not enough answers.

But Ginny, it turned out, could partly answer one of them. "It's a funny thing," she said, "but I heard some of the boys talking about it yesterday. Yon fella, the one's not your friend, he seems to have dropped out of sight these past few days, right outta circulation. There's people looking for him, but he doesn't show."

"Which boys?"

"Well, now, it would have been . . . let me see . . ." Ginny drained her glass, splashed four fingers of John Jameson into it and reached for the ice. "It would have been some of the boys up the club."

"Rafferty's team?"

"Aye. Or lads of their persuasion." She drank. "You wanna be careful, handsome. You may think it's good crack, playing off these characters one against th'other. But they play rough, you know."

"It hadn't escaped me," Bolan said dryly.

"That Connolly, the ugly one he is. If it's beating folks up or puttin' the boot in, he really enjoys that. And Rafferty's just the opposite: He's the cool one all right. With him it might just as well be a game of chess—only when a piece is taken off the board and put back in the box, it's a pine-wood box with brass handles and they take it away in a hearse. He can't forget 1916, that one, even though he wasn't born then."

"Ginny," Bolan said, "I need you to do something for me."

"Jus' now," she said, her voice beginning to slur a little, "there's a lotta things I wan' you to do for *me*! Why don' we . . . ?"

"I'm serious. Could you find out something for me?"

"Try me, lover boy."

"Could you find out from your friends whether this guy calling himself Simon Gage has in fact made a deal yet and sold the secrets, and if so to which side? Could you do that for me?"

"Oh, aye," Ginny said. "I might at that. There's a wee fella, Danny McClusky, not a political at all. He might be in the know. He runs with the hare an' hunts with the houn's, if you take my meanin'. Being a harmless little lad, nobody pays him any mind, but he keeps his ears open, see."

"The information's worth money to him," Bolan said.

"Fair enough. Give me a little time. Call me the day after tomorrow, okay? At this number." She took a small notebook from her purse, scribbled seven figures on it and handed it to him. "Afternoon, between five an' seven, okay?"

As Bolan took the paper, folded it and stowed it in his inside pocket, a bell shrilled in the hall. The madam went to answer it and let in a fluffy blonde with heavily mascaraed eyes, followed by a nervous-looking middle-aged man carrying an umbrella. As the door, with its red and blue glass panes, swung shut, the grandfather clock struck two.

Suddenly Ginny raised her arms above her head and yawned. "Les' make tracks, honey," she said. "We can take the rest of the bottle up with us."

Wall-to-wall Axminster carpeted the corridors in a pattern of flowers and fruit. Number four was chilly, with an oasis of scorching heat around an old-fashioned gas heater burning beneath the mirrored mantel. The massive headboard, the clothes closet, the washstand and the dressing table were made of bird's-eye maplewood. A modern sink and a bidet lurked discreetly with the john in a curtained-off alcove.

As soon as the door closed, Ginny reached behind her and unzippered her dress. She shook her shoulders, and the pale blue material swished from her arms and dropped in a shimmering pool around her feet. She was wearing a wired strapless bra in the same shade, matching silk panties with frilled legs and dark thigh-high nylons.

She manipulated the fasteners at the back of the brassiere and her breasts sprang free. She unbuckled one of her boots and drew its gray suede length from her leg, unrolling the stocking after it. "Go in there, you, and get your clothes off while I get rid of this other boot," she said thickly.

Bolan went. "I can't get the bloody thing off. There's something wrong with the buckle," Ginny called. "The damn thing's stuck. I . . . Ah, the hell with it. What's a boot between friends?"

He heard a long sigh, a sudden creak of the bed. He twitched aside the curtain. Miss Ginny McDade, naked except for one suede boot, a nylon and a pair of blue satin panties, had fallen back on the covers and passed out cold.

Bolan heaved a sigh of relief. He was thankful that Ginny's intake of alcohol had spared him what might have been an embarrassing refusal, and a rejection, for her, that could have been wounding.

She had more than earned her money, had even risked her life getting him out of the club. There was no reason why she should lose out because she had, from her point of view, picked the wrong guy. He left twice the sum she had asked for beneath the highball glass on the night table.

Then, picking up her legs, he swung her fully onto the bed and pulled the covers over her. She muttered something unintelligible but remained unconscious. Bolan hoped she would remember to contact her friend Danny McClusky.

He switched off the light, made himself as comfortable as he could in an armchair by the fire and pulled his jacket over his shoulders. He would be gone long before she was awake.

## 14

The wind rose during the night. When Mack Bolan left the house on Antrim Road shortly after dawn, it was blowing half a gale. The fruit trees and flowering shrubs in the expensive suburban gardens were leaning toward the hills, and above the descending series of roofs dropping toward Belfast Lough he could see whitecaps marching across the water from the Holywood shore.

As he stood waiting for the lights to change at the intersection where the taxi had stopped the night before, he heard his name called.

Bolan swung around. Ten yards behind him a small, battered gray car had pulled up. The nearside door was open, and the driver was leaning across from the wheel.

The car was a Volkswagen; it could have been the mirror image of the one that had burned in the vacant lot. The driver was Deirdre O'Mara.

The Executioner approached the vehicle. "Come inside a minute," she said. "It's desperate cold with the door open."

"You must be joking," Bolan said.

"Ah, come on," she said. "I'm not working for Rafferty just now. It's off duty I am. What are you concerned about? Gunmen behind the seat?"

"I'm concerned about gunmen. Period."

"All right. I know what happened last night. It was nothing to do with me. Please believe that. And for God's sake get in, man."

The Executioner slid into the passenger seat and slammed the door. "Why should I believe you?" he asked. "After all, it was your introduction that got me sapped first, then shot at. Thanks very much."

"I don't see how impostors can complain if—"

"Look, I know about that now. I'm no impostor, nor is my buddy. It's the guy who's going around asking for money who's phony."

"The explanation had occurred to me," the woman said. "That is one of the things I wanted to talk to you about."

Bolan rubbed his eyes. Too little food, not enough sleep, too much to drink in the call of duty—his eyes felt like ball bearings running in sand. "Baby," he said, "you'd make a lot more sense if you were the far side of a cup of hot, strong, black coffee."

Twenty minutes later, in a café near the city hall, warmed after a second scalding cup, he asked, "Okay. For starters, how did you happen to be at that intersection just when I was waiting to cross over?"

"That's easy. I was following you ever since they dumped you in the Botanic Gardens last night. Until you went to the club, that is. After that... Well, we have contacts among the cabdrivers. But there's lots of things I don't know. That is why we must talk. But first let me tell you what I do know."

She lit a cigarette and drained her cup. "My father and my grandfather were with the Army. You know that. I was brought up in their ways and in their thinking. Which is to say I was trained in the south. Now there's a lot of folks up here think the Army has gone soft, has lost its sting. So they're all set to make their own private army and get on with it."

"Rafferty, for example?"

"For example. He's dedicated, but he's shortsighted. And the Staff in Dublin, the old guard that is, they may appreciate his motives, but they don't want any truck with those prepared to sacrifice a long-term strategic gain for a short-term political advantage. So they've disowned Rafferty. He's out on his own. But they like to keep an eye on him just the same."

"Got it!" Bolan saw light. "So they asked you...?"

She nodded. "Officially, I'm kind of a liaison. I run messages and suchlike for Rafferty. But my allegiance is to the south. I keep them up-to-date on what goes on in the Rafferty camp. They don't like the way he works in with the underworld here, for one thing. They think he's too quick with the firearms."

"You can say that again," Bolan agreed.

"We have been fighting a long time, and in some quarters we are almost respectable. We might even achieve our aim—a united Ireland—not too far in the future. But if these idiots goad the Protestant extremists too far, there'll be big trouble. They'll get us our bad name back, and we shall have to start over."

"You said you were told to follow me...?"

"As you were the second man within a few days to offer arms from someone called Simon Gage—one looking for money, the other not—it's not surprising we were suspicious. Then, when you went to the Unionists at the Ulster Hall..."

"Look," Bolan said, "I guess I better tell you the whole story. I'm not really selling arms at all. It's all a cover..."

For the second time in twelve hours he explained Gage's self-imposed mission, and his supposed part in it, to a woman.

"I must say I like the man better for knowing he's not a traitor to his own side, even if it's a side I hate," she said. "So far as the business at the club is concerned, I'd no idea they would go so far as to try and shoot you. I hope you believe that.''

''But you knew they were going to attack me if I'd gone where they said, in Mullen's Passage?''

''I did so. But I thought it was just to rough you up a little, not to kill you. Because that's the plan now. I heard Rafferty giving the orders. You're under sentence of death.''

''I don't get it,'' Bolan said. ''Rafferty couldn't possibly have known that I never intended to go through with the arms deal. And even if there were two Simon Gages, that doesn't seem serious enough to—''

''He did know that you went to the Unionists at the Ulster Hall,'' Deirdre said. ''But that's not the real point. Whether you're the real or the fake doesn't interest him anymore. And the same goes for the other man and the arms. The important thing is, you penetrated his organization. And when you're clandestine *and* breaking away from the established leadership, that matters. He's wanted by the police, the UDV and the British army. The Prods would love to lay their hands on him. He's even afeared the Staff might turn him in on some kind of deal. So he has to spend all his time underground because of the price on his head...and you have seen him. Not only that, you have also seen Tom M'Quade, his number two, and Jamie Craig—''

''Jamie Craig?''

''The wee foxy fellow they use as a go-between.''

''Ferret-face!''

''Call him what you like, he's a dangerous man. And as far as the three of them are concerned, not only did you kill some of their mates, but you know too much. That's why you've got to go.''

Bolan was frowning. ''You must have heard all this after I left the club. Yet I thought you said you were tailing me....''

She stared at the cigarette she was mashing out in an ashtray. "Once I knew you had gone into that . . . house, there was no point. I mean the place is well-known. I asked a colleague to keep watch until dawn, and in the meantime I returned to the club."

"I'd hate you to think . . ." he began.

"You really don't need to explain," the woman responded. Her cheeks were very pink.

Bolan closed his mind to his suddenly stirred emotions, to the nagging suspicion that the bogus Gage might already have done his deal, that unknown to Deirdre O'Mara the Mourne arms dump was already part of Brognola's IRA conspiracy.

He persuaded her to meet him for a drink in the Grand Central early in the evening, then went out into the city.

TWO HOURS LATER, Simon Gage drove through the city center, past the shipyard and down the southern shore of Belfast Lough to Craigavad and Holywood. His date with Mulligan and the pastor was at a place called the Crawfordsburn Inn, a superior club with wall-to-wall royal-blue carpeting, white woodwork and panels picked out in gold.

They met in a small private lounge upstairs furnished with chintz armchairs, a Jacobean bureau with empty drawers and a gilt sunburst mirror. Through the open window Gage could hear the bounce of tennis balls on a clay court.

"Don't quite know what to make of your offer, sport," the Reverend Kevin McComb said. "Charlie Mulligan here has filled me in on the details, but I'm inclined to think . . ." He shook his pale head. "Dicey. Very dicey."

"It seems fairly straighforward to me," said Gage, who knew nothing of the previous offers in his name. "Either you take me up on it or you don't. Either you can use the stuff or you can't."

"Oh, but it's not as easy as that. It's not easy at all. One does have one's image, you know. In certain cases one's support has to be *implicit* rather than *explicit*. You see what I mean?"

Gage saw. McComb preached action, but his hands were kept cleaner if he could persuade others to actually take the initiative.

"I mean," McComb said carefully, as though he had read the Englishman's thoughts, "I'd gladly go a couple of rounds in the ring with any of these Republican bastards, or take 'em on no-holds-barred if it comes to that. But one does have to think of one's cloth. And, er, cut one's coat accordingly, ha-ha."

"Quite," Gage said.

"You see, old chap, when it comes to guns... Well, of course personally I think the only way to deal with these Commie subversives *is* to fire off a few rounds. Give 'em a taste of their own medicine. But while I can say that privately to you, I can hardly say it publicly, can I?"

"You seemed to be doing so last night."

"Ah, you mean my silence-the-ignorant bit at the Ulster Hall?" The clergyman bared yellow teeth. "Always goes down very well, that. But you will have noticed I was careful not to say *how*. I do firmly believe Charlie's right and we have to, by hook or crook, rid ourselves of these callow longhairs and the Papists who've latched on to them. Kiss the country goodbye otherwise. But our function after all, vis-à-vis the laity, is an advisory one."

"Yours but to reason why," Gage could not resist, "and theirs to do or die?"

McComb looked at him hard. "I don't know that I'd put it quite like that, sport," he said.

Gage remembered he was supposed to be playing the role of a right-winger who thought the army wasn't being tough enough. "What I can't understand..." he began. "I mean these students, the Reds, the so-called civil rights pinkos. Why would they ally themselves to the, er, Papists?''

Mulligan spoke for the first time. He laid a finger alongside his nose. "Exploiting the situation, jumping on the bandwagon, the way they always do," he said. "Someone's feathering their nest there, you may depend on it.''

He went across to the window and closed it. The tennis players, Gage saw, were still wearing sweaters: the wind blowing down the lough was cold. "So have we decided what...steps...are to be taken, then?" Mulligan asked.

"I've explained our position to Mr., uh, Gage. You did say your name was Gage?" McComb asked.

"That's right. Captain Simon Gage."

"Just so. Well I'm thinking, Charlie, the best thing we can do is send Captain Gage to see our friend Connolly, don't you agree?''

"The very man," Mulligan said. "He'll be at the Nirvana this afternoon, too, will he not?''

"He will.''

"It being a Saturday. Right. Well, here's what you do," Mulligan said to Gage. "There's this friend of ours, Morrie Connolly. He's by way of being a bookmaker. He'll be at the dogs this very afternoon. If you go and see him, and take him a note I'll give you, I'm sure he'll be able to help you.''

"The point was, *I'm* trying to help *you*," Gage said.

"Agreed, agreed. Just a figure of speech Mr., er, Gage. My point is, Morrie has a finger on the pulse. He knows exactly who wants what, and where, and how best they can use it. A valuable man indeed." Mulligan picked up a document case, went to the bureau and produced pen, paper and an envelope. He exchanged glances with McComb, and Gage thought he saw the pastor give an imperceptible nod. Mulligan wrote a few words, addressed the envelope, licked the flap and stuck it down firmly.

"I put the address of the track on the outside," he said, "though any taximan in town will know the place. Ask at the members' enclosure for Connolly. We're quare and grateful to you—but he's the fella for action after all!"

Back in the city, Gage met Mack Bolan in Geraghty's Wine Lodge at noon, and Bolan informed him of the maneuvers of his phony namesake. The soldier whistled. "No wonder they kept asking me my name," he said. "That's buggered up our plan a bit, hasn't it? What should we do now? Call the thing off, the whole bloody thing?"

Bolan shook his head. "Not on your life. Let's see what *they* plan to do." He took the envelope from Gage and slit it open. "If you'd been doing what you said you were doing, Mulligan would be safe enough assuming you'd not open it," he said. "But since you have no intention of selling out the arms dump, we can't lose anything by seeing what he wrote."

There were two lines of neat handwriting on the single sheet of paper. The message, which was unsigned, said:

The bearer of this note says his name is Simon Gage. Am sure you will do your best to look after him well.

Bolan nodded. "That's the tip off, the giveaway—'says' his name is Simon Gage! It's letting Connolly know that, in their opinion, it's you who's the phony. And 'look after him *well*'—that's an order to get rid of you, I'd say. Tell you what, though. Let's keep the date. Only I'll go in your place."

"Oh, no," Gage protested, "I couldn't let you—"

"Look, Connolly won't know what you look like anyway. He'll only be familiar with the impostor, right?"

"Yes, but—"

"You can't afford to get your regiment mixed up in local crookeries," Bolan said persuasively. "Your CO told you the army can't mess with politics. I can look after myself, I promise you. And I promise, too, that I'll pass on anything I find out concerning Osborne's murder.''

Gage finally agreed. ''But you're not really doing this for Derek, are you?'' he asked. ''It's something to do with your own undercover work, isn't it?''

Bolan smiled. ''I promise you I'll pass on anything I find out,'' he repeated. ''Anything at all.''

The Nirvana greyhound racing track was a fair distance out of town. The tiered seats in the oval stadium were crowded with people eager to make a killing at the track.

In the long tunnel leading to the members' enclosure, the rising wind blew old betting slips, bus tickets, crumpled cigarette packages and sheets of newspaper past Bolan more quickly then he could walk. Morrie Connolly was pointed out to him in the members' bar.

He was younger than the Executioner expected, a tall and beefy thirty-year-old with a coarse-featured face and small, mean eyes of a very pale blue. Black hair grew low on his forehead and covered the backs of his hands. He was holding a pint tankard of beer by his side.

As Bolan approached, Connolly plucked a cigarette butt from behind his ear and slapped his pockets in search of a match.

The Executioner did not normally smoke, but it was part of his cover. ''Light?'' he said, holding out his own lighted cigarette.

Connolly took it from him, held the glowing end to the charred tip of his stub, and squinted up at Bolan from beneath his eyebrows. ''Who the hell are you?'' he growled. ''What do you want?''

Bolan reached out and took back his cigarette. He dropped it on the floor and ground his heel on it. ''Mr. Connolly?''

''What of it?''

"Mulligan told me to come and see you."

"Mulligan?" Connolly said. "I know a dozen Mulligans."

"Charlie Mulligan. I met him at the Ulster Hall rally."

"So fuckin' what?" The bookmaker's manner was offhand to the point of being offensive. You took it or you left it: he was giving nothing away.

"He said you might be able to help me."

"Help? Look, mister, I don't help nobody. Piss off. You're wastin' my time."

"Well, then, I might be able to help you." Bolan kept his cool with an effort.

Connolly pushed himself upright off the bar. He was taller than the Executioner. Reaching out with one huge hand, he grabbed a fistful of Bolan's raincoat, bunched it and drew the warrior toward him. "When I fuckin' need the help of some faggot Yankee," he said menacingly, thrusting his face close to Bolan's, "I'll fuckin' tell ye. I don't know who you are, mister, comin' in here with your lah-di-dah voice and—"

"The name is Gage," Bolan said coldly, twisting the black-haired fingers away from his raincoat with his own steely hand. "Do you mind?"

"What did you say?" Connolly snatched his hand back in astonishment.

"Gage. Simon Gage. U.S. Army. I'm seconded to the British regiment stationed out at Lough Neagh."

"You don't say! In the army, is it?" Connolly had fallen back a pace, to Bolan's relief. The man's breath smelled.

"Yeah. I have certain intel Mulligan thought you could use." Bolan glanced around the bar. Most of the drinkers had flooded out as the PA system announced the start of another race. "It concerns explosives, firearms and the like," he added in a low voice.

"It concerns explosives, firearms and the like," Connolly mimicked in an exaggerated nasal twang. "You mean you can get us fuckin' shooters?"

"There's a secret dump I know about."

"Well, well, well." Connolly backed off and scrutinized the Executioner through half-closed eyes. "Charlie usually sends me a little note... But no matter. We're always short of guns."

"Yeah, that's what I imagined," said Bolan.

"What d'you mean by that?" The hood was suspicious.

"I mean nobody seems to dare use them. Not because they're scared, of course, but because I guess there's so little ammunition for so few guns."

"We do all right." Connolly knitted his brows. "What are you gettin' at, then?"

"I'll give you a for-instance. That officer who was shot the other day up the Falls."

"What about it?"

"Well, your boys only fired a single shot. I know they got him but—"

"What the hell d'you mean?" Connolly interrupted furiously. "Why do you think the bugger was done, at-all?"

"Search me. Maybe some kind of protest because the army's looking after the Catholics too well?"

"That's what you were supposed to think, asshole. 'Twas the bloody Papishers themselves done it, to make folks *think* it was us. To put the blame our way." Connolly paused and then said sullenly, "So don't say it was my boys, or I'll knock your fuckin' teeth in!"

One more dead end, Bolan thought, for the real Gage. Everyone said the other guy did it, because Deirdre O'Mara had already told him she was sure Rafferty had no hand in the killing. And now they were pulling the second degree of subtlety: the other guy did it to make you think it was me. After that, it was I did it to make you think it was the other guy doing it to make you think it was me. It could go on forever. Bolan wondered if he would ever get the chance to land a good right across to Connolly's jaw.

Looking at the brutal face, with its heavy blue shadow, he thought he would probably smash his own knuckles before any damage was done to the jaw.

"About those shooters, what are you proposin'?" Connolly asked roughly.

"I don't propose anything," Bolan said. "I told Charlie. I think the government should get tougher. Much tougher. If they won't act, you guys'll have to act yourselves—more than you've done so far. Being attached to the British army, *I* can't do anything. But at least I can put you in the way of this dump. For chrissakes, what do you have to do to get people to accept a free gift in this country? I should have thought you'd jump at the chance."

Connolly nodded several times. "Yeah," he said slowly, "that's just what you would think, innit?"

Bolan looked at his watch. "Tell you what," Connolly said. "I think you better have a meet with some of the boys. Do you have the info—the stuff about guards an' that—on you?"

"No. I have to check back at the camp and—"

"That's what I thought. Tonight, then?"

"Okay. As long as it's not too early," Bolan said, thinking of his meeting with Deirdre O'Mara.

"Nine o'clock. Be at the Massereene Hotel, Corporation Street, at nine. Come to the back room, and we'll see what we can do for you." Morrie Connolly drank the remainder of his pint in a single draft, dropped his cigarette butt into the wet glass and strode from the bar without another word.

Bolan left the streaking dogs and the roaring crowd of the Nirvana behind him and returned to the city center. He had to pick up the prints from a roll of film he had had developed and make his call to Ginny McDade before he met

Deirdre at the Grand Central. He didn't know how long that meeting would last, but he was certain of one thing: he wasn't going to be anyplace near the back room of the Massereene Hotel in Corporation Street at nine o'clock!

In this the Executioner was mistaken. In fact, he was going to be at the Massereene long before that.

## 15

Bolan went back to his hotel to fetch the Nikon, and spent an hour taking pictures to substantiate his cover. There was still tension in the air, more security checks than usual at the entrances to restaurants and department stores, more army patrols at the railroad stations and around the city hall.

He picked up the prints from his first roll of film, stuffed them in his pocket without looking at them, then went to a post office to call the number Ginny McDade had given him. There was no reply.

He called again at five-fifteen. Zero.

At five-thirty he went to the Grand Central for his meeting with Deirdre O'Mara. She hadn't arrived, so he ordered a drink in the lounge and sat down to read the evening paper.

The previous night's civil disorder filled the front page. After the Ulster Hall demo there had been two confrontations. The biggest, when the Ulster audience had clashed with Catholic militants in the Falls Road area, had started when a party of organized Republican vigilantes had attacked the more vociferous of the Unionists inflamed by Mulligan and McComb's rhetoric. There had been more than a hundred people injured.

The second incident had been smaller but bloodier. It had erupted by the apartment block where Derek Osborne had been killed. Students from the Ulster Hall had picketed the street, protesting on behalf of the Catholics who had been forced to leave their homes in the block.

First there had been no more than an exchange of insults. Then a second body of demonstrators, more belligerent than the students, had arrived to attack the Protestants. Finally a small body of hoodlum Unionists had fought with the picketers. Soon after the army had arrived with riot trucks and water cannon, but there had been many casualties, most of them serious, and seven people, three of them students, were on the critical list at the Royal Hospital.

Bolan sighed. His mission, his vocation, had always been to smash the predators, to rip the guts out of the sharks, to silence the snarling hordes of animal man so that at least some of the decent, ordinary folk in the world could walk the streets free from fear. Today his efforts seemed insignificant. He felt like a kid trying to stem the flood with a bag of sand.

It was, he knew, a never-ending task, and one that would remain unfinished when his own time came. Yet others would pick up the standard after he had fallen, the good fight would continue, and if there was no final victory in sight, at least there were battles to be won. There was always hope.

But here in this drab city the whole battle order seemed to be reversed. If you read the paper, you'd think it was the decent, ordinary folk in the minority. Bolan felt as though he were in the middle of a whole population gone crazy: four hundred years, forty decades, twenty generations...and they still hadn't learned how to live in peace together!

Bolan laid down the paper, walked out into the lobby and called Ginny again.

No reply.

He returned to the lounge and sat down at his table.

No Deirdre.

A quarter of six. He picked up the paper again. It was feared that rioting could break out tonight, though on a larger scale.

A dope test on a favorite that had lost spectacularly at Leopardstown had proved positive.

The Dutch foreign minister had resigned over a call girl scandal.

Keiron Winslow-Mowbray, a Dublin industrialist, had urged the Council of Europe to subsidize weapons research in EEC countries.

Bolan ordered another drink and read further.

During the night there had been seventeen fire alarms; eleven of the fires had been the work of arsonists.

Explosions had disrupted three council meetings that day in County Armagh and one in Fermanagh.

Thirty-nine people had been convicted in Belfast courthouse that morning for insulting behavior and fined varying sums.

At six-ten, Bolan started the crossword puzzle, watched from the adjoining column by the heavy-jowled, mournful face of Keiron Winslow-Mowbray, Dublin industrialist.

Six twenty-five. Bolan began to worry.

Suddenly he got to his feet and went in search of the hall porter and a cab.

Deirdre O'Mara might simply have decided to stand him up, of course. She could have been given some urgent briefing that prevented her from joining him. She could have left a message he hadn't received.

Or something might have happened to her.

There was no message at Reception. Bolan decided he had to satisfy himself that the last alternative was a nonstarter. And for this he had only one lead: he'd go to the guy who had put them in touch originally and ask for her address. If he didn't have it, there was nothing the Executioner could do.

The pub was less crowded in the evening. It was almost dark, and the huge bar had somehow a more homey look with the colored lights garlanding the ship's prow reflected along with the bottles and glasses above the chased glass of the windows.

Blue Suit was standing in his usual position by the steps to the cellars. "Miss O'Mara?" he said in answer to Bolan's question. "Sure I've no idea who you're talkin' of— Oh, so it's you, sir! The turkey sandwich man himself! Well, now, I couldn't say it's where the lady *lives*, you know. But an address to find her at, I could give you."

The house was one of a row of small detached villas at the far end of Ballysillan Road. Immediately behind it, the land rose to the steep cliff of Cavehill and the rounded hump of Black Mountain.

Wind howled in unseen wires as Bolan hurried up the neat concrete path to the front door. There was a light in the front room, and the familiar gray VW was parked by the curb outside.

The door was opened by an elderly woman wearing an apron. "Miss Deirdre?" she repeated. "I'm afeared you've had your journey for nothing, sir. She left here soon after five. A wee man called for her with a message from a Simon Gage...."

Bolan stared. "Pardon me," he said. "Maybe there's some mistake."

"No mistake," the woman said firmly. "I'm not deaf. I heard the wee fella myself. An urgent message from a Simon Gage, he said. She was to go some place—the Marine, I think it was—and if she liked he'd lift her there hisself, for he was goin' that way anyways."

"The Marine?" Bolan repeated. The name meant nothing to him. "And she went off with him?"

"She did."

"He didn't say anything else? I'm sorry, but this is very urgent."

"He did not. Just something about this Mr. Gage having some information for her. That was all I heard."

"You wouldn't know where or what the Marine is?"

She shook her gray head. "I would not. 'Tis just a name to me. It was in Corporation Street, I think the wee man said."

"Corporation Street?" Bolan echoed. "It wouldn't have been *Massereene*, would it? The Massereene Hotel in Corporation Street?"

The door was already closing. The woman shrugged. "Well, now, the wee fella spoke so fast... It might have been. And then again, it might not."

Bolan was already on his way back to the waiting taxi. It had to be Connolly. Gage wouldn't have a reason to contact Deirdre, and to decoy the woman with the use of his name. What would the Unionists want with her?

Either they wished to get to Bolan or maybe Gage through her; or else she was considered a valuable enough target in herself. And they would certainly know of her, if her father and grandfather had been as prominent in the movement as she had said.

In either case he had to follow the only lead he had in an effort to find out what had happened to her. He gave the cabdriver the address of the Massereene Hotel.

It was beyond belief that there would be no connection between the decoy summons and his own rendezvous, which was to take place in the back room of that same hotel later in the evening.

The hotel was a gray stone building sandwiched between a warehouse and a brick block full of lawyers' offices. Faded gilt lettering spelled out the name on the windows fronting the street. On the double doors at the top of the entrance steps, the hands of generations of traveling salesmen had rubbed away varnish, stain and wood, so that the surface surrounding the brass handles was as bare and clean-picked as a bone washed up on the seashore.

Inside, an old man in shirtsleeves pored over a copy of the evening paper in a cubbyhole at one side of a dark staircase.

The Executioner decided to keep the cards close to his chest. He would act as though he were arriving for the meet with Connolly—only a couple of hours ahead of time. He supposed he could play that dumb.

There was no need to.

"A meeting with Mr. Connolly and his friends?" the old man repeated. "Ah, then you'll be Mr. Kelly, then?"

"Yeah," Bolan said recklessly. "That's me, Kelly."

"Then there's a message for you. Mr. Connolly's gone up to the mill. He'll be back just before nine, he said. But if you'd time enough you were to go on up there."

"Sure," Bolan said. "The mill. It's, uh, some time since I ... You wouldn't happen to know...?"

"It'll be Cleary's, the one they talk of buyin'," said the old man. He gave Bolan an address between Shankill and Crumlin roads, then turned back to his paper.

"One more thing," Bolan said. "Was Mr. Connolly with other folks when he left?"

"Just the lady an' wee Bert Currie and Mr. Flanagan and the rest," the old man replied, wetting the tip of one finger and turning a page. "Quare and tense she looked, too. Happen she'd had some kind of shock."

Bolan turned and raced down the steps and set off in search of another taxi.

The janitor picked up the bill Bolan had left on the desk and stowed it in his pants pocket. "Funny," he said aloud, "thon fella didn't *sound* like one o' the Kellys. Must be the Yankee branch."

BOLAN GOT OUT OF THE CAB where the gray length of
Crumlin Road twisted its way up into the hills, and walked
three blocks to the mill. There was an air of expectation in
the streets. Small groups of men gathered on the corners,
drifted toward streetlamps, joined other groups, split and
reformed, and kept up all the time a continuous sullen
murmur of conversation that was the more menacing because of its restraint.

Most of the windows were shuttered, some with crude
homemade barriers nailed across the opening. The tension
was palpable.

These men were waiting for something, anything. They
had been fed on anticipation. And if they didn't quite know
what it was they were waiting for, they would use the first
excuse that presented itself to release the violence that was
in them.

Most of the houses had small flagstaffs projecting between windows on the upper story. On commemoration days
and national holidays, Bolan had been told, either the British Union Jack or the orange, white and green Irish tricolor
would hang from these, to flaunt the occupants' sympathies. Some of the neighborhoods were so sharply divided
that one side of a street would be Protestant, the other
Catholic.

There were no flags to label the area tonight, no means of
telling which side these men were on, Unionist or Republican. A mob was a mob; they all looked alike. But as an obvious foreigner the Executioner was the target for a hundred
muttered threats, a hundred surly growls as he hurried
through.

For once in his life he felt genuinely uneasy. Although the
Beretta was safely in its quick-draw rig beneath his left arm,
he hadn't felt so vulnerable, hadn't experienced so cold a
pricking at his nape, such tenseness in the muscles of his
exposed back, for a very long time.

He was relieved to locate the street he was looking for. The mill occupied the whole of one side, a huge nineteenth-century industrial facade in red brick. Across the road, a terrace of two-story workmen's cottages had been abandoned to the rats, the weeds and the local vandals. There wasn't a single pane of glass, a single unsplintered door in the whole row.

As he drew closer, Bolan saw that the mill, too, was a casualty. At some time or other it had suffered a disastrous fire. Below the parapet, gaping windows showed the night sky between beams that had once supported the gutted roof. Lower down, rubble and charred rafters filled the blackened remains of what had been the administration block.

Had the janitor at the hotel given him a bum steer, or was he in the wrong street? He was about to turn back when he noticed in the light of the street's single lamp a thin coating of wind-dried mud on the cobbles of an alley at one side of the building.

There were freshly made tire marks on the greasy surface.

Glancing over his shoulder to check that he was unobserved, he stole into the entry and made it toward the rear of the block.

The mill was L-shaped, and the section in back seemed to have escaped damage in the fire. Twenty-foot arched windows pierced the entire side. These must have spanned two separate floors because a thread of light showed at the top of one, although the lower half was dark.

Half a dozen cars were parked in the yard enclosed by the ell. Beyond them yawned the dark mouth of a loading bay. Bolan checked out the rest of the yard. The remaining sides were walled in, barbed wire topping the brickwork. Moving as silently as he could, he crossed the cobbles and stepped into the bay.

Lancing the beam of a pencil flashlight into the blackness, he saw the platform at the inner end, with some of its timbers splintered and rotting, barred doors behind it, a rusted pulley in the roof.

And at one side there was a small pass door leading to the undamaged wing. Bolan switched off the beam and pushed. The door opened to his touch.

Inside there was an impression of space. In the faint illumination filtering through the huge windows, he saw sheeted islands of machinery massed against the dark.

After the sullen rumble of the city outside, the silence of the abandoned mill was oppressive. The air was dank and chill, with a sour, flat odor of greased metal hanging over everything. Oil-smooth highlights slid over the contours of the looms as he switched on the flashlight once more and threaded his way across the shop, winking coldly back from casings and plates and shafts. Finally he found a darker patch marking the position of a doorway.

He walked through.

Steely fingers materialized out of the darkness to clamp over the wrist of the hand holding the flashlight. A circle of cold metal bored into his neck just below the ear.

"All right, mister," a hoarse voice growled. "Drop the glim, the hands high in the air, and let's see who we have here."

Mack Bolan had felt the cold steel of a gun muzzle against his flesh often enough to be familiar with the sensation. This wasn't a gun muzzle: it wasn't a ring of metal with a hole in the center; it was a solid disk. He would bet his life on it.

He did bet his life on it.

Allowing every muscle in his body to go suddenly slack, he slumped floorward, dropping below the menacing steel circle, pulling his flashlight arm free of the watchman's grip.

There was no shot. Just a stifled curse.

At the floor level the Executioner's watchspring muscles uncoiled to project him violently up as he whirled to face his adversary, the Beretta already drawn and in his free hand.

He was right: it wasn't a gun; it was a short iron bar.

It flashed viciously down to crack against his forearm, temporarily paralyzing the ulnar flexors and forcing his hand to open so that the autoloader dropped and skated away beneath one of the machines.

He swung the flashlight at the guy's eyes, but the bar whipped up and knocked it away. The pencil tube fell to the floor, and the light went out.

Bolan seized the man's arm, lowered his head and sank his teeth into the sinewy wrist.

The watchman yelled, the bar clattered to the concrete floor, and they were on equal terms in the gloom. Bolan twisted away from a raised knee, took a kidney punch that knocked the breath out of him and prepared to unleash a selection of the dirtier tricks of hand-to-hand.

The flat of the hand to a jugular, a fist with the forefinger and pinkie jutting forward to blind the eyes, a hacked shin, a punch low in the belly and a hard hip ground against the genitals were enough to stagger the guy on his feet and let the Executioner rush him back against one of the sheeted looms. He seized the guy's head and banged it against the molded casing.

All at once a curious strangled sound puffed from the guard's lips and his arms fell away from the Executioner's back.

Bolan figured it for a stall, the same ruse he had used. Then he realized his hands were warm and wet, the palms covered with what he knew was blood.

Unknowingly he had slammed the guy's head against part of the machine with an upward-pointing metal projection, and this had pierced the tarp sheeting and penetrated the skull.

Bolan lowered the body to the floor. He hadn't intended to, but he had killed the man. That was the way it went sometimes. He wiped his hands on the dead watchman's jacket.

He was crouching, thinking about searching beneath the machines until he found his Beretta, when he heard the scream.

It was a high, shrill scream, suggesting outrage and fright rather than pain. But it was a feminine scream.

It galvanized the warrior into action. The gun could wait. He sprinted for the doorway where the watchman had jumped him. The scream had come from that direction, but somehow filtered, diluted; it hadn't sounded as though it had come from the floor above.

There were stairs beyond the doorway. On the upper floor he found himself in a warren of small offices and cubicles that had once housed pattern-makers, keepers of samples and color-matchers, for the mill had once been part of Ulster's decaying linen industry. A single electric bulb burned in the last room, and Bolan saw that the strip of light he had seen earlier issued through a gap between two old army blankets that were nailed across the window.

At the far end of the room, faded lettering on a rust-spotted enamel plate beside double doors announced that this was an emergency exit, to be used only in case of fire.

Bolan discerned a low rumble of male voices that seemed to come from an area off the lower part of the stairwell.

He crept downward, treading lightly, keeping to the side of each step. A biting draft stirred his hair as he approached the exit doors leading to the yard. One of them was slightly open, but the stairway continued down to a basement level. The current of air was blowing from there.

Frosted glass panels allowed a faint illumination to filter through double doors blocking off the basement. Pushing one open, he found himself in an unlit storeroom. The voices came from a rectangle of light at the far end. Bolan catwalked across, flattened himself against the wall and peered through.

The floor level dropped once more.

Beyond the opening a gallery led to a narrow flight of steps, and at the foot of these a huge storage area stretched away into the darkness. The light came from a single powerful bulb hanging over a tableau grouped twenty feet from the steps. A dozen men stood in a half circle around Deirdre O'Mara, who was sitting on a broken chair with her arms bound behind her back.

Behind them the dark wall rose to loading doors that must lead off the bay on the floor above. Stacks of rotting bales wrapped in sacking bulked in the shadows outside the pool of light below the lamp.

"... sure it doesn't matter what happens to the bitch," a harsh voice was saying as Bolan sidled onto the gallery. "It's O'Mara's brat, is it not? After that bastard an' his ould man, any whore from the same seed's not worth the sawdust you fuckin' spit in."

"All right, all right." This was Connolly, tall, dark and menacing, holding up a hand in the center of the group. "It's business first, lads. We're here to find out where we can lay our hands on Rafferty and M'Quade, remember."

The ages of the men ranged from twenty-five to fifty. "Lay our hands, did ye say, Morrie?" one of the younger ones asked, giggling. "Thon's a right fine idea, I'm thinkin'. Is she a good thing, d'ye think?"

"A good thing? Is she hell?" another guffawed. "Aren't all Papishers the same, sure? Go down the whole street today, then it's off to the bloody confessional and a free seat in paradise tomorrow! Look at the boobs on her. You think they got that way without a good few Papish hands—"

"Shuddup!" Connolly roared. "You can find out for yourselves in just a minnit. Right now we want to find out about bloody Rafferty." He turned and approached the chair, reaching out a black-nailed hand for the woman's hair. The ropes that lashed her wrists together and cut into the soft flesh of her upper arms also drew her shoulders back so that the features of which her captors had been making such lascivious comments thrust forward.

Deirdre's chin was raised defiantly, and her eyes, though scared, were not cowed.

Connolly twisted his fingers in her hair and dragged her to her feet. "We'll have a bit of fun with you later," he said. "Treat you like the little Papish slut you are. But first there's a few questions you're goin' to answer."

"Have your fun," the woman said contemptuously, "but don't expect me to play parlor quiz games with the likes of you."

Connolly turned his hand over so that the palm and the fingers that were clenched in her hair faced upward. Her head was forced back and down so that she faced the ceiling, back arched and knees half bent in an unnatural position.

Bolan heard the man say softly, "Come on now. We know Rafferty's lot is plannin' something dirty for next week. We know there's a council meetin' tomorrow. Where is it at? And what street are Rafferty and M'Quade hidin' out in now?"

O'Mara said nothing. Bolan could see tears, started by the pain of the fingers dragging at the roots of her hair, spilling from the corners of her eyes.

Connolly brought his arm slowly toward the floor, forcing her body into an even tighter curve. While she was held there, bent into an arc like a bow, he raised his other hand and slapped her once, twice, three times, four times, forehand and backhand, across the face. The blows had very little force, but the sound of them rang through the cavernous storeroom like the cracks of a whip.

Bolan looked frantically around him. For the sake of the mission he ought to hear more; on humanitarian and personal grounds he had to rescue Deirdre.

The gallery was eight or ten feet above the level of the floor. Two battered oil drums stood off to one side. Beside them, a large pulley with a hook attached lay on its side. From its wheel two thick ropes curved slackly up into the shadows of the lofty ceiling. The pulley must have been part of the gear they used to transfer stores from the loading bay high in the opposite wall. But there was nothing that would be any use at all as a weapon.

Connolly was talking again. "It's a matter of choice, you see," he said. "We're goin' to do you anyway. All of us are going to have a turn. It's up to you to choose whether or not you get beaten up first. Because you're going to answer those questions."

He passed his hand familiarly between her legs and up the swell of her belly. The half circle of men shuffled closer. Bolan could hear their breath rasping in the dankness of the cellar.

"Hey, Morrie," one of the older ones called, "what say we have a wee feel of the shape of things to come, eh?"

"All *right*, McNulty," Connolly rasped. "Just wait a minnit, would you. Now, bitch—" he brought his brutish face down near hers "—which is it to be? What do you have to say?"

"What I have to say," Deirdre panted, "is that…it's kind of you…to prove…that my father and grandfather were right…about the kind of people you are."

Connolly slapped her again, harder this time, and she gasped with pain. He had raised his hand a second time when the sound of footsteps clattered down the concrete stairway behind Bolan.

"That'll be Kelly," someone said.

The Executioner dived behind the oil drums and crouched as Connolly and his cronies turned toward the gallery. A man hurried through the open doorway and ran down the steps. "There you are, then," he said. "Sorry to be late, Morrie, but I had trouble with that old fool at the Massereene. He didn't want to pass the message on. Said he'd already given it to someone."

"Shit!" Connolly said. "What in hell happened?"

"Don't ask me. Some prick came in and the old idiot *asked* him was he Kelly—and the guy said he was, so he got the message."

"Jesus! Suppose he comes here? We'll have to finish them off, but. Who could it be, for Jay's sake?"

"How should I know?" Kelly said irritably. "But you should bloody well have posted a lookout anyway. Anyone could get in."

"There is a fuckin' lookout. Gullery. You didn't see him as you came through the machine shop? He didn't challenge you?"

"I'm telling you there's nobody there."

"Bugger's sneaked off to smoke a ciggie or have a pint!" Connolly was furious. "Mahon, go you to the entrance and catch him when he comes back. I'll give the bugger a lesson he won't forget. You better take young Harrison with you. O'Dwyer, Wilson, you two take a look around the dump in case this sod from the Massereene got here already. If you see anyone, do him up."

"Ah, Morrie," one of the men complained, "sure we'll miss all the fun with the skirt—"

"Stow it. You'll get your fun later. Now do what you're fuckin' told and piss off."

The four men climbed the steps. As they left, the newcomer, Kelly, turned momentarily to watch them go. Bolan, doubled up in the shadows behind the oil drums, was astonished.

The overhead light threw the man's features into sharp relief: glittering eyes and an angry mouth over a lean, wiry frame.

Kelly was the man who had started the fight in the bar—the man Bolan had last seen the night before, leading the most violent of the anti-Unionist demonstrators attacking the Ulster Hall....

Bolan shook his head. What kind of a double game was this? Whose side was Kelly really on? A supposedly militant Catholic who was a welcome visitor at the inner councils of the Protestant extremists? There was a parallel, somewhere here, with the thinking behind the plot Bolan was briefed to smash.

The IRA disguised as British soldiers, attacking their own people; a Unionist pretending to be a Republican fanatic?

Or vice versa?

There was no time to think about it now. Kelly was speaking urgently.

"It's for next week, and it's something big," he said. "But that's all the wee two-timer Danny McClusky could tell me. Else he was too scared to come across with more."

"If he was, we'll scare him more and get it out of the little sod," Connolly said. "Is it concerned with the Mourne stuff?"

"It is."

"Then we've got to get to Rafferty and choke it out of him." The gang leader had released Deirdre's hair, and she had straightened herself painfully and was trying to regain her breath. Now he stepped up until his face was mere inches from her own. "For the last time," he snarled, "before we stick the electrical wires into you, where is this meetin'? And where do those two Papishers hang out?"

"Go to hell," the woman panted. "And that's where you will go, too, if the Church's teaching—"

Her words broke off abruptly as Connolly drew back his fist and slammed her in the solar plexus with all his force.

She jackknifed forward, retching, the air whistling from her lungs as she pitched down onto her knees.

"No bitch of a murderin' Papist is goin' to tell me anything about bloody religion," Connolly shouted, dragging her to her feet and preparing to hit her again

Bolan exploded into action.

It was suicidal. He couldn't possibly achieve anything. Even if they weren't armed, it was nine to one; he would have no chance, could do Deirdre no good.

But he was physically incapable of hiding there in the dark while she was beaten up, tortured and probably raped. It was a basic gut reaction.

Deirdre O'Mara was no leather-clad heroine of a blood-and-guts TV serial, expert in the arts of karate and kung fu. To see her, bound and helpless, being coldbloodedly worked over overcame his rational evaluation of the odds.

It was the thought of Kelly and the Ulster Hall that gave him the idea. Same means, different end.

Seizing the thick ropes running through the pulley, he backed off to the gallery entrance. If both were fixed at the other end, he might be able to make it. But if one of them merely ran over another pulley, he would simply hurl himself to the ground. It was better than doing nothing, though.

Connolly had hit Deirdre a second time, higher up, on the chest. His fist was cocked again.

The ropes ran up into the shadows of the roof. Grabbing them as high as he could reach, Bolan raced across the gallery, lifted his feet over the low railing and launched himself into space.

His weight dragged the ropes taut. They held.

Direction good; elevation perfect.

Swinging like a pendulum, he shot across above the cellar floor and felt the heels of his boots thud against Connolly's head just behind the ear.

The big man fell, sprawling amid the splintered wreckage of the chair. Carried on by his own momentum, Bolan landed on a concrete shelf below the loading bay doors on the far side of the cellar, and immediately pushed himself off again, like a swimmer turning for a second length, to start the return journey.

This was the tough part, for the muscles in the lower part of his right arm were still numbed from the blow he had taken from the iron bar.

Kelly's mouth was open in astonishment, the other men had frozen, Deirdre was swaying on her feet and Connolly had just struggled upright as the Executioner swung through the pool of light for the second time.

Grimly hanging on to the rope, he scooped up Deirdre with his left arm and kicked out again at Connolly as he passed.

The sole of his boot scraped the Ulsterman's face, smashing the nose sideways.

Bolan's right arm was shrieking with the pain of his damaged muscle, shuddering with the strain of supporting his own weight and Deirdre's, and for a moment he doubted he would make the gallery. But at last the arc was completed. He let go of the rope, and the two of them dropped to the floor.

Staggering, he whirled around and played his only card. "All right, Sergeant," he shouted. "You keep them covered while I get the girl away!"

The assurance in his voice was such that he almost made it. The men, who had begun racing toward the steps, halted uncertainly, peering into the shadows beyond the pool of light. And then Connolly, foaming with rage, yelled, "Don't believe the sod! It's a bloody try-on. The bugger's on his own. Away and after them now...."

Deirdre O'Mara was tottering on her feet, struggling to drag air back into her savaged lungs. Desperately playing for one second's respite, two yards advance on the pursuers, Bolan snapped again, "You're to shoot the first man that sets foot on those steps, Sergeant. And shoot to kill."

It was then, amazingly, miraculously, that a cool voice spoke from behind the oil drums.

"Right, sir," it replied crisply. "We'll give 'em a couple of rounds just to show we mean business...."

And two shots from an automatic rifle cracked out to ping against the lowest of the concrete stairs.

**16**

"But who was it, for God's sake?" Deirdre O'Mara demanded. "How many of them were there and how did they get there?"

They were two blocks away from the mill, and she was still bemused.

"I told you," Bolan answered. "After I'd cut the ropes, while you were rubbing the circulation back into your arms, I went back to the basement to see if could I help. The whole gang was standing down there like caged lions, waiting to pounce! And whoever it was, was just sitting tight—holding them at gunpoint while we got away."

"You didn't see them at all?"

"Uh-uh. They were in the shadows behind those drums. I'm pretty sure it wasn't anyone from the British army; That voice sounded local to me. Familiar in a way, too, but I can't place it. At least you don't have to thank the hated Brits for your release!"

"I'd thank anyone who helped me get free of that...that *animal*," Deirdre said. "You couldn't see how many they were?"

"Not a chance. If you ask me, there was only one guy. He fired a couple of shots to make his point, and then sat tight. He said there was nothing I could do. My best bet was to get you away as soon as I could. I never heard any other voices."

"How was he going to get away himself?"

"I asked, of course. He just said not to worry, it was all under control. The way he said it, I believed him."

"When do you suppose he came in?" Deirdre asked. They were hurrying down a street that led to Shankill Road, avoiding the groups on each corner, waiting for a chance to cross over, so they could cut back up toward Ballysillan and pick up the VW.

"He must have come in after Kelly," Bolan said. "Maybe he was tailing Kelly. But he must have been outside the dark storeroom soon after Kelly's arrival."

"Of course," she said. "The four men Connolly sent out to search. He must be a smart operator whoever he is!"

They had found the quartet—Mahon, Harrison, O'Dwyer and Wilson—all unconscious, neatly in a line, outside the mill's emergency exit as they had left, each one expertly bound and gagged with lengths of rope and parts of his own clothing.

"I'm not so much interested in who he is," Bolan said. "Like you, I'm happy to accept his help with thanks and leave it right there. But I'd sure appreciate knowing *why* he was there at just that time...."

A sudden burst of shouting erupted from somewhere over the low roofs of the houses on the eastern side of the street. Glass crashed, and there was a rush of feet. A moment later whistles blew. A flat, hollow explosion, followed by two more farther away, split the night. Within seconds the depressing skyline was silhouetted against a pulsating red glow as flames leaped up behind the chimneys.

Bolan took Deirdre's arm as they approached a corner. This time she didn't snatch it away. Men were running toward the fire, pounding past in groups, cursing as they went. The shouting had swelled in volume until it was now a continuous and menacing roar.

"Bravo," Deirdre said bitterly. "I suppose that's another houseful of our people 'persuaded' to move out of the district with the help of threats and petrol bombs and mob violence.''

"Forget it," Bolan said. "A couple of blocks away the same thing could be happening in reverse. Your 'people' haven't exactly been noted for their tolerance in the past."

"Och, you're as bad as the others, the pompous, self-righteous British who—"

"Be quiet!"

Gripping her arm fiercely, he dragged her into the shadow of a doorway. For the past few minutes he had been glancing over his shoulder. Now his attention concentrated on a pair of dimmed headlights advancing slowly along the street they had just left, on the far side of Shankill Road.

"What is it?" she asked, struggling to free her arm.

"Our friends, I'd bet."

"You mean Connolly and the others?" Suddenly she was very quiet.

"Yeah. Our rescuer isn't going to wait in the mill all night. He's going to give us a reasonable time to get away from there, and then he's going to split, still covering them. If he's as efficient as I think he is, he'll have an escape route all mapped out."

"And after he's gone?"

"After he's gone they'll be so angry, being bested, that they'll stop at nothing to get their hands on him . . . and on us. Don't forget they have half a dozen cars among them."

"So you think . . . ?" She nodded toward the car at the intersection. It had stopped, but nobody got in or out.

"They'll search the neighboring streets, hoping to pick us up. They know you have no car. They'll suspect I don't have one."

As Bolan spoke another car, traveling slowly, nosed its way down Shankill Road. Before it reached the intersection, it veered across to the wrong side of the roadway and stopped at the corner by the car they had been watching.

Two men got out and walked over to the passenger side of the first vehicle.

"You're right. It *is* them." Deirdre's whisper was urgent. "There's the little one came for me: I think his name's Currie. And Flanagan. I recognize him."

Bolan nodded. The men leaning down to speak to the passenger in the first car were giving orders; arms were raised and circled, fingers pointed. A third car crawled up the hill, blinked its lights at the other two and continued slowly on its way. The Executioner thought he could distinguish the powerful bulk of Connolly tensed beside the driver.

Flanagan and Currie returned to their car. The driver mounted the sidewalk, spun the wheel and wrenched it around in a U-turn to follow Connolly. Below them, the flames burned brighter against the night sky, and the howling of the mob was drowned by the bells and sirens of advancing fire trucks and riot wagons speeding up from the city.

"What are we going to do?" Deirdre murmured.

Bolan was watching the remaining car. "Depends on them," he said. "If they turn up or down we're okay. But if they head straight over, as they probably will..." He shook his head. "There are a few folks around, and the lighting's not so good, but they could hardly miss us."

The car jerked forward, hesitated in the center of the intersection, then drove straight for them.

In the doorway, Bolan felt behind him for a handle. The door was locked. Abruptly he swung to face her, covering her body with his own and flattening her against the door. As the lights of the car silvered the cracked paintwork, Bolan lowered his mouth to hers.

Behind his back the car ground past in first gear. The short hairs on his nape prickled for the second time that night. He could feel the beating of her heart through his jacket, and the pounding of his own in the pulse of the wrist laid against the woodwork.

The light swept over them, passed on, and the sound of the engine diminished.

Bolan raised his head. "It'll take them about a hundred yards to realize nobody in their right mind would be courting a girl up here with a riot going on in the next block," he whispered.

Her heard a faint screech of brakes, a metallic clunk as gears were engaged too hastily. Somebody shouted.

Bolan seized Deirdre's wrist. "Run!" he urged.

They dashed back to Shankill Road and sprinted downhill toward the flames. Behind them the contralto whine of the car's reverse ratio slid up the scale as the driver backed up hurriedly to the intersection.

Fifty yards farther on, another narrow street ran parallel to the one they had just left. Bolan dragged Deirdre after him, and they raced away from the riot.

They heard the car shudder to a halt and then roar forward. The Executioner darted a glance over his shoulder. He could see the headlight beams as they began the swing around the corner. He looked ahead again...and almost missed a step in midstride.

It was like witnessing a movie trick shot done with a mirror: the twin yellow eyes he was expecting to turn into the street behind them were in fact sliding into view around the corner of the intersection ahead. A second car had entered the street from the other end....

Bolan pulled up short, dragging Deirdre to a halt. The headlights were a hundred fifty yards away, moving slowly toward them. It didn't have to be one of Connolly's cars of course, but assuming it wasn't was too much of a long shot to risk. In any case, fifty yards behind, the car chasing them was now in the street and accelerating.

"All right," he snapped. "In here '

He punched open a low gate hung on brick posts and ran across a flagstoned front yard to the door of a small house. Light showed behind the door's frosted glass panels. Bolan twisted the handle and shoved.

The door opened at once and spilled them into a narrow hallway ripe with the odor of cooked vegetables. In a room on the left, a collarless man in shirtsleeves was illuminated by the flickering green radiance of a television screen. "Who the hell are you?" he demanded angrily. "What d'you think you're doin', bustin' in here like this?"

Deirdre squeezed the Executioner's arm warningly. "It's the polis," she said in a breathy imitation of a local mill girl. "They're wantin' for to put oor Frank in the Crumlin Road Jail."

The man had a small black mustache. The mouth below it had been half open, waiting for a pipe that was raised halfway. Now it closed with a snap. "Ah," said he, "that's different. Give them half a chance an' them fellas would put their ould mothers inside. C'mon this way."

He ran past them, opened a door at the end of the hallway and beckoned them to follow. Outside the house in front, doors slammed and they could hear the sound of raised voices.

Beyond the kitchen the rear door opened into another yard, which was crammed with rolls of used linoleum, threadbare carpets and piles of newspapers tied with string. The houses in these streets were built back to back, and the wall separating this yard from the one beyond had been partly demolished, leaving a clear way through to the opposite house in the next street.

Deirdre was about to run through when their host turned and barred the exit with an arm. "Just a minnit there," he said suspiciously. "We know you're on the run. All right. But let's hear a wee bit more about yous before we allow yous through… Who're you for, then? Where do you hang up your hat of a Sunday?''

Once more Bolan allowed the woman to answer. "I don't wear a hat, only a sash," she said in her put-on accent. "It was left to me by me father."

The man moved aside. "Aye," he said. "Though it's hardly a subject for jokin'. Go you to the door at the far end of th'other yard now. That's ould Annie M'Crae's place. Turn right inside the parlor and there's a closet leads through into the next house. Thon's an empty yin, an' you can away through intil the street."

"Thanks, mister," Deirdre said. "What about Mother M'Crae, though?"

"Pay her no attention. Th'ould dear's deaf and half blind. She's used to folks comin' and goin'." He turned around as a shadow fell across the frosted glass of his front door and someone began thundering on the knocker. "Go on now," he whispered. "An' good luck to ye."

As they dashed across the yard, they heard him shout testily, "All right, for Jay's sake. I'm comin', I'm comin'. Hould it a minnit, can't ye? I'm in the blasted privy!"

There was an oil lamp burning in the back room of the house at the far end of the yard. An old woman with a black shawl over her head sat crocheting by an ancient kitchen range that shone with black lead. She didn't even look up as they hurried past her door, turned into the parlor and made for the closet. "Someone's always running away from someone in this area," Deirdre whispered. "The houses all connect up like rabbit warrens."

The empty house on the far side of the closet stank with mildew, and the floors crunched with rotted plaster that had fallen from the walls. They slipped through a splintered front door that stood open to the sidewalk and found themselves in a long, featureless cross street.

As they began the trudge up to Ballysillan and the noise of rioting faded slowly behind them, Bolan asked, "How did you know the mystery password?"

"The password?"

"To convince the old guy we were on the level. All that about the sash."

"It's not a password. 'The sash me father wore,'" she quoted. "It's a song, the battle cry of the Protestant Orange Order—named after William of Orange, who won the Battle of the Boyne in 1690 and started the persecution of the Catholics here. They wear orange sashes on parades."

"And you were letting him know...?"

"It's a fair bet that any house in those few streets would be Protestant. He wanted to make sure we were on his side. It was a way of letting him think we were—" she blushed "—without actually lying."

Bolan made no reply. He was thinking of what he could report to Gage.

**17**

Zero progress. That was what Mack Bolan was going to have to report to Captain Simon Gage when the two men met at Bolan's hotel late on the last night of the soldier's seventy-two-hour furlough.

The Executioner had little hope that Gage himself would have anything more positive to add.

Zero progress, that was, in the identification and tracking down of Derek Osborne's killer.

In the case of Bolan's own mission, the picture was not so bleak.

The IRA was planning "something dirty." There was to be a council meeting to finalize the details the next day, Sunday. The plan was to be put into operation the coming week. And the Unionist extremists wanted in some way to cash in on it. This much he had learned from Connolly and Kelly during the brutal questioning of Deirdre.

Could there by any doubt that the "something dirty" was the massacre of Catholics, falsely attributed to the British army, that the meeting was to work out the timing and logistics, or that the Osborne killing, as he had originally believed, was the supposed excuse, the hook on which the whole evil scheme was to be hung?

But he couldn't tell Gage this without revealing the details of his own assignment.

And—this was the supreme irony—he could get no farther himself until he asked Deirdre O'Mara exactly the same questions as those posed by Connolly.

"The way I see it," he said, "the key to the whole question lies with this Danny McClusky that Kelly and Connolly were talking about." A harmless wee lad, Ginny McDade had said, who ran with the hare and hunted with the hounds. . . . Nobody paid him any mind, but he kept his ears open.

And Kelly had said that his intel on the IRA coup had come from McClusky, and that it was "concerned with the Mourne stuff."

"The key to what question?" Deirdre asked, taking her eyes momentarily off the road to glance at Bolan.

"The key to all the questions," he said, "and the answers they were trying to beat out of you in that ruined mill."

"They interest you so much, these questions and answers?" Her voice was suddenly cold.

"They interest me insofar as they have a bearing on the inquiry Gage and I are carrying out," Bolan said carefully. "That is to say, finding the killer or killers who murdered his friend Derek Osborne."

"I don't see how they *can* have any bearing on that. The officer was shot last Wednesday morning. I already told you, my associates had nothing whatever to do with that. And I don't see what a meeting that takes place tomorrow, four days later, can have to do with it either."

"What the meeting is to discuss may have a great deal to do with it. Your people—or at least those under Rafferty's control—are planning something even Connolly described as dirty. If you could just—"

"I only know that there is a meeting. Period," she snapped.

"Where?"

"If you're so anxious to know, why don't you pull my hair and slap my face until I tell?" She was really angry now.

"If that was all I wanted," Bolan said gently, "I could simply have stayed hidden at the mill, waiting, and listened to what Connolly and his thugs forced out of you."

There was a short silence. She shot a red light and narrowly missed a bus. "I'm sorry," she said at last. "Of course I am grateful that you rescued me—at considerable risk to yourself—but I cannot see that this puts me under an obligation to give away secrets to a foreigner. And a friend of a British army officer at that."

"Not an obligation," Bolan agreed. "In my profession you don't go looking for rewards."

"What is your profession?" she asked sharply. "For if there's one thing I'm sure of, you're no more a news photographer than I am. And all this talk of helping Captain Gage in the hope of getting a photo-scoop is so much eyewash. Are you working for the British government?"

"No," Bolan said.

"The American government, then?"

"Not exactly. You ask too many questions yourself," Bolan said. "And you don't give enough answers." He cursed himself for his slip of the tongue. In his eagerness to pry out of her the information he needed so vitally, he had spoken as his real self and not his cover self. He said, "Working for anyone or no one, I can promise you that many lives will be saved if I have the information I need. And your organization could get the blackest reputation of its whole existence if I don't get it."

"No way." She shook her head. "You should know by now that neither threats nor violence will make me betray the Army. As for reputations, for many, many people the Army never has been black at all. You're talking like an Englishman."

Bolan didn't know what to do. He admired her devotion to her cause. But her obstinacy was as infuriating as it was frustrating. How could he convince her?

Only by telling her the real reason behind his determination. But even if that was possible, did he know her well enough to trust her with the secret? If she mistrusted him, why should he have any more confidence in her? She claimed to be keeping an eye on the trigger-happy Rafferty for the "Staff" in Dublin. But which section of the IRA really commanded her loyalty? And suppose Rafferty's massacre plan was already known to—and approved by— the old guard in the Irish capital?

No, there were too many factors over which he had no control. The way it was so far, taking her fully into his confidence might blow the whole deal.

"Look at it this way," he said, trying another approach. "You tell me I'm on Rafferty's hit list, that the order has gone out for my execution. By now I'm probably on Connolly's hit list, too, if only because I got you away from the mill. Do you approve of this, so far as Rafferty is concerned? Does the Army?"

She turned to look at him again. "Frankly, no. Violence there must be, sometimes, in any revolutionary organization. Freedom is not won without blood being spilled. But not in this way, not for this reason—or for no reason. We have to accept the necessity of killing, even of assassination. But of our bitterest enemies, not of bystanders who happen to get in the way or see someone they're not supposed to see. At least, that's the Staff view."

"And your view?"

She steered the VW neatly into a space in Bolan's hotel parking lot, braked and cut the engine. "If my view was any different," she said finally, "I'd not be here, would I? And by now, likely you wouldn't either."

"No, I guess not. I'm sorry." Bolan sighed. Each of them was prepared to go outside the law, but only if his or her moral code required or permitted it. Their aims were very different, but from a personal point of view, was there all that much difference between their separate, private standards of behavior?

"This man McClusky," Bolan said abruptly. "Had you heard of him before? Do you know him?"

"Danny McClusky? Sure everybody knows him," Deirdre replied. "And Danny knows everybody. Knows their business, too, which may not always be good for him. But he's harmless enough, so everyone lets him be. He's a runner or something for the bookies."

Fighting the Mob stateside, Bolan had often enough come across the same scenario. A go-between, a stoolie, a seller of information who played a minor role in a major league. Such a guy could be tolerated by both sides: the police because he was a useful source of tip-offs on nonsyndicate crime, the Mob because he could keep them abreast of police thinking, and both because he could be used to spread disinformation they wanted "unofficially" leaked.

Such a man was worth more alive than dead to both sides.

Until he happened upon some piece of information concerning one side that was too hot for him to handle....

Danny McClusky knew about the Mourne arms dump, and it seemed he knew what the IRA planned to do with it. Kelly, who like McClusky himself appeared to play both ends against the middle, said that what he knew scared him so much that he wasn't even prepared to talk about it.

Bolan was not surprised. He knew how it was going to be used, too. All the evidence pointed that way. But unlike McClusky, he didn't know where and when.

"We've got to find him," Bolan said.

"Who, Danny? He'll probably be at the Ambassador later, though I doubt you'll want in there again. He could be at Geraghty's now, or the Union or even the Massereene. He might be stuffing himself with peanuts and chips and olives over a single draft beer at the American Bar in the Midland.''

''Geraghty's closes in a half hour, and anyway I have a meet here with Gage at ten,'' Bolan said. ''You know where this McClusky lives?''

She shook her golden head. ''But he stays sometimes with his mam in a village out at Nutts Corner, near the airport.''

''If he's scared, that could be where he's heading. We'll go there later. He must be located. It's vital.''

''*We*'ll go there?''

''If you really don't know what Rafferty's meeting is about—and if you refuse to find out—he's my only chance of stopping something monstrous.''

''So tell me what this something is.''

''I can't. Not until I'm certain you're on my side. Not until you've discovered for yourself how low—Well, let's say until you've made up your own mind without any pressure from me. And I think you will, if you help me find McClusky.''

There was something in the man's voice, some inner conviction she found totally persuasive, that finally convinced Deirdre to go along with his request, despite her suspicions, despite her reservations concerning Bolan's own role.

''Very well,'' she said. ''I'll wait here in the car for thirty minutes while you talk with your officer. After that, I'll drive you wherever you want. But if the man's late, or if he keeps you longer than that, I'm away.''

''Late?'' Bolan said lightly. ''A captain in the British army?'' And then, in a more serious tone, he said, ''Don't worry, I'll be back within half an hour. Thanks.''

She didn't have to wait that long.

Bolan went into the hotel and called the number Ginny McDade had given him from a pay phone in the lobby. No reply.

He went up to his room.

Captain Simon Gage was not late for his appointment with the Executioner. In fact, he had arrived early.

He was sitting in an overstuffed armchair by the night table with the top of his head blown off and most of his brains splashed over the flowered wallpaper.

He had been shot at point-blank range with the silenced Beretta 93-R Bolan had lost beneath the looms in the machine shop of the abandoned mill. The gun was lying on the blood-spattered bedcovers.

Bolan had no doubt that the killer would have worn gloves so that the warrior's own fingerprints would remain undisturbed on the weapon. And he had been seen in public with Gage in a dozen places over the past five days.

And both of them had been seen at the Ulster Hall, where two dead men had been found onstage after the Unionist rally—one shot by Gage himself, but with this same Beretta.

And each of them had been asking indiscreet questions in pubs all over town, one in the Protestant, the other in Catholic neighborhoods....

Neat.

Some kind of sectarian quarrel, as far as Homicide was concerned?

Bolan snatched up the Beretta and shoved it into his shoulder rig. He grabbed the Hasselblad and the Nikon and got the hell out of there—via the fire exit at the end of the passageway outside his room.

## 18

Fallen leaves swirled in the headlight beams as Mack Bolan raced the Volkswagen up the curving driveway that led to Simon Gage's regimental headquarters on the shores of Lough Neagh.

Wind threshed the lakeside alders and scattered occasional drops of rain across the screen as he braked in the parking lot reserved for officers and ran for the long, low building at one side of the requisitioned mansion that served as the mess.

Deirdre remained in the car. It would be unwise—from both their points of view—if a known IRA sympathizer was to be seen on a British army base.

Gage had been dressed in nondescript civilian clothes, and during his investigations he had carried no identification. So it would be some time before the homicide cops made a definite identification and contacted the army authorities. Bolan wanted to get there first and tell his story, or as much of it as was useful, before an official report was made. And before the carefully planned setup linked him with the captain's murder.

Bolan's press pass got him past the guards on the door and into the adjutant's office. Arranging to see Colonel Alleyn took longer. He was asked to wait in the visitors' anteroom while an orderly was sent to find out if the CO was available.

The adjutant ordered him a drink from the bar. Before it was served he was called to the phone. It was five minutes before eleven o'clock.

Bolan looked around him. He was alone in the room, and the only noise he could hear was the rustle of flames from the log fire below the copper hood of the chimneypiece. Somewhere behind him the wind rattled a window in its frame. Through an open door he saw a group of senior officers murmuring together at one end of the mess bar.

A steward in a white jacket brought the drinks.

Bolan remembered the man from his first visit, when he was arranging to accompany Osborne's routine patrol in the city.

Recognition was mutual: not many Americans frequented the mess. "Blowing up for a dirty night, sir," the steward said conversationally.

"Looks that way," Bolan replied. "Tell me, there's a man I met here who I'd very much like to see again. He was drinking at the bar the first time I was here. Do you by any chance remember him—tall, thin character with glittering eyes? A major in the gunners, I think."

"Major in the gunners, sir?" the man repeated. "Now that you mention it, I believe I do. You wouldn't remember which day it was, would you?"

"Sure. It was last Tuesday. Sometime before dinner."

"Ah, yes, of course. Tuesday it was. He was with that poor young Mr. Osborne. Came in about four-thirty and had to wait here in the anteroom until Mr. O. came off duty after his patrol. They dined together in the mess."

Bolan's pulses quickened. If the riot-inciting, two-faced Kelly was directly tied in with the murdered officer... It was something to think about—something that would seem to confirm his idea that the killing of the officer *was* the first step in the IRA plot.

Something that might even tailor Kelly, the man playing many different roles, for the killer slot?

"I guess you wouldn't recall the major's name or where his unit's stationed?" he asked.

"No, sir. I'm afraid not," the steward replied. "But I can easily find out for you, if you like. Just wait while I fetch the mess visitors' book."

The Executioner sipped a Bushmills liqueur—Ulster's single-malt gift to the drinking fraternity—and listened to the wind moaning in the chimney.

The steward returned in a few minutes with a wide leatherbound volume. They put it on the table and leafed through the big pages columned with names, ranks, units and locations of mess guests.

"Here we are then," the steward said. "Sunday, Monday—Cor! That's funny!"

The page bearing the details of guests who had visited the mess the previous Tuesday had been neatly razored from the book.

SURPRISE NUMBER TWO: Colonel Alleyn accepted Bolan's story at face value.

Understandably he was both distressed and outraged at the news of Gage's murder. But he made no attempt to verify it or make further inquiries while Bolan was there. "Silly young fool," he said angrily. "One more good officer lost, for what? I told him. You heard me, dammit, you were here." He shook his head. "Poking his nose into local politics. Bound to end badly. Probably found out too much. Killed to keep his mouth shut . . . and the body planted in your room, trying to pin the murder on you. Keep you quiet, too, while you try to get out of that one."

The Executioner forebore to say that Gage had actually been killed in his room, that they had a meeting there, that the murder weapon was his own Beretta. Alleyn was not as angry as he had feared at the news that Gage had disobeyed orders to play detective, less angry still at Bolan's admission that he had helped out in the hope of a scoop.

Bolan didn't get it, but he wasn't going to complain.

He would very much have liked to confide in the colonel, but that was impossible. He had to stick with his cover.

"What next?" Alleyn asked. "Shoot a few more street-fighting scenes? Our man on the inside of the riots, that sort of thing? Interviews with the Provisionals not much use, I suppose. They're eager enough to talk, but no pictures, eh?"

"I figured I might continue to follow Gage's lead, at least for a day or two," Bolan said carefully. "There may be nothing in it pictorially, but I kind of feel that I owe it to him. He was quite a guy."

"Stout fella," Alleyn agreed. "First-class shot. King's Prize at Bisley. Best to leave it to the law, though. They'll pick up his killers in the end. Osborne's, too." He sighed, and then added, "Talking of pictures, though, you'd get jolly good ones from the air, I'd think, if they continue hotting it up the way they were last night and the day before. Bit of a new angle, what!"

"From the air, sir?"

"Yes, yes. If you could fly, you know, low enough—and slow enough—I'd say there'd be a chance of some really original shots."

Bolan frowned. "I'm sure you're right. But ...?"

"I mean," the colonel said with studied casualness, "if you were to get hold of some machine like that little Venom autogyro they're trying out at Aldergrove." He took a pipe from his pocket and began stuffing tobacco into it from an oiled silk pouch.

"A Venom?" the Executioner echoed.

"Funny little craft. Like a wheelchair with rotors. Dare not stand up, or you get your bloody head cut off! But jolly useful for recon, if you ask me. Can't think why they don't put a guard on it. Thing's standing all by itself in an old bomber pan outside the perimeter track.''

Colonel Alleyn lit a match, sucked in flame and puffed smoke. "Still, no business of mine, eh? My job's just to keep the fighters apart! Nice of you to drop in, Belasko. Appreciate you thinking of me first. Poor Gage."

He rose to his feet, shook hands briefly and strode from the anteroom in a cloud of blue smoke.

THE CAR THAT HAD BEEN TRAILING the Volkswagen since they had left Ballysillan Road pulled out from behind a screen of bushes as they left the regimental HQ. It was a large closed car, and there were four men inside.

It drew level with the VW between the airport and the long descent to the city around the flank of Black Mountain. Deirdre was driving again, and Bolan was relating his interview with Colonel Alleyn.

The big sedan forged slowly ahead. As the rear window drew level with the driver's window of the Volkswagen, the window was wound down. A blued steel barrel projecting from a perforated cooling jacket was thrust toward the smaller car.

"Look out!" Bolan shouted.

For the second time that week he wrenched the steering wheel violently from Deirdre's hands, cranking it as hard as he could to the left as the gun muzzle belched flame.

They were going faster, and the abrupt change in direction played havoc with the VW's centers of gravity and steering geometry.

The car's nose slid toward the nearside of the road, while its tail, ballasted with the weight of the engine, jerked upward.

The car flipped over onto its roof, slammed into a grassy roadside bank, spun around twice on the shoulder and then zoomed into the air to drop back on its crumpled wheels again in a plowed field on the far side of the verge.

Bolan's desperate grab had been just in time. The killer's deathstream, intended for him and the woman, had sprayed into the rear of the sedan as it turned over. But the man handling the SMG, intoxicated with the thunder of his lethal toy, was convinced the Volkswagen had crashed because he had succeeded in his mission to eliminate the occupants. The big car sped away toward the city.

Still strapped into their seats, saved by the rigidity of the solid bodywork, Bolan and Deirdre opened their eyes. The inside of the car was pungent with the aroma of gasoline. After the appalling clatter of the smash, the silence was intense.

Bolan unbuckled his seat belt and extricated himself from the wreck. Nodules of glass from the shattered windshield showered to the ground as he stood upright. He had suffered a cut on the forehead; Deirdre O'Mara had bruised her ribs against the buckled wheel. Otherwise, astonishingly, they seemed to be unhurt.

The roof of the VW was badly dented, the nearside front fender was smashed and a headlight was missing. A tire was flat. But apart from the windshield and one side window the rest of the vehicle seemed relatively undamaged. "This kind of maneuver is becoming monotonous," Bolan said. "Just for laughs, try the starter."

She turned the key. The starter motor whined. There was a screech of metal, followed by a metallic thump.

Deirdre took a pencil flashlight from the glove compartment and handed it to the Executioner. He walked around to the rear of the car and unlatched the louvered hood. It came away in his hand and clanged to the ground. Inside, the thin beam of light showed him where the steel-jacketed SMG flesh-shredders had ripped through the fan cowling and mangled the cooling blades of the turbine. The float chamber had been sheared off the body of the carburetor, the distributor cap was smashed and gasoline splashed from a broken lead on the tank side of the pump.

"Damn!" Bolan said feelingly. He stepped back from the car and looked around him. Somewhere above the clouds there was a moon. In the faint light he could make out ragged hedges, trees, the rounded summit of the mountain above. On the far side of the road, the land fell away toward the distant illuminations of the city, but there was no sign of any houses nearby. The raindrops carried by the wind blustering up the slope fell more thickly now.

Bolan walked back to the front of the car. "This Nutts Corner village where the McClusky woman lives," he said, "how far is it from here?"

"A mile. Maybe less." Deirdre was sitting in the back seat. "But we can't call there now. It's after midnight. You know country people. Even if the old woman was awake, she'd say nothing now."

Bolan sighed. "I guess we better just sit it out until daylight then. We'd lose too much time trying to get help or going back to the city. It really is urgent."

"Thank the dear Lord we landed with our tail to the wind," she said. "With no screen, we'd be quare and cold facing the other way. Come on in. It's cozier back here."

He got in and sat beside her, realizing suddenly that she was trembling all over. Being a theoretical revolutionary was fine, but two murderous attacks on a car she was driving, the gunfight in the vacant lot, Bolan's escape from the execution squad in the club, the brutal elimination of Gage and her own nightmare martyrdom at the abandoned mill—the cumulative effect of all these, he was aware, had finally proved too much for her. Somewhere inside Deirdre, continued exposure to violence had burst an emotional dam: she was no longer able to maintain the pretense of keeping it together.

A person, even the toughest of people, can only take so much. Instinctively he put his arms around her. She came to him at once, willingly, gratefully, sobbing now uncontrollably, the tears that rolled down her cheeks shining in the diffused light of the moon.

It was a long time before the racking sobs ceased.

## 19

A new day had dawned, and the wind had freshened again; it was rocking the car on its springs and flattening the tufts of coarse grass at the side of the road when Bolan at last emerged from the Volkswagen, stretching. On the hillside somewhere below, telephone wires moaned a high descant, and smoke from the chimneys surrounding the shipyard gantries streamed out across the slate roofs of the distant city.

How many of those roofs, Bolan wondered, hid the men plotting death and destruction of their fellow beings, the conspirators determined to worsen still further the hatred and suspicion and distrust that had for so long soured the atmosphere of that city?

"We'll go to the McClusky house now," he called. "I'm still certain this man has the key to one hell of a lot of headaches. But if he's scared, he may be tempted to run, and we have to get to him before it's too late."

Deirdre kept a zippered leather weekend case containing a change of clothing in the VW's trunk. While Bolan stretched himself in the cold dawn wind, she took off her crumpled skirt and sweater and dressed in black stretch pants, knee boots and a heavy ribbed fisherman's jersey, which she covered with a black rain slicker.

Bolan slipped the flashlight into his pocket, picked up his camera case and took her hand. They set off for the village, leaving the VW in the field

The McClusky cottage was at the far end of a single street comprising a church, three pubs, a post office and general store, and two rows of whitewashed single-story dwellings.

An elderly woman with a lined face and a black shawl over her head opened the door as soon as Bolan knocked. "Wee Danny's away," she said severely, "and yous the second foreign lot askin' already today, an' the sun not risen an hour."

"I'm sorry," Bolan said. "We especially wanted to see him before he left. But you say his other friends already passed by? They were looking for him, too?"

"Aye. Four on 'em, in a great big black car, they were. Can't say I liked the look of yon fellas neither. But then Danny has some quare friends all right, always did."

"You don't happen to know where Danny has gone, Mrs. McClusky?" Deirdre asked. "It's most important we find him as quickly as possible, you see. We have...news for him."

"So had th'others. Or so they said. He's gone where he always goes when the boyo's in need of a little rest. It's no joke workin' as a runner for that Connolly fella, the bookmaker over to Belfast."

"It's hard to find a quiet place these days," Deirdre said sympathetically. "Which one does Danny favor?"

"He's gone where he always goes, across the border to Bundoran. I told them an' I'm tellin' yous."

"Does he always stay in the same place?" Bolan asked. And he knew, instinctively, almost before she replied, what the answer would be.

"Sure he does," the woman said. "The Excelsior Temperance Hotel, across the road from the supermart in Mount Street."

THEY BOUGHT a large-scale tourist road map, a copy of the *Belfast Newsletter*, a bottle of milk and some bread in the general store. Out of the wind behind a drystone wall, they sat down in a small field beside the lane that led from the village toward the airport. Deirdre broke the bread in two and handed one portion to Bolan. Then she pried the cap from the top of the milk bottle and drank.

Bolan's brain was speeding. Questions and answers slotted into place as neatly as the green lines of digital display unrolling across a VDT screen.

Danny McClusky was a regular visitor to the Excelsior. The Excelsior was the safehouse drop where Bolan had picked up the papers and gear organized for him by Hal Brognola. Conclusion: there was some connection between Brognola and McClusky.

McClusky worked as a runner for Connolly; he also acted as informer for the IRA extremist's paramilitary group. He ran with the hare and hunted with the hounds. Conclusion: McClusky was on the make, probably on the take, and clearly owed no loyalty to anyone.

Brognola had heard of the Rafferty plot through his Belfast contact, who had been subsequently killed by a car bomb. McClusky knew about the plot, was so scared by what he knew, that he was in fear of his life and on the run. Conclusion: McClusky could be, not a double but a triple agent; he could be the contact who had originally tipped off Brognola's man, running for the Excelsior bolthole now in the hope that his Brognola connections could get him out.

Run a check now on cars . . . and Catholics.

A black stretch limo had acted as command car when Bolan was first ambushed as he landed in the creek near Bundoran. The killers who had fired on them and wrecked the VW last night had been in a black stretch limo and so had the "friends" looking for McClusky this morning. Conclusion: the leaks were two-way, not only channeling intel in Brognola's direction but also feeding it out from his end.

"There's another thing," Bolan said aloud, though his ruminations so far had been in silence. "The guy behind the gun last night—did you see who it was?"

Deirdre was munching bread. She nodded, her face crumpled into an expression of distress.

"Ferret-face," Bolan said. "Your friend Rafferty's henchman, Jamie Craig. A dangerous man, as you said."

She made no reply. Wordlessly she handed him the paper. SLAIN GIRL WAS NIGHTCLUB QUEEN, he read below the fold on the front page. And then:

Police investigating the murder of the red-haired woman whose body was found early yesterday in a private hotel off the Antrim Road have established that the victim was Miss Frances Virginia McDade, 28, of Cookstown, Co. Tyrone. Miss McDade, who described herself as a model, was well-known in Belfast nightclub circles.

The nearly nude body was discovered by a hotel servant. A nylon stocking was tied tightly around the neck, and the woman had been severely assaulted.

Police are anxious to interview an American journalist named Michael Belasko, who is believed to have been the last person to see Miss McDade alive.

"The bastards!" Bolan said. His face was ashen. "That poor kid...just because she helped me. Your gallant patriotic friends, I suppose?"

"Not anymore," she said passionately. "Not after this, not after the attack on us last night, not after Gage. They're no better than the brutes had me up at the mill. No, not anymore: So far as Rafferty's concerned, it's the finish for me."

"It could be exactly that if we're not damn careful. You've been seen with me. They knew it was your car las† night after all.'' He shook his head. ''With the Protestant extremists, your IRA extremists, and now the police after me, too, I've got one hell of a chance of finishing what I set out do!''

''Just what did you set out to do?'' Deirdre asked softly. ''You told me you weren't really selling arms, but *I* don't believe this detective story you and Gage cooked up either. Anymore than I believe you're a real newspaperman.''

After all they'd been through together, Bolan felt he owed her the truth—at least as much as he could reveal.

''The detective story was on the level, as far as Gage was concerned,'' he said. ''I latched on to it because it fitted in with my own plans. And because, although he didn't know it, the killing of his friend was part of something I'd sworn to stop.''

''And that something...?''

He told her the whole story, omitting only the fears that, if it succeeded, the Rafferty plan would wreck Anglo-American collaboration on the XP-29 project.

That wasn't likely to be a motive that would appeal to her. She could believe him a lone crusader, she could believe him a U.S. field agent, she could imagine him working for some screwball peace movement. It didn't matter: he was gambling on the fact that the story was horrifying enough to carry her without supplementary detail.

He was right.

''My God, but that's *terrible*!'' she gasped when he had finished. ''Imagine the effect! British troops fire on a Catholic crowd! Return of the Black and Tans! The uneasy truce between our Republicans and the Brits would explode into violence. Our extremists would act, and the Unionists would have an excuse to be tougher still and cancel the few concessions we've won so far.''

Bolan nodded. "And the death of Gage, after the Osborne killing, will lend more support still to the Army revenge theory."

"They've got to be stopped!" Deirdre said fiercely. "I see what you mean now about blackening the name of the Army. The Staff will go crazy when they hear of this—"

"They won't have time to hear of it," Bolan cut in with a brusque movement of his hand. "The countdown has already started. It began with Osborne's murder and gained momentum with the killing of Gage. It could happen anytime. If there's not to be total chaos in Ulster, we've got to stop it ourselves."

"But you don't know the day or the time of the attack?"

"I don't know when they plan to raid the Mourne dump either, or which particular Catholic gathering is to be the target."

"How can we find out?"

"By locating McClusky before the guys in the black limo do. I told you. I'm certain he's the key, and I believe he knows all those things. And I believe he's running because he also knows Rafferty is aware that he knows, and aims to shut his mouth at all costs."

"But according to his mam he was the best part of an hour's start on us, and the black car almost a half hour."

"We know he's heading for Bundoran, and she told us he's driving an easily identifiable car—a small red MG roadster."

"But there's dozens of routes he could take from here. And this isn't going to make it any easier for us through the roadblocks." She handed him the newspaper again.

Bolan glanced at the front page for the second time. The lead story reported sectarian violence in Belfast and Londonderry, rioting in Armagh, firebombs and confrontations with the army in several small towns near the border. The second headline stated that Dublin industrialist Keiron

Winslow-Mowbray, a prominent member of a Franco-German-Irish electronics consortium, was to stand as a candidate for the Euro-Parliament. The now-familiar heavy features stared up at Bolan out of the newsprint. He frowned, raising questioning eyebrows at the girl. She pointed to the Stop Press.

One paragraph, overlinked and printed askew in the blank space, was headed: AMERICAN SOUGHT IN SECOND MURDER HUNT. Beneath it, the smudged lettering read:

Body of British army captain Simon Gage found dead of gunshot wounds in hotel room occupied by U.S. newsman Michael Belasko. Police wish to interview Belasko in connection with this and Antrim Road killing as they believe he may be able to help them with their inquiries.

"'Help them with their inquiries,'" Bolan quoted bitterly. "That's the Brit way of saying, 'We know the bastard did it.' We've got to get out of here and after Danny."

"We don't even have a car," Deirdre said.

"Just one moment," Bolan said slowly. "We may not even need one. It's an extraordinary thing. I thought at the time the guy was practically propositioning me to steal it. There can't be an connection, of course. But just the same..." He fell silent.

"Steal what?"

"A miniature autogyro," Bolan said. "From the airport down the road."

## 20

A cloudbank racing up from the southwest threatened to blot out the early morning sun as Bolan and Deirdre O'Mara arrived at Aldergrove.

The lane skirted the far side of the field, a mile away from the main entrance. Army details patrolled the perimeter in APCs and Land Rovers, but there was a twelve-minute gap between each patrol, and Bolan reckoned that should be enough for them to do what had to be done.

They had no difficulty locating the autogyro. It was, as Colonel Alleyn had said, in an old hardtop pan outside the perimeter track—a diminutive shape pegged down under a tarp between a Cessna executive jet and a beat-up Piper Cherokee that looked as if had just escaped a Sahara sandstorm.

The pan was no more than fifty yards from the road. It was no problem for them to slip beneath the wire and make the asphalt circle immediately after the army vehicles had passed, because the track dipped toward the lake and they were almost immediately out of sight. And once sheltered between the two larger ships, Bolan and Deirdre could work undisturbed.

The tarp, unlaced, bellied out in the wind, and they had to stow it behind the nosewheel of the Cherokee. After that it was simple.

The Wallis Venom stood little higher than the Executioner himself. The wide, outrigged undercart—its wheels no bigger than those of a motor scooter—supported a curious, spidery machine. In front, a faired cowling enclosed two seats in tandem and the controls. Behind this was a 130 hp, air-cooled, flat four Rolls-Royce engine driving a four-blade "pusher" propeller. And a long way aft was the rudder, slung between two single lengths of spaceframe tubing. A small missile was slung beneath the cockpit.

The two blades of the rotor were mounted on a metal pylon directly above the rear passenger's head and connected to the engine drive shaft by a pulley.

Bolan walked around the tiny ship, examining the exhausts curling away from each cylinder bank, and the cooling vanes and flexible tubes that led to the propeller and rotor head.

"Nice," he said admiringly. "A bit vulnerable with everything out in the open air, but maneuverable as hell, I'd say."

Deirdre was examining the cockpit. There were two biker-style crash helmets on the front seat; the controls were one hundred percent conventional. She frowned. "I'm not sure I understand the difference between an autogyro and a helicopter," she said. "The way this looks, I could fly the thing myself."

"Different principle," Bolan told her. "In each case the rotors act as a wing to keep the thing in the air. In a chopper, the blades change pitch and act also as motive power, dragging the ship *through* the air. But the autogyro rotors are freewheeling, and only rotate when the plane is moving. It has to be propelled by an ordinary propeller like this." He nodded at the four-blade prop. "In other words, this baby can't stay up there on rotors alone. Which means it can't hover the same way a chopper can, but you can maneuver it around the sky more freely."

He looked at her sharply. "Did you say you could fly?"

"Surely. I took my pilot's license at a club near Dublin, started on powered ultralight deltas, graduated to Cubs and finally made the A and B on the real thing. You want me to fly this?"

Bolan made a lightning decision. "Yeah," he said. "You know the country. I'll navigate and handle the weapons."

She nodded and climbed into the front seat, dragging a helmet over her blond hair. The stick was as she'd expected. The few instruments—fuel, oil, horizon level, airspeed indicator and altimeter—were mounted vertically on a panel in front of it.

Bolan slung the Hasselblad around his neck, clipped the folding carbine stock onto his Beretta and climbed in behind.

The engine burst into life with a clattering roar. The little ship trundled forward onto the perimeter track and accelerated as the rotors above Bolan's head started to twirl.

Deirdre eased back the stick and lifted off in less than eighty yards.

Over his shoulder, Bolan saw the next patrol pull up, men in camouflage fatigues and steel helmets out of their vehicles and running, an officer shouting orders.

The next moment the autogyro was dipping toward the lake, and the clatter of the rotors was drowned by the roar of a Boeing 757 taking off from the main runway not far behind them.

The land tilted and slid away as they skimmed the water toward the distant humps of the Sperrin Mountains. They stood clear and sharp in patches of green and russet and ocher against the pale western sky.

They had worked out a rough flight plan while they had waited for the patrols to pass. Lying beneath a screen of bushes with the map spread out on the ground, Bolan had traced McClusky's possible routes to Bundoran, a straight-line distance of some eighty miles, although by road it looked more like one hundred or even one hundred ten.

"As the guy goes there often," Bolan had said, "he probably has valid papers, a good reason for each trip and a crossing point where the guards know him. For my money, that would be the route around the northern tip of Lough Erne and then west to Ballyshannon. The border there is only a few miles from Bundoran."

"Unless he knows they're after him," Deirdre had said, "in which case he might take a roundabout route to try and shake them off."

"A point," Bolan had conceded. "But do you think the Rafferty gang is going to follow him all the way? Once they're sure where's he's heading, won't they just phone or even radio ahead and get some of their buddies out to block the road?"

She had bit her lip. "That would be more like Rafferty, all right. And he's plenty of followers in the border region. Would that not be a stronger reason for him to take the smaller country roads, but?"

"It could be. But those roads are kind of empty, and a red MG roadster isn't all that common in those parts, I'd guess. They'd be able to keep track of him just by asking."

"So you think he'll opt for the fastest, straightest route he knows best?"

Bolan had nodded. "Being scared, I figure he'll want the hell out the quickest way possible and forget the planning."

In either case, they had assumed McClusky would have taken the M-1, Ulster's only high-speed freeway, west to Dungannon. The choice then lay between the direct, minor-road route south of the Sperrins to Dromore and Ballyshannon, or the longer but faster road via Enniskillen— the way Bolan himself had entered the country.

"Starting from here," Bolan had said, "it's ten miles to the freeway. Then he's only got another twenty before it ends. On the minor roads he's not going to average much more than thirty. He can't be much more than ten miles beyond Dungannon now, and once he's out there we have three times his speed and we can fly straight."

"Yes, but we can't stop at an intersection and say, 'The red car, which way did he go?'"

"If we haven't located him or the black limo by the time we're halfway to the border on the direct route, we'll zigzag between the two," the Executioner had decided.

On the far side of Lough Neagh now, following Bolan's directions for Dungannon, Deirdre yelled over her shoulder, "All very well chasing this man, but who's chasing *us*? We did steal the plane, remember." She glanced down at the patchwork of fields sliding past below—they were flying no higher than five hundred feet—and asked, "Can they trace us by radar?"

"Not a chance." Bolan leaned forward and shouted in her ear. "We're way below the screen. And unless they knew the route we were planning to take, they wouldn't have a hope of detecting us from a recon ship."

Deirdre nodded. She was handling the tiny autogyro well. Lacking the power sense of a regular chopper, it was at the mercy of air pockets, thermals, turbulence, floating like a leaf on the wind. But she kept it straight on course, using a flick of the rudder here, a few degrees of boost there, to combat the air currents and follow the roads while Bolan scanned the traffic below with a pair of Zeiss binoculars he had found in a pocket behind the front seat.

They had been in the air twenty minutes, and the lough was no more than a streak of silver beneath the darkening sky behind them, when they reached the fork where the two routes diverged, at a village named Bellygawley.

But Danny McClusky had made better time than they had expected. It was forty-two minutes before the warrior sighted the red roadster, and they were already quartering the twelve-mile stretch of country separating them, paying special attention to the network of country lanes in between.

It was the fifteenth red car Bolan had seen among the dun-colored army convoys, farm pickups and sparse civilian traffic; the third convertible and the only MG.

The moment he located it, he discovered that he had been right . . . and wrong.

McClusky *had* taken his customary route, the most direct one; he had made it as far as a place called Lack, within sight of Lough Erne.

But Rafferty's men in the stretch limo hadn't radioed ahead to call out supporters to bar the road; they had followed the red roadster themselves, and this was where they had caught up with it. The MG was canted over in a weed-grown drainage trench near a deserted farm, and the black sedan, which had forced it there, was angled into the roadside just ahead. There was nobody in sight.

Bolan touched Deirdre's shoulder and pointed downward. "I'm afraid we may be too late," he shouted over the rotor clatter. "Circle lower. They must be in those buildings, unless there was a third car."

There wasn't.

As she maneuvered the autogyro down almost to rooftop level, men in cloth caps ran from the crumbling stone building. There were three of them, two with handguns and a third carrying a long tube over his shoulder with a conical projectile attached to the front end.

"Swing her away," Bolan yelled urgently, "with all the boost you've got!"

Deirdre turned a questioning face toward him.

"That's an RPG-7," he shouted. "Russian rocket grenade launcher. It can hit a moving target at 300 yards. Get out of range *quick!*"

Even as he spoke and the Venom soared away, the man holding the launcher's two pistol grips pivoted their way, and a long tongue of flame belched from the rear of the tube.

The missile, leaving the weapon at three hundred feet per second, opened stabilizing fins as the rocket motor cut in and trebled the speed, streaking its fiery tail toward the autogyro. Fortunately the five-pound HEAT grenade veered at the last moment, and Deirdre's reactions were perfect. The Venom banked and sank while the warhead zipped on to autodestruct in a ball of fire at the planned distance of 922 yards.

"Put her down over there—" the Executioner indicated a roofless barn behind the farm buildings "—we might not be so lucky a second time."

She nodded. The autogyro floated sideways and down again as a second missile was fired. It hurtled over the slate roof of the farmhouse, passing as close to the Venom's undercart that they could hear the snake hiss of the rocket motor, and exploded with a dull roar in the top branches of a row of leafless elms on the far side of a plowed field.

After that they were momentarily hidden and out of range. Deirdre grounded the ship on a slope of sheep-cropped grass within easy reach of an open gateway beside the road. "Good thinking," Bolan approved. "Only a few yards and we're on the hardtop, ready for a lift-off and a quick getaway."

Holding the Beretta, he vaulted from the cockpit and told her, "Stay put and keep the engine idling while I check out the terrain, okay?"

The farm followed an established Irish peasant tradition. A smallholder built a house. When it deteriorated, instead of having it repaired, he built a second adjoining it, keeping the damaged first part as a barn. When the second dwelling in turn crumbled, a third was built, the second became the barn, and the original building was allowed to rot away. It was not unusual in the county to see a series of four or five similar structures, each in a worse state of repair than the one preceding it, until the last—in fact, the first built, maybe generations ago—was no more than a pile of stones marking the position of the original walls.

It was near this oldest part of the complex that the autogyro had landed. Bolan leaped over the low wall and approached the gable end of the cow barn beyond it. He could hear shouting from the far end of the row, and someone was running up the road on the far side of a hawthorn hedge.

Peering through what had once been a doorway, he held his fire. More men would be advancing around the rear of the farm. It was then that he heard the scream.

It was a man's scream, starting low and rising hysterically up the scale to end in a sobbing, pleading babble. It was a cry of fear, of anticipated pain rather than a shriek of agony. Bolan had no doubt that it was uttered by Danny McClusky.

He heard a harsh voice rasp, "'Tis no good creatin', Danny boy. You know the rules. We know yous a lyin', cheatin', twistin' little bastard. Didn't you just confess that yourself, sure? Well, now you get what's comin' to you."

"No!" the terrified voice screeched. "No, no, no, *no!* Please, boys, please. I didn't mean no harm. I was only obligin'. Shoot if you must, but for the love of God not the drill! Not the bloody *drill!*" Once more the words ended in a scream.

Bolan felt the hair on his nape prickle. He knew of the barbarous punishment both sides of the underground Ulster war inflicted on informers. Instead of killing a traitor outright, they smashed both of his kneecaps—which meant, besides weeks of agony, that the man would never walk again. This "kneecapping" was done at point-blank range with a large-bore revolver. Or, if the avengers were not disposed to be "merciful," the victim was held down while each patella was shattered with an electric drill.

The informer was alive, but Bolan wanted him in a condition to talk. Before McClusky was reduced to a gibbering wreck, the warrior hurled himself into action.

The man behind the hedge was between him and the gate where the Venom was parked. Folding down the foregrip, Bolan raised the Beretta to his shoulder and blazed two withering bursts through the spiny branches.

He scored with the second. He heard a strangled cry, a stumbling clatter as the extremist fell, the sound of a firearm skating away across the hardtop.

Bolan raced for the rear of the tumbledown ruin. The elm hit by the rocket grenade was on fire. Teased out by the strong wind, the flames would soon set the whole row alight. He didn't have much time: firefighters from the nearest town would be on the way before long. There was already a long feather of smoke stroking the sky toward Lough Erne.

Clumps of brier, stacks of rotting lumber and rusted oil drums dotted the rough ground behind the farm buildings. Two more men were dodging from cover to cover. One was carrying the SMG that had blown Deirdre's Volkswagen off the road.

Rising from behind the spilled stone walls, Bolan hosed a thundering stream of death across the yard, stitching a flesh-shredding figure eight between the scattering gunnies. The hardguy with the SMG managed a single burst that almost blinded the Executioner with granite chips and plaster dust as the slugs caromed off the stonework near his head. Then the thug stumbled to his knees with his chest cored by 9 mm boattails, blood spurting into the dust.

The second hardman dropped, rolled, hoisted himself up behind a pile of lumber and spit fire the warrior's way from a heavy Tokarev TT-33 automatic. Bolan dropped flat to escape the hellstream, but sprang up again instantly, against all the expectations of his enemy. He stood totally un-shielded in the open as he held the Beretta two-handed in front of him and chugged three parabellum passports to oblivion in the killer's direction.

Surprise meant hesitation. And hesitation cost the guy his life. In the tenth of a second before his trigger finger re-acted, he lost the top of his head in a flying fan of blood and brains.

When the gunfire had ended, Bolan heard the rumble of the Venom's engine, a distant crackle of flames and then, sibilant and sinister, the unmistakable whirring of an elec-tric drill. It was followed by one of the most terrible cries of agony Bolan had ever heard.

He jumped down from the wall and raced around the far corner of the house. McClusky screamed continuously, an animal sound, inhuman and frightful.

Bolan never knew whether Rafferty's henchmen consid-ered three guards sufficient protection against intruders, or whether they were so intent on their brutal task that they didn't hear a thing.

The four men in the stretch limo must have called in lo-cal talent, because apart from the three hoods Bolan had wasted outside, there were still five men in the empty front room of the old farmhouse when he burst in.

Four of them were crouched, holding McClusky's wrists and ankles so that he was spread-eagled on the dusty floor. The fifth man was Ferret-face. He held a pistol-grip elec-tric drill that was connected up to four heavy-duty truck batteries, and he was bending over McClusky's left leg.

The pant leg had been ripped away, and the spiraled van-adium-steel tip of the drill, rotating at 5000 rpm, was plunged into the tortured man's frenziedly jerking leg at knee level.

McClusky was shrieking mindlessly, his writhing, bucking, contorted body spattering the floor with blood and bone splinters.

There were four shots left in the Beretta's magazine. Bolan had no compunction. He wasted the quartet of hoods holding McClusky down—one shot for each, coring the skulls of the two nearest, fisting through the chests of the guys holding the victim's arms. It was done so quickly that Ferret-face barely had time to swing around, snarling, before the Executioner was on him.

He was still reaching for the gun in his hip pocket when the Executioner's bulk crushed him to the floor. Bolan snatched the drill and rammed the point against the IRA man's chest.

He squeezed the trigger recessed in the pistol grip. The drill tip whipped into motion with a thin screech. Bolan leaned on it with all his force, coring the man's ribs and pulping his heart.

Ferret-face's eyes opened wide in disbelief. As the irises rolled upward under the lids, he gave a coughing grunt, blood pumping from his nostrils and open mouth. His body went limp.

Danny was still screaming, thrashing from side to side. Bolan raced to the autogyro where there was a first-aid box clipped to the side of the rear cockpit.

A morphine injection and a makeshift dressing applied by the horrified Deirdre reduced McClusky's wild mouthings to an intelligible mumble, and between them they carried him to the Venom. The elms were blazing fiercely, and the bray of fire trucks floated to them on the blustering wind.

Bolan left the bodies, the RPG-7, the drill and the other weapons. With some difficulty they maneuvered the injured man onto the Executioner's knees in the autogyro rear seat. "We'll get you to a hospital," Bolan said. "You'll be looked after. But first there are some questions you have to answer."

"Bundoran," McClusky muttered. "Bundoran... Excelsior hotel...look after me...there."

Deirdre looked at Bolan inquiringly. "There's a supermarket parking lot across the street," he said. "We could land there and lift off again if we're quick before the Garda arrive."

From Lack to Bundoran was a little over twenty miles, no more than a fifteen minute flight in the Venom, allowing for certain evasive measures along river valleys in the border area.

Cloud covered the whole sky now, reducing the ocean to a leaden gray dotted with whitecaps. Visibility was poor. Bolan found no problem locating the supermarket three blocks inland from the esplanade, but as soon as the autogyro began its descent, he saw that something was wrong.

The Excelsior Temperance Hotel had been reduced to a smoldering black bulk crisscrossed with charred timbers from which spirals of smoke rose from the remaining walls. The firefighters had gone; the hotel was gutted.

When they were at roof level, Bolan picked out the burned wreck of an ancient Morris station wagon in a lane beside the hotel site. Part of the windshield was still in place, the laminated glass behind the steering wheel punctured by three unmistakable bullet holes.

The extremists worked fast.

Bolan had discovered the answers to his questions during the short flight. Now, as the effects of the morphine accelerated, Danny McClusky was lapsing into a comatose condition. "We'll unload him in the parking lot," Bolan said to Deirdre. "There's nothing we can do here now. There's nothing more he can tell us, and there'll be someone there who'll call an ambulance."

He stared at the rows of parked cars as the autogyro touched down and traveled a short distance along one of the traffic lanes.

A uniformed attendant ran up waving his arms.

"This man is badly hurt, and he needs immediate hospital treatment," Bolan yelled when the man was near enough to hear. "Help me get him out of this and onto the ground, okay?"

He waved aside the man's questions until McClusky, still moaning faintly, was laid out on the asphalt lot. For the first time Bolan realized the little man was the same physical type as Ferret-face. "Phone for an ambulance at once," he ordered.

"Yes, but how did...? I mean what the divil are you...?"

"It's urgent," the Executioner snapped. He climbed back into the machine. A crowd of rubbernecking shoppers had already gathered around the Venom.

"Hey!" the attendant shouted. "You can't just drop outta the sky like that, leave a wounded person here unattended and then go—"

The autogyro rose like an elevator and flew away inland, toward the border.

IT WASN'T UNTIL LATER that afternoon that Bolan was able to explain to Deirdre the significance of what he had learned from the injured McClusky on the flight to Bundoran.

It was simple enough when it was all laid on the line, but it looked hellish complex when only half the picture was visible.

Rafferty did know about the Mourne dump; the fake Gage had sold him the whole story. McClusky had acted as go-between, so he knew the story, too. Out of loyalty or fear he had hedged his bet by tipping off Connolly's Unionists as well.

What Connolly didn't know was the diabolical use to which the arms and uniforms stolen from the dump were to be put. McClusky had, however, passed this on to Brognola's spy in Bundoran, which was how Bolan had come into the story.

It was Bolan's activity in Ireland, along with that of the real Captain Gage, that had put the IRA wise to McClusky's treachery, which he had confessed under torture before he was kneecapped.

That still left questions unanswered, such as why Bolan had been expected when he had landed at the secluded inlet. But he now knew the most important points: that the raid on the dump was planned for that very night, and that Connolly's gang, knowing this but ignorant of the reason for it, aimed to attack the IRA and hijack the arms once they had been lifted.

The Executioner also knew the grim details of which Catholic gathering had been selected for the "British" army attack.

All he had to do now was to get over there and work out some way to stop it....

But there were also slight local difficulties to be overcome. It hadn't occurred to the warrior that, flying back into Ulster, he might be mistaken by the UDV for an IRA infiltrator.

Nevertheless he was.

The autogyro came under fire as it skimmed the treetops.

The first Bolan knew of the attack was when heavy-caliber slugs punched holes in the metal fairing of the Venom's nose.

He swung around in his seat and saw that the guerrillas were hidden behind a hedge, presumably to guard a country road that led inland from the border. A "commandeered" Humber FV-1611 armored personnel carrier was maneuvering in the unused field so that the man behind the ring-mounted 12.7 mm machine gun could keep his sights on the autogyro. Half a dozen men in battle fatigues were deployed around the APC, some with SMGs, some with Kalashnikov assault rifles.

Deirdre threw the miniature machine into a tight turn, dropped twenty feet and then soared up under full boost. Bolan was half standing in the cockpit, blazing down at the UDV irregulars with his Beretta. Deirdre gestured frantically in front of the controls, and he saw that the needle on the fuel gauge rested on zero.

Two of the men had fallen, but the machine gun was still firing. Tracers streaked perilously close to the rotors.

There was only one thing Bolan could do. If they touched down within a couple of miles, the APC, traveling at 40 miles per hour, would pick them up within ten minutes. The vehicle had to be taken out of action, and there was only one way to do it. He turned to the missile control.

The two-seat military autogyro flown by Deirdre was an experimental prototype not yet in series production, and the warrior knew nothing of its offensive capability.

He had obviously noticed, in their haste to "borrow" the machine and lift off from the airfield, that there was a small rocket-fired missile slung between the undercart outriggers. He thought the weapon was a miniaturized Malkara or Rockwell Hellfire antitank weapon, but he didn't know if the warhead was a dummy or real. The only time he had been out of the cockpit since they had first lifted off was during the battle at the farm and, very briefly, to unload McClusky. He hadn't had time to examine the armament on either occasion....

Now was the time to find out.

The sight and firing button were located at one side of the cockpit cowling for operation by the rear seat navigator.

As the APC's heavy machine gun spit flame again, the louvered slits above the vehicle's hood slid into view across the eyepiece.

Bolan thumbed the button.

The Venom lurched upward as the rocket motor in back of the missile fired. The cigar-shaped projectile leaped forward, towing an incandescent tail, and streaked for the armor-plated Humber. Bolan had a momentary view of the UDV men scattering across the hillside, and then the missile hit. It wasn't a direct hit: the nose cone struck the ground between the front and rear wheels.

But the warhead was no dummy.

There was a bright flash against the green slope, then an orange fireball tinged with brown smoke that rolled skyward. The dull, thumping concussion of the explosion was audible over the snarl of the engine behind them.

When the smoke cleared, Bolan could see that the APC had been blown over onto its side, the platform chassis a tangle of twisted steel. A wheel had been blown off, and flames licked the underside of the six-cylinder 120 hp engine.

It was enough. The Humber was not one hundred percent destroyed, but it certainly couldn't follow them when the autogyro came down.

The gunner's lifeless body had been ejected from the turret. The two guerrillas nearest the vehicle had fallen. The sheared wheel, having burst through the hedge, was rolling down the lane.

Two men remained. One, armed with an SMG, was running for the shelter of the hedge; the other was coolly firing an AKM from a kneeling position.

Bolan, too, was kneeling—up on the seat, his head dangerously close to the rotors—spraying a deathstream of bullets over the men below.

He took out the guy with the SMG first, because the weapon had the potential to do more damage. Then, as holes appeared in the autogyro's rudder and lead speared the flexible tubes and caromed off the cooling vanes a little too close for comfort, Deirdre kicked the machine into a tight curve and dropped to thirty feet while the Executioner laid waste the gunman's chest with the last few rounds in the Beretta magazine.

She coaxed the Venom to the brow of the hill, flying only a few feet above the ground, now, and they sailed out above a slant of moorland covered with heather and stacks of peat.

Suddenly the engine spluttered, coughed, caught again as she banked first right then left to use the last cupful of fuel in each carburetor, and then died.

The four-blade propeller feathered, the rotors slowed, the land was falling away beneath them. She had to put down immediately, whatever the surface, because once the rotation of the blades fell below a certain critical speed the ship would stall and they would drop like a stone.

It was a rough landing.

The wide undercart stopped the autogyro from tipping over on the steep slope, but there were rocks among the heather. A former snapped, and the machine skidded fifty yards before it slewed sideways and came to rest with one wheel in a deep trench and a rotor buried in the dark pile of peat that had been excavated from it.

When they climbed out of the crumpled nose of the aircraft, Deirdre stared at the bullet holes, the fragments of steel spars, the pierced tube and said shakily, "My God, we were lucky to make it this far!"

"Not lucky," Bolan said. "We were fortunate to have a great pilot." He put an arm around her shoulder. "All we have to do now, is find some kind of transport that will take us quickly to the place where the Mountains of Mourne sweep down to the sea!"

She was looking down the heathery incline toward a green valley where smoking chimneys rose through a canopy of trees. "That's a village called Derrygonnelly, I think," she said slowly. "If it is, I have friends there. Friends who could supply a car."

"Let's go," Bolan said. "How far is it from there to the target area?"

"It must be all of ninety or a hundred miles," she said. "We have to follow the shore of Lough Erne all the way to Enniskillen and then drive across Fermanagh to Ballygawley. We have to follow the border where it skirts the tip of County Monaghan, which is part of the south, and then go right across Armagh and Down before we reach the sea."

"As long as we get there before dark."

"We may not. Most of the roads are slow and twisty, and we must be three miles from Derrygonnelly, all of it rough country without even a dirt road. Plus it may take time to locate my friends."

"We'll make it," the warrior said with confidence.

GETTING THERE WAS NOT EASY. It took more than an hour to make the village, another was wasted waiting for Deirdre's friend to show, and then a suitable car had to be found and fueled. Before they had driven a mile, it began to rain. By the time they reached Enniskillen, the rain had turned into a downpour, and was blowing across the road in almost horizontal gusts. There were several official army roadblocks along the Monaghan border, and two unofficial UDV checkpoints in Armagh.

Bolan drove the elderly Mercedes diesel, providing details of the intel he had gleaned from the injured McClusky while they were in the autogyro.

"Did the poor wee man know the way Rafferty and the boys were going to get to the dump?" Deirdre asked when

Bolan had finished. "Or was that only to be decided at this council meeting?"

"By car to Newcastle and then a motor launch to the caves."

"Did you say there was an army boat on permanent alert down there?"

"So I was told. McClusky says it'll be sabotaged."

For a moment she was silent. The rain lashed across the windshield quicker than the wipers could clear it. Bolan was obliged to slow down to a crawl.

"There's lots of caves on that coast. Your dump wouldn't be in the old smugglers' grottoes north of Glasdrumman, would it?" Deirdre asked.

He slanted her a quick glance. "Yeah," he said quietly. "That's where it is."

"Well, for God's sake!" She shook her head. She laughed. "We used to play there when we were kids. I know them like the back of my hand!"

"You could take us there?"

"I could. And a better route than theirs, too. They'll be sure to run their launch ashore on the strand, in a wee cove off to one side. And then they have to climb the Iron Man's path, and that's desperate difficult, even in daylight. But I can run you into an underground cavern that's open to the sea. The boat rides through a channel out in the cliff, and then there's stairs out in the rock, up to the cave the smugglers used."

"What boat?" the Executioner asked.

"Seamus Flaherty's boat. It's kept in the harbor at Ardglass."

"Who is Seamus Flaherty, and how do you know he'd lend it to us?"

She laughed again. "Sure, a boy I grew up with. We used to live next door to each other."

"How do you know we could borrow the boat?" Bolan repeated.

"It's there for the taking. Any of us can have it, any of us that used to hang around together."

"Where's Seamus now?"

She bent her head. "Doing a job of work," she said evasively.

Bolan let it drop. He wasn't there to blow the underground members of the "official" IRA. "Ardglass is farther away than Newcastle," he said. "Could we get there in time to catch them while they're still getting the stuff out? Before the Connolly gang attacks?"

"We might."

"Do you know this Iron Man path?"

She shook her head. "Only the caves themselves, and the way in from the blowhole in the cliffs. They all have local names. Do you know which one the arms are in, and where the guards are?"

"There are no guards," Bolan said grimly. This was the most staggering of the disclosures McClusky made. "That's why I have to go myself. It's kind of a double bluff. Gage, the real Gage, wasn't going to let on to a foreigner, but McClusky told me that those decoy blockhouses, the ones the whole world knows are fakes, really are the entrance to the arsenal!"

Deirdre stared at him. "But the smugglers' caves . . . ?"

"The stuff is stored in the caves all right, but the way to get at it is through the blockhouses. Only there's no direct way through. It was all walled up to prevent hijacks. In the event of an emergency, the Brits are instructed to blow their way back in and unload the arms via the blockhouses."

"So the route through the caves—?"

"Was never intended to be used. It would take far too long. But it exists just the same. That's why Rafferty is using it. McClusky said they voted against a frontal attack on the blockhouses in case the guards—they do have guards there—outwitted them and gave the alarm. Also they might not blow in the right place. And finally, from the sea, they can take all the time they want.''

"Did he tell you where Rafferty's massacre of our people was to take place?''

"A Catholic fete and sports meeting at a church school outside Tandrages, near Armagh. Mainly women and children. It's near enough the regimental barracks at Newcastle to make it believable as an army reprisal raid.''

"Oh, my God,'' Deirdre said.

Bolan braked to a halt. A trestled barrier blocked the road, and the Mercedes was surrounded by civilians wearing berets and plastic camouflage capes shiny with rain. Another UDV block.

A thickset man walked up to the driver's window and asked for their papers. The man had no right in the world to do so, but he was holding a Colt Commando SMG—looted, the Executioner guessed, from a British SAS depot—and there was no point in arguing.

"How do I know yous a photographer?'' the man growled.

"I can show you my Nikon, a Hasselblad—''

"Any sod can buy a camera. Can you prove it?''

"I guess I can.'' Bolan kept his cool with an effort. Vigilantes could be dangerous. "Here's my press card, my accreditation and,'' he said, suddenly remembering, "a batch of the pictures I shot.''

He felt in the camera case and produced the wallet of prints enlarged from the first 35 mm roll he had exposed. He had never bothered to look at them.

As all the photos had been taken from the Protestant side of the fence, most of them in company with a British army patrol, they seemed to satisfy the UDV irregular. He handed them back, ordered the barrier to be moved aside and waved them through.

A little later, beneath an arc lamp at the exit from a village, they were stopped at a genuine military checkpoint. It seemed violence had broken out again in Belfast and security was being tightened all round. There were several cars in front of them. While they waited their turn, Bolan leafed idly through the photos he had taken.

Youths throwing stones at an army patrol, RUC cops under attack, the demo in back of the Ulster Hall, damaged buildings, a Molotov cocktail exploding against a barrier. The earliest photos, the first six on the thirty-six-frame roll, had been taken that first morning when he had accompanied Osborne and Gage on what had turned out, tragically, to be more than a routine patrol.

The pictures showed the barricade, the opposing mobs, the unrepentant Protestant pastor, the gaunt face of the empty apartment block— The empty block? The fifth floor, and the army patrol in the street below? He remembered light flashing on a moving pane of glass. He had captured the image on the eight-by-ten print.

The fifth-floor balcony: a bright patch and a dimly seen figure behind it.

That was the fourth frame. On the fifth and sixth, the figure was no longer dim. He was out in the open, firing a gun.

Unknowingly Bolan had photographed the murderer at work.

The face was familiar, too. Bolan couldn't believe it.

As a visual clincher, there was proof actually in the car itself. On the back seat of the Mercedes there was a copy of that day's paper. It wasn't the same paper as the one they had read that morning—this one was the *Irish Times*—but the front-page stories were the same: riots in Belfast and Londonderry, two murders, with an American sought; a horse-race scandal; the Dublin industrialist who was a candidate for the Euro-Parliament. Photo inset.

When they were safely past the checkpoint, Bolan stopped beneath a streetlight. He switched on the pencil flashlight and reached for the camera case: in a side pocket there was an 10x magnifying glass. He examined the prints, the jowled face of the man with the gun on that balcony, the inset newspaper photo.

The news photo wasn't the same as the one in the *Belfast Newsletter*. But it was the same man: the Dublin industrialist who was a leading light in a European arms and electronics consortium. And this time he was standing by a black Mercedes 600 stretch limo.

The man with the gun on the balcony in Bolan's prints.

Derek Osborne had been shot by Keiron Winslow-Mowbray.

And the solution to that puzzle also dropped into place the missing piece that completed a much broader picture.

Through incomplete intel, Hal Brognola had gotten the story the wrong way around.

Anglo-American collaboration on the XP-29 project was not at risk by chance, as a by-product of a crazy plot by IRA extremists; that plot had been deliberately engineered, encouraged and financed *because* it would louse up any hope of collaboration.

Winslow-Mowbray and his consortium were callously using the Irish situation, and the rabid fanaticism of Rafferty and his followers, for their own financial gain. Because if the deal fell through a lot of development work that would otherwise have gone to American aerospace firms would now come their way.

It was almost dusk and the rain had stopped, although ragged clouds still sped low across the darkening sky.

"I know Rafferty's not leaving Newcastle until after dark," he said, "but I'm worried about getting there on time in a small boat on a night like this. Because they've *got* to be stopped.''

"Don't worry about the weather," Deirdre said. "There may be a bit of a sea running, but the wind has dropped." She reached into the back of the car for her slicker. "I've as much interest in stopping this as you, and we're still five miles short of Ardglass. So put your foot down, man, dear, and go!"

**21**

The next two hours were among the most eventful of Bolan's life. They arrived at Ardglass after dark to find the place a kaleidoscope of movement and color. A country fair had taken over the center of the little town, and they were forced to leave the car in a side street and continue on foot. They shouldered their way through the crowd, shoving and jostling. Openmouthed faces, laughing, shouting, screaming, swam past them in the light of the flares. The nutty fumes of roasting chestnuts and the sickly sweet odor of candy floss wafted past them; the screeches of children riding a roller coaster drowned the wheeze of a barrel organ.

Then they were away and running for the sea, clattering down narrow lanes, crossing a parking lot and feeling the cold pressure of the wind on their faces as they turned a corner and reached the waterfront.

Deirdre hurried along the dock, past rows of small boats straining at ropes creaking to the swell. Bolan followed her around a stack of wicker pots pungent with pitch and rotting bait, then out along a floating boardwalk that projected into the harbor. The planking, rising and falling with the moored dinghies to which it was lashed, led them to an odd-looking craft.

She was fifteen feet long and broad in the beam, a squat green shell with high bow and stern posts and a half deck that ended just forward of the dog-kennel engine housing midships. The bulkhead blocking off this fore-part was fitted at one side with the wheel, compass and other controls, and on the other with a narrow door that led to the sail locker. There was no windshield, and the stern half of the boat was open.

Bolan looked dubious. "You figure we can make it in that?" he asked.

She pushed the hair out of her eyes. "Of course we can," she panted. "I've been out in her often enough. She was built as a miniature whaler, kind of an experiment, someplace up in the Faroes, I think. But they found she was too small. Dear knows how she got down here: She was lying about, beached, for years, just a hulk for the kids to play in. Then young Flaherty got hold of this two-hundred horsepower diesel and fixed her up."

"A sail locker," Bolan observed, "but no sail?"

She shook her head. "Just the diesel. She doesn't even have a mast that I know of. She's tough, but. That's why we're using her tonight. And there's a quare old turn of speed to her: She'll make twelve to fourteen knots if you push her."

She jumped down into the cockpit and hauled a canvas cover off the engine housing. Bolan leaned down to grasp the handle that cranked the heavy flywheel starting the engine. Over the narrow beach that ran around the stern he could see masts, rigging and crosstrees rocking in the light of the street lamps lining the dock. The moon was up, silvering the shallow slate roofs clustered around the port. Looking the other way, he saw rough water just outside the harbor mouth in the moon's shining path.

For a moment Deirdre had misgivings. Even at its moorings the old whaler was lifting and falling sickeningly. By the time Bolan had started the engine, released the painter and shoved them off into the middle of the port, the boat seemed suddenly small and very fragile. Deirdre tossed her head and shrugged. She had done it often enough before: what difference did a few waves make?

The rollers were marching in between the harbor's two piers at fairly long intervals—they could hear them thundering on the shore beyond the seawall sheltering the dock—and it was not until they were well clear of the warning lights on each breakwater that the realized how rough it was.

Under the whine of the wind, the old boat lifted its blunt nose to the crest of every wave, hung suspended for a moment, then crashed down into the trough with a thwack that sent the spray flying and jarred their teeth in their head. But by then the duckboards were pressing the soles of their feet once more as they rose to the next one.

As soon as the whaler churned out from the lee of St. John's Point, they were at the mercy of the sou'wester sweeping up the Irish Channel, and the full fury of the weather seized them.

Bolan had handed the wheel over to Deirdre; she was the one who knew the coast. He was looking over the stern at the lights of Ardglass, clustered like shining fruit along the dark branch of the coast, when suddenly they slid away and out of sight. The boat had dropped into a trough. He swung around and stared in amazement at the wall of moonlit water rearing over them.

At the instant it was threatening to engulf them, the whaler slewed and then seemed to climb almost vertically up the slope. The vicious, curling tip of the comber hissed past, only inches below the gunwale, and then they were on the downward tilt, the wind snatching Bolan's breath, whistling in his ears, and howling across the foam-flecked surface to lick tongues of spume from the waves.

"I thought you said the weather had calmed down!" he yelled, staggering forward and then crouching behind the bulkhead beside his companion.

She was hunched over the wheel, wet eyes bright in the moonlight, anticipating the unwieldy craft's every movement with swift motions of the spokes, tiny variations in the opening of the throttle. Her doubts had vanished in the challenge of the job at hand. She turned and smiled at him.

"I said the *wind* had dropped," she called. "But I warned you there'd be a bit of a sea running."

"I wouldn't like to be out in what you called a big sea," Bolan countered. "And there still seems to be plenty of wind to me."

"Ah, c'mon now, she's not a point over Force Eight," Deirdre replied. "These seas are about eighteen foot, trough to crest. It's when they're shorter you're in trouble. Your bow lifts before your stern's down. Break the boat's back before you can whistle."

The whaler corkscrewed through a crest crumbling into foam, hung giddily in space, then plunged down into a trough to smash against the swell of the next wave with a shock that sent showers of spray exploding into the air. Drenched with icy water, Bolan yelled against the wind, "Deirdre, do you really think we can make it in this weather?"

"Certainly. We're heading out across Dundrum Bay here. This is the worst we'll get. But the land curves around to meet us again after Newcastle. We'll get a bit of shelter from the mountains then—and there's slack water off Glasdrumman where we have to turn and run in before the wind. It's deep there, too. The Mournes drop straight into the ocean. That's why the smugglers used— *Watch out!*"

A mountainous wave rose at them crosswise, canting the boat alarmingly on her beam. At the same time another breaker speeding diagonally across its face broke with a noise like a shellburst over the stern, cascading a torrent of seawater into the cockpit.

Bolan picked himself up from the swilling duckboards to hear Deirdre shout, "Bail, man! Bail! Get that water out of here or we'll be done for entirely next time we hit a sea like that!"

Bolan grinned to himself. There came a time when everybody's cool went overboard. Water swirled around his knees. Beneath the rear thwart he located a two-gallon gasoline can with the top sawn off and began to bail vigorously as they plowed into the howling gale.

Deirdre O'Mara was wrestling with the wheel, teeth clenched on her lower lip as she steered the bucking whaler up and down the gigantic seas.

The next thirty minutes were hell. Bolan didn't offer to take the wheel himself, for although he was stronger, Deirdre knew the coast and he didn't. Working steadily, he saw the lights of Newcastle rising and falling over the crests; he watched the dark, smooth outlines of the Mourne Mountains blot out the stars over the southwestern horizon, and when at last they put about and ran before the wind, he watched the huge combers, marbled gray and gold by the moon, sweep past on either side as they lurched shoreward.

The boat, squatting low in the water now that she was half awash, alternately buried her nose and her stern in the following waves as the twin screws—now laboring, now racing as they lifted clear of the sea—thrust her remorselessly on.

Many times, as they sank endlessly into some trough, Bolan marveled that they rose again; many times, as the whaler shuddered under the onslaught of an extra-large roller, he was convinced she would disintegrate or capsize.

He was relieved when the nightmare ended. Not because he was afraid—natural hazards had no power to frighten the warrior—but because he had been unable to contribute anything in the war against the elements.

He continued to bail, the muscles of his arms and back straining, until at last he realized the buffeting had resolved itself and the boat was now merely bobbing in the water.

The dark masses of water no longer crumbled into foam on every side. The shriek of the wind had died to a whistle. He looked up from his backbreaking task. They were close in under the mountains; he could make out the glint of a rock face beneath their bulk. On either side he could hear the distant thunder of surf.

If he strained his eyes in the pale moonlight, he could see the pulsing line of phosphorescence where the breakers dashed themselves against the cliff.

But straight ahead, in the freak area of slack water Deirdre had told him about, the sea simply rose and fell, sucking at the rock.

The old boat was carried forward, slowed, then surged on again, apparently straight at the cliff. Deirdre gave an exclamation of triumph. There was a sudden acceleration, the drop of a curtain of darkness as moon and stars were extinguished, and then a slow spreading of unearthly green light as they floated out into the center of an enormous cavern. The whaler had carried them safely through into the old smugglers' retreat.

Bolan could see why they had to sail past the opening in the cliff and then turn to run back into it. The split in the mountain, created at the dawn of time by some gigantic fault, had been hollowed out by the incessant lapping of the ocean. But the channel leading out ran along the axis of the fault and emerged facing almost due south: it would have been virtually invisible, and certainly impossible to navigate in this weather, approaching as they had from the north.

Deirdre uttered some triumphant exclamation, but Bolan could not make out the words because the first syllable that passed her lips was caught up to echo in a vast rock

chimney above them, distorted and magnified as it reverberated around galleries of dripping granite to merge with
the suck and slap of the water and the muffled roaring of
wind somewhere above.

There were no waves in the cavern, but the boat rose and
fell as the sea ebbed and flowed—maybe eight or nine feet,
Bolan reckoned, watching a weed-slimed ledge sink into
view each time the whaler reached the zenith of its climb. He
scrambled onto the deck, kept his balance with difficulty
and leaped for the rock shelf as the unwieldy craft rose.

Next time around he grabbed Deirdre as she jumped. She
stumbled and landed on her hands and knees, almost falling back into the water.

The roof of the huge cave closed in to the width of the
original fault forty or fifty feet above their heads, and above
this slanting cleft the moon was visible in a jagged strip of
night sky. It was the moonlight, refracted from the pale
veins and outcrops in the rock, that pierced the gloom with
a thousand glittering points of light and flooded the surface of the water with its strange radiance.

Bolan switched on the pencil flashlight. At the far end of
the ledge, the beam lit a flight of narrow steps hacked from
the rock wall. "There are four hundred and seventeen of
them," Deirdre whispered as they gazed at the stairs that
spiraled upward. "Prepare for a tough climb!"

The Executioner was in shape but by the time they were
ninety or one hundred feet above the water, with more than
half the stairway still to go, he stopped to catch his breath.

Deirdre stood on a step behind him and twitched his pant
leg, pointing downward. Moving with the swells, the whaler
had pulled free from its mooring and floated out into the
center of the cavern. She had clearly struck some rocky
projection under water, for the weathered planking at the
bow had a jagged hole.

As they watched, the splintered, waterlogged nose buried itself ever deeper, and the stern rose into the air until the boat was standing on end. For an instant she remained like that, then gently she rolled over and slid beneath the surface.

Bolan sighed. "No round trip by boat. Whatever happens now, we have to find your beach or discover some route that leads through to the surface."

Ten minutes later they were standing on an unprotected platform carved from the granite at dizzying height above the basin. Bolan was thankful he had not been one of those long-ago illegals forced to tote cases of French brandy or casks of rum up that punishing stairway.

The great cleft in the rock sloped steeply at one side of the platform. An experienced mountaineer with pitons, rope and mallet might have been able to wedge himself into the chimney and inch himself up into the open air. For Bolan and Deirdre there was only one way to go: along a rock tunnel that yawned blackly on the other side.

Shining the light down onto a surface that was dry and floored with sand, he took her arm and led the way into the dark.

In the sudden silence, the gentle lapping of the waves far below sounded like the breathing of some great subterranean beast, sleeping after a satisfying meal.

## 22

The wide low-roofed cave was walled with whitewood shelves and dividers that were arranged as neatly and orderly as a regular army PX.

Fatigues, camous, dress uniforms, berets, steel helmets, boots and groundsheets were packed away according to size. Stenciled crates full of FN automatic rifles, machine pistols, grenades and packages of C-4 plastique stood islanded in the center of the underground arsenal. The light cast by oil lamps, placed at intervals throughout the cave, revealed the barrels of hundreds of rifles in wooden racks and sent the shadows of the men in the cave dancing across ammunition boxes, CS cartridges and field telephones, which were displayed like the stock of some bizarre supermarket.

An occasional gleam signaled the presence of mortars and antitank weapons farther back in the shadows.

Rafferty, M'Quade and half a dozen other men were loading items into sacks that were piled at the entrance to one of four tunnels leading out of the cave.

A heavyset jowled man wearing expensive fisherman's waders and a sheepskin coat was directing the operation. "About thirty should do," he said. "Uniforms, guns, helmets, ammunition belts and grenades. To exaggerate would make it less believable." And then he said to Rafferty, "Of course, if you want a few automatic weapons for your own use later, or maybe a mortar or two, there's nothing to stop you from adding them to the cargo. But time is short, and you can always come back for more now that you know the way in.''

''Whatever you say, Keiron,'' the IRA extremist replied. ''You're the boss tonight. Start gettin' the stuff down, fellas, soon as the sacks are filled. Shooters first, boots and uniforms last, when you're tirin'.''

Keiron Winslow-Mowbray had prominent eyes and a wet mouth. ''Come on, chaps,'' he urged, the jowls quivering. ''We don't want to get caught on the strand when the tide goes out, do we?''

TWO HUNDRED FEET AWAY, in another of the linked series of caves acoustically isolated from the arsenal, Bolan and Deirdre O'Mara emerged from the tunnel mouth and were jumped instantly by men who materialized from the darkness.

A gloved hand was clapped over Deirdre's mouth, and she was pinioned in a bearlike hug. When the Executioner swung around at the sound of the scuffle, a sock filled with sand hit him on the nape with agonizing force, and he went down.

He was dragged half conscious along a passageway to a smaller chamber that was dimly lit by a single miner's lamp.

A very tall man stood outside the circle of light, his shadow gigantic on the rock wall and roof. When he picked up the lamp and held it high, Bolan saw that the man was Morrie Connolly. ''Here's a couple of rats we found in the hole, Morrie,'' one of his captors said.

''Rats, is it?'' Connolly said. ''I'm thinkin' it's rats in a trap all right.'' Peering at Bolan and the woman, he added, ''Well, well, well. If it isn't the Papish bitch and her knight fuckin' errant!''

''Deirdre, I told you the loyalists are renowned for their courtesy and the elegance of their manners,'' Bolan responded.

"Manners, is it?" Connolly said. "I don't think it good manners at all to bust into a private meeting, the way you did in yon mill, and take away the guest of honor." Abruptly he slashed Bolan a backhand across the face with all his strength. Bolan staggered. Connolly's strength was formidable.

"Now that *you*'re our guest, mister," Connolly said, "I think it's up to us to teach you a few manners yoursel'." He looked around the circle of faces and said crisply, "All right, hould him boys!"

Two men sprang to Bolan's side, each seizing an arm in a police grip so that if the warrior struggled his arms would break at the elbow.

Connolly balled his right fist and punched it gently into the palm of his left hand. "This is for the dunt you gave me swingin' on that rope," he said. He drew back his arm, measured the distance with his eyes and slammed a paralyzing blow to the Executioner's solar plexus.

Bolan's body, rigidly pinioned, was unable to jackknife forward, and his knees rose slowly toward his savaged diaphragm until he was entirely supported by the goons. Soon his heels lowered to the ground again, and air began groaning back into his lungs.

"Kelly," the gang leader said, "you and Flanagan tie up the girl and gag her. We'll come back and have a little party with her when we've done the Papish whorehounds." He settled his weight evenly on spread legs, swiveled at the hips and dealt Bolan a terrible blow over the heart. Bolan's body jerked, and the man holding him staggered a little to one side.

"That's for trespassing at the mill," Connolly said, stepping close to him and flexing his black-haired fingers. "And this is for spoiling our fun with the bitch." He reached down, grabbed and squeezed. Hard.

Bolan barely managed not to scream, loath to give his tormentor the satisfaction.

Connolly smiled, staring into the Executioner's contorted face. He increased the pressure until the muscles in his forearm stood out rock-hard.

"The rest," Connolly said finally, "is because I enjoy beatin' the bejasus outta buggers who won't mind their own business."

He began to inflict a systematic beating.

Bolan started to lose consciousness. He heard Deirdre scream once, and then he was overcome by a crescendo of pain.

A little later, panting, Connolly dropped his blood-smeared hands and brushed the sweat from his forehead with one forearm. He reached up a forefinger and thumb and seized Bolan by the chin, tilting his gory face up to the light. Only the whites of his eyes showed beneath the lids.

"All right, fellas, you can let him drop," Connolly said. "We'll have no more trouble from this one."

CONNOLLY'S ATTEMPT to hijack the arms stolen by Rafferty's wildcat IRA group was well enough planned but ill-timed.

The Unionist paramilitary had arrived in daylight, on a fishing boat "borrowed" at gunpoint from a Protestant sailor in Kilkeel, near the border. Return of the boat—and the sailor's future—depended on his silence, he had been told.

Knowing the time and location of the raid, but ignorant of the route to the caves or their relation to one another, they had beached a little farther down the coast and waited for Rafferty and his men to arrive in Winslow-Mowbray's oceangoing cruiser. After that they had simply followed the IRA renegades up the Iron Man path, some of them dispersing among the smaller caves once the IRA started to work on the cache of supplies, others returning to sea level to set an ambush among a tumble of giant boulders that protected the cove from the big waves rolling in from the southwest.

Connolly's mistake, and the flaw in his timing, lay in the fact that he had not taken into account the product.

The plan was to attack simultaneously from the shore and the caves behind the arsenal when the majority of Rafferty's men were actually on the precipitous zigzag of the Iron Man path. Given that the two sides had about the same firepower, it might have worked well enough, with the Republicans decimated in this pincer assault while they were out in the open on dangerous terrain.

But they weren't carrying crates of brandy and casks of rum on their shoulders. They were ferrying arms down to the cruiser. Including grenades.

Instead of being sitting ducks, they had a distinct advantage as they positioned themselves high up on the windswept ledges of the path.

Winslow-Mowbray was already on the beach when Connolly, from the caves above, gave the order to attack on his walkie-talkie. Rafferty, halfway down the cliff, threw himself flat when the first gunshots flamed from among the boulders below. Two of his men fell, one tumbling screaming to the rocks at the water's edge.

But the IRA leader had already shouted his order to his troops ahead and behind him, and each man carried a sack of MK-2 grenades. A shower of them were lobbed from above, and the blasts burst left and right, ripping flesh from bone and pulverizing the guts of the ambushers with flying steel and rock chips.

Winslow-Mowbray reached the cabin cruiser drawn up on the tiny crescent of beach at the head of the inlet. Now a dazzling beam lanced the night from a spotlight mounted at one side of the wheelhouse windshield. Swinging across the cliff face, the finger of brilliance stroked the boulder barricade, pointing out the few terrorists who had not been decimated by the hail of grenades.

Rafferty and M'Quade showed no mercy. They showered a stream of death over those who had survived the grenade attack.

At the top of the winding path above them, Connolly, Kelly and Flanagan cut down four more of the Republicans with handguns before an MK-2, expertly thrown by M'Quade, smashed the life from Flanagan and left Kelly slumped against an outcrop with his intestines spilled across the rock steps. Connolly, who brought up the rear, escaped back into the warren of caves.

BOLAN RECOVERED CONSCIOUSNESS in total darkness. Every part of him hurt like hell: his groin was on fire, his ribs ached and his face felt swollen. He was no superman. His resistance might be stronger, but he could be knocked out, made to feel pain as much as any human being. What was different about the Executioner was his astounding power of recovery—partly due to his superior physical condition, partly to an iron-clad determination and resolve.

He rolled over, discovered that his limbs were unbound and stumbled to his feet with a suppressed groan. His outstretched hands met a rock wall. He explored it until he found an opening, staggered through, felt his way along the tunnel beyond.

The tunnel branched. Instinctively he went left. He was unaware of it, but he was being drawn by the faint odor of extinguished oil lamps, and following the faint breeze that was soothing his lacerated face.

The darkness was lightening imperceptibly. He could hear the harsh thunder of surf breaking someplace in the distance. The tunnel turned. For a moment he was lost in another cavern, then he sensed the salt breeze, stronger now, and a louder indication of the sea. He veered across the rock floor, found the tunnel and walked in.

The warrior didn't know why he had been left behind, alive, and neither bound nor gagged. Perhaps they hadn't expected him to regain consciousness. He didn't know what stage the raid—or the hijack—had reached. He only knew he had to stop it. At all costs.

A short passageway opened abruptly on his left. It didn't lead in the direction his senses told him he should go, but there was light at the end of it, a rectangle of moonlight half blotted out by the huge silhouette of a man standing with his arms outspread to press, palms outward, against the two walls of the tunnel.

Connolly.

He was standing in what was a natural window overlooking the Iron Man path, his plan in ruins, his men blown away, his own life in danger.

Anger welled to the surface. The desire for revenge did not figure often in the Executioner's private code. It did now.

"It's just you and me now," Bolan snarled. "Man-to-man."

Connolly whirled, startled. Bolan launched himself at his enemy. Hand-to-hand combat in his condition would have to be quick, short in duration and now.

His right foot shot out, the steel toe of his boot slamming into the outsize Ulsterman's groin.

The bully didn't even have to time to retaliate. As Connolly folded forward, his face contorted in agony, Bolan summoned all of the strength left in his battered body and put it into an uppercut that started near the floor and ended in a paralyzing smash to the gangster's jaw.

Connolly straightened with the force of the blow and catapulted backward through the opening in the rock.

Bolan followed, carried on by the impetus of his attack.

Connolly landed eight feet below on the slanting ledge cut from the granite and settled there briefly. Then, overbalanced when his heels hit jarringly on the pathway, he fell. By the time Bolan's feet struck the rock, the giant had plunged to the roaring breakers that creamed and frothed around the jagged outcrops three hundred feet below.

The Executioner barely saved himself from pitching over the edge. While Connolly's death cry was still carried on the wind, Bolan turned and battled his way upward toward the opening in the cliff face that led back to the tunnels linking the smugglers' caves.

He passed the disemboweled carcass of Kelly, the eyes no longer glittering, and the remains of Flanagan. He penetrated the caves. But the lamps in the storeroom were no longer lit: the IRA plunderers had taken their booty and left.

Bolan went down to the inlet on the lee side of the rocks. It was a perilous journey. The shallow, uneven steps were pitted with black shadows in the moonlight, their surface slippery with spume carried up by the wind. On one side was the yawning abyss, where a false step would plunge Bolan to an instant death.

He passed several more bodies on the way. As he was warily negotiating a craggy outcrop that would bring him into full view of the beach, Bolan saw that the sacks of stolen arms and uniforms were piled on a shingle above the high-water mark. Rafferty and his men were passing them up to the cabin cruiser whose stern was still half afloat in the spent seawater welling in past the natural breakwater sheltering the cove.

Bolan weighed the situation. He was unarmed: the Beretta had been taken from him when he had been intercepted by Connolly's men. The corpses on the pathway had been stripped of whatever weapons they had been carrying.

How many of the IRA kill squad were left? It was clear there had been a battle and Connolly's gang had lost; it was also evident that Rafferty had suffered losses. The Executioner didn't know how many men there had been to begin with. In any case, the wildcat extremist would have no difficulty finding more men to carry out his diabolical plan once he got the merchandise away. Correction. *If* he got away.

Because Mack Bolan wouldn't let him. Once that cruiser was afloat with the British army uniforms and arms, the slaughter of innocents was inevitable.

And there was only Mack Bolan, unarmed and in bad shape, to stop it.

Most of the sacks had already been loaded. Rafferty, M'Quade and Winslow-Mowbray had arrived with eight men—six to locate, repack and transport the material down the Iron Man pathway, two to keep watch by the boat. Connolly's gangsters had accounted for half a dozen men. There remained only the three principals and two IRA soldiers.

It took Bolan ten minutes after he had gained the foot of the path to satisfy himself that this was all. But there was still no sign of Deirdre. Was she a prisoner aboard the cruiser? Had she been murdered by the Unionists? Had she been left, bound and gagged to die alone in the lightless caverns far above?

But now there was no time to think about it. The mission came first.

Only a couple of sacks remained to be heaved aboard. M'Quade and one of the IRA men were straining at the cruiser's sharp bow, shoving its stern out into the rising tide. Rafferty and Winslow-Mowbray were in the wheelhouse. The fifth man picked up the two sacks and staggered toward the boat.

Two things happened to even the odds.

Bolan heard Deirdre O'Mara's voice, raised more in scorn or anger than in fear, from the cruiser's cabin.

As he looked across the strand he saw a camera case lying open among the wrack at the high-water mark.

Picked up during a cleanup after the battle, it had presumably been discarded because it contained no weapons. The two cameras lay where they had been thrown, half buried in soft sand. A 35 mm SLR Nikon...and a Hasselblad.

Bolan had no doubt that the case was the one he had been carrying when he'd been jumped by Connolly's goons. If he was right...

He wormed his way along the base of the cliff until he could reach the cameras. It was his Nikon all right. And the Hasselblad? He popped open the back plate. Nobody had troubled to check it: the four 9 mm rounds were still in place.

The cruiser was afloat. The engine started. The screws thrashed. The last man heaved the two sacks on deck and clambered aboard. Winslow-Mowbray spun the wheel to maneuver the craft in a tight circle sternfirst so that she would be headed out to sea when he opened the throttle.

Bolan ran among the boulders sheltering the inlet, leaping from rock to rock, the Hasselblad slung around his neck.

As the cruiser's stern slid past below, Bolan scrambled to the top of a huge granite outlier that overhung the inlet. He jumped.

The warrior landed on deck with a shock that jarred the breath from his lungs. Recovering quickly, he spun around to face the last IRA man aboard, a man with a sawed-off shotgun aimed to fire from the hip.

At a distance of ten feet, knowing he couldn't miss, Bolan pressed the Hasselblad's trigger button without raising the viewfinder-sight to his eye.

The shot echoed within the confines of the rocky cove.

The goon was hurled backward into the water before he could fire a blast.

The shot had alerted the other IRA hardguys. Bolan ran forward and dived for cover behind a dinghy slung amidships. For a moment the curly head of M'Quade appeared in the light from the wheelhouse as he raced toward the stern. "Big man," he called, "you trespass too often. And trespassers will be prosecuted." A shot from a heavy-caliber automatic rang out, and splinters flew from the dinghy's timbers as the slug cored through the wood close to Bolan's head. "If you interfere in matters that don't concern you," M'Quade cried, "you must pay the penalty."

Two more shots rang out, and now three shafts of moonlight penetrated the gloom beneath the upended tender. Bolan had crawled under the little boat on elbows and knees; he rose into a squatting position on M'Quade's side of the craft, raising the Hasselblad to eye level. "That goes two ways, M'Quade," he said softly.

The double report reverberated throughout the sheltered cove. Bolan's 9 mm skullbuster took away the side of M'Quade's head and splattered a screen of blood over the side window of the wheelhouse. Bolan rocked back on his heels as the Irishman's slug severed the camera strap and seared a furrow across the flesh of his right shoulder.

M'Quade fell into the sea. Bolan stifled a curse as the man's gun went with him. There were two rounds left in the Hasselblad, and three terrorists to deal with. He rose to his feet and burst into the wheelhouse. Winslow-Mowbray had scuttled below at the first sign of trouble; the second IRA soldier was at the wheel. There was no sign of Rafferty or Deirdre O'Mara.

Bolan didn't hesitate. The steersman was part of a gang sworn to massacre women and children in the name of a cause that had become perverted. He wasted the guy with one of the remaining rounds and ran for the companionway leading to the saloon.

Rafferty was sitting on a divan next to Deirdre O'Mara, the barrel of the D-3 Colt Cobra in his right hand pressed to her temple. "Put that machine on the table, you," the breakaway chief said to Bolan, "or the lady, like Clementine, is lost and gone forever. After that we'll talk."

Bolan slid the Hasselblad, with its single remaining bullet, onto the table. There was just one thing he could do. "Talk about what?" he said.

"Sure your own part in this affair," the IRA chief replied. "And hers. Is it some carnal relation you have then? For I cannot accept the idea of betrayal, see. And otherwise I'm unable to see why she should be a traitor to the cause. She'll be court-martialed anyway and probably shot. But I'd like to know first."

There was another divan facing Rafferty on the other side of the cabin. The Cobra's hammer was not cocked. There were two pressures on the revolver's trigger, and then the hammer had to go back and spring forward again before the firing pin was hit. These were the variables Bolan had to estimate before he acted.

"Okay, let's talk," he said, slumping onto the opposite divan. He allowed himself to fall heavily, as if the cushion was lower than he expected, his knees jerking up to counterbalance the fall of his back. If he could pluck the small, flat-bladed throwing knife from the strap at his right ankle while he was in this temporary jackknife position, could he throw it fast enough to hit Rafferty before the man could fire the revolver?

The gamble paid off. Rafferty didn't see the knife until it was already in flight. He pulled the trigger, but before the hammer fell the blade had sliced into his right eye, puncturing the eyeball and piercing the brain, and Deirdre had dived to the floor. The shot went through the ceiling and up into the wheelhouse.

Rafferty fell sideways, fluid from his ruptured eye mingling with blood and brain matter on the cushion of the divan.

Bolan lifted the woman from the floor. "They f-f-found me tied up where Connolly had left me," she said in a trembling voice. "If you hadn't c-c-come..."

"It's okay, honey. It's over," he said soothingly. "Go on up and take the wheel now before we capsize. I have business to attend to down here."

Keiron Winslow-Mowbray was sitting on a bunk in the small sleeping cabin in the cruiser's bow. The cabin shone with polished teak and brass and Waterford crystal decanters on a silver tray.

Bolan held Rafferty's revolver in his hand.

"Who are you? What are you doing here? What the hell do you want?" the industrialist blustered. "What the divil are you on about? You can't come here—"

Bolan raised the pistol until the muzzle was lined up with Winslow-Mowbray's forehead.

He squeezed the trigger.

# EPILOGUE

The cruiser was no more than a quarter of a mile offshore, and Bolan had barely disposed of the dead, when they were caught in a searchlight beam and ordered to stop by a coast guard cutter. The boarding party, to the warrior's astonishment, comprised Simon Gage's commanding officer, Colonel Alleyn, and a fat man in uniform with fingers like sausages.

"Allow me," Alleyn said, "to present Major McGeehan, of a rather special branch of the Intelligence Corps..."

Bolan's astonishment showed on his face. "I don't get it," he said blankly.

"You're puzzled because you're looking at it from the wrong end, as it were," Alleyn said. "For us, Derek Osborne's death was practically the end of the affair. For you it was the start. The GOC, Northern Ireland, you see, was increasingly worried about certain aspects of the violence here. It seemed to follow too much of a set pattern, to be too well organized, to be merely an outbreak of people's resentment—even allowing for the inflammatory effect of evil men like Mulligan and fools like McComb. So we called in a special investigator."

"Enter Major McGeehan," Bolan stated, looking across at the fat man who sat complacently watching the lights of Newcastle rise and fall off the cruiser's port bow.

"Exactly. Major McGeehan was asked to find out whether the riots were Catholic inspired, Protestant inspired, or perhaps due to Protestants masquerading as Catholics—or vice versa. Being an Ulsterman himself, Major McGeehan was able to submerge himself in the, uh, subcultures of the city, perhaps better than you were, and it wasn't long before he came up with something."

"No kidding!" Bolan murmured, eyeing Deirdre.

"He found," Alleyn said, "that the people behind the disturbances were neither Provisionals nor Orangemen proper, neither civil rights fighters nor Republicans, but a certain fanatic section of the Orangemen deliberately fomenting trouble in such a way that it *looked* like the IRA."

Deirdre exclaimed aloud. "Of course! That man . . ."

"Kelly," Alleyn nodded. "One of a number of old-fashioned agent-provocateurs. You saw him a couple of times, Belasko. Two incidents out of many. He would dress himself to look as 'Republican' as possible, then go to Protestant bars and pick fights because the Unionists there wouldn't talk to him. When the students or the labor movement or the civil rights people held nonviolent demos, Kelly would get together a similarly dressed crowd, with similar banners and slogans, and be as violent as possible, attacking the police and everyone—as you saw at the Ulster Hall. The result would be that people would come to associate the Republicans, the Catholics, with violence and unreason, and finally the great mass of ordinary, decent Protestants would be persuaded the extremists were right."

"Rafferty and the IRA extremists were cashing in on this, I guess?" Bolan said.

"They were about to. That's why the offers of arms from the Mourne dump were so eagerly accepted by both sides. But you can imagine how Major McGeehan and I felt when—just at this critical moment—you arrived to help poor Gage play private eye. And you'll understand why I poured cold water on his scheme.''

Bolan nodded.

''As for your bright idea of passing your two selves off as a second wave of arms salesmen...'' Alleyn shook his head. ''It was too much. Finally we decided to let you go ahead and use you as a kind of smoke screen, a decoy behind which McGeehan could carry on his own work with less chance of being blown.''

''That's why you practically talked me into stealing that autogyro, right?'' Bolan stated.

''Did I do that?'' Colonel Alleyn asked innocently.

''And you of course,'' Deirdre cried suddenly, turning to the fat man, ''you were the anonymous rescuer at the mill?''

McGeehan smiled. ''Well, now,'' he said, ''I'd just hate for you to think that every Protestant in Ulster was like yon rubbish. I was followin' Kelly, you see, and once I saw where he was at—well, it was the obvious thing to do, givin' the both of you a wee bit of a hand there.''

''It's a bit late,'' the woman said awkwardly, ''but, thank you.''

''We are aware of of the action that took place at the arsenal,'' Alleyn informed them. ''We have IR night vision equipment on the cutter.''

Bolan accepted that he and Gage had been used. And it was a relief that the Brits were happy enough, this time, not to be involved in a sectarian fight. He also realized that neither Alleyn nor the major knew about the Winslow-Mowbray side of the plot, so the question of U.S. interference, or the necessity for it, need never arise.

Mission accomplished.

But there was still one question that puzzled him. ''Tell me one thing, sir,'' he said to Alleyn. ''Who was the man who was using Simon Gage's name?''

It was McGeehan who answered. "Well, now, I'd have thought you guessed that," he said. "It was Derek Osborne, of course."

"*Osborne!* But why?"

"For the basest of reasons, I'm afraid," Alleyn said sadly. "He was a gambler. He had debts with Connolly's firm. He was doing it for money. And he used Gage's name, I suppose, to keep his own nose clean. Once he had sold out his regiment and his country he was killed, no doubt, to keep his mouth shut. Or because one side or the other found out he'd double-crossed them.

"Ah, yes," Bolan said blandly, "that must be the reason."

Like hell. More likely it was because the plotters needed a dead Brit, an officer, to lend credence to the idea that the planned massacre was a revenge operation. And who better than the man who'd sold them the means to realize their plan . . . because it had to be dead secret and dead men tell no tales.

As THEY WALKED across the tarmac after landing at Aldergrove, Bolan turned to Deirdre. "That welcome party I got when I landed near Bundoran. How the hell did they know I'd be there?"

"They didn't. You were in the wrong place at the wrong time—a simple case of mistaken identity. One of our operatives rolled over information concerning an arms deal. Intel reported the traitor would land that morning . . ."

He cupped her chin in his hand. "There's a hymn that starts 'Fight the good fight with all thy might.' Too bad we're fighting different battles on different sides."

"Too bad," she echoed. "But one day, things may be different. When Ireland is one. Until then?"

"Until then," Bolan responded as he handed her into the waiting car.

Then he turned and walked off into the night.

# Available NOW!

## DON PENDLETON's
# MACK BOLAN

# TROPIC HEAT

The probing tentacles of the drug network have crept far
enough into the streets of America. The only solution is
to cut the cancer out at the source. The only man equal
to the task is Mack Bolan!

SB-9R

---

GOLD
EAGLE

For the millions who can't read
Give the Gift of Literacy

One out of five adults in North America
cannot read or write well enough
to fill out a job application
or understand the directions on a bottle of medicine.

You can change all this by joining the fight
against illiteracy.

For more information write to:
Contact, Box 81826, Lincoln, Neb. 68501
In the United States, call toll free: 800-228-3225

The only degree you need
is a degree of caring

# TAKE 'EM FREE
## 4 action-packed novels plus a mystery bonus

## NO RISK
## NO OBLIGATION TO BUY